Oh! Where Are Bloody Mary's Earrings?

Oh! Where Are Bloody Mary's Earrings?

by ROBERT PLAYER

HARPER & ROW, PUBLISHERS
New York, Evanston, San Francisco, London

A JOAN KAHN—HARPER NOVEL OF ENTERTAINMENT

 For information address Harper & Row, Publishers, Inc., 10 East 53rd Street, New York, N.Y. 10022.

STANDARD BOOK NUMBER: 06-013353-8

LIBRARY OF CONGRESS CATALOG CARD NUMBER: 72-9100

To Eira

Contents

This story is a figment of the author's imagination. A few of the characters are entirely fictitious; the others have been so long in their humble graves or marble tombs as to be now beyond all harm.

TUDOR PROLOGUE

It began long ago, over four hundred years ago. All Spain lay brown and parched under a July sun. Only in the north, in the round blue harbor of La Coruña, could an Atlantic breeze ripple the water, gently lifting the pennons, gonfalons and banners of the big galleon.

They called her *El Espíritu Santo—The Holy Ghost.* She rode like a feather upon the waters and yet somehow seemed neither very holy nor very ghostly. Rather did she seem like some huge scarlet flamingo. Her hull and her high carved fo'c'sle were streaked with scarlet; her pennons were also mainly scarlet; the three hundred sailors swarming in her rigging wore scarlet livery; flying above all was the great standard of Spain, itself an affair of gold and black and scarlet, of lions rampant, of castles and Hapsburg eagles—all quartered together.

The Holy Ghost—beheld in awe and wonder from the crowded quays—had been built, painted and furnished to take the future King of Spain to his marriage with the Queen of England. Outside the harbor the Lord Howard was waiting with a hundred and fifty English sail, to escort *The Holy Ghost* to Southampton—as was hoped. As was hoped, for all up the English coast, at Plymouth and Brixham and Lyme, landing places had been prepared should the Spanish King feel sick.

Deep in the galleon's hold was the baggage of all the grandees of Navarre, Aragon and Castile, of a horde of young hidalgos.

There were marvelous chests and coffers; there were leather bags crammed with jewels, crammed with the pearls and gold of the Spanish Main; there were daggers, collars and corsages, goblets, buckles and caskets; there were also chalices and tabernacles and rosaries and pectoral crosses—all gifts to such priests as had adhered to Mary Tudor and the Faith. There were odds and ends to be thrown away on English whores. Also down there, among the creaking timbers, was a gift to the Queen—Spanish bullion that would need ninety-seven big wagons to drag it from Southampton to the Tower of London.

There was something more. It was rumored that the King's own cabin, with two noble swordsmen outside the door, contained the greatest treasure on board. That cabin, high in the stern, ran the whole width of the galleon so that Philip, for hours on end when the melancholy sat upon him, could watch from magic casements the foam of the ship's wash trailing far astern.

At one end of the cabin was Philip's bed with its coverlets of cloth of gold, and with the arms of Spain upon the tester. At the other end was the silver altar. It was upon this altar, just before the ship sailed, that the Cardinal of Toledo had placed the Body and Blood of Philip's Savior. It was before this altar that the confessor, a Hieronymite monk, said mass each morning as the sun came up over the calm sea.

Alongside the jeweled pyx was a plain casket of ivory. When the men's hammocks were slung below decks, then Ivan Pétya, the King's Russian valet, would tell all the secrets of that royal cabin. Pétya had been trained in Kiev, in the service of a prince of Muscovy. He had found his way by devious routes—he was a devious man—first to Byzantium, then to Venice and so to Madrid. He knew everything there was to know about intrigue and corruption and sex—and politics. He was now a double agent, "practicing," as the phrase went, against both England and Spain, against both Philip and Mary. He would tell his friends below decks, while they hung upon his lips, all there was to know about the King's Ganymedes and mistresses—and indeed rather more than all. And then he would tell them about Mary Tudor—not about her lovers, but that she had none, that she was plain and barren and frigid, that only through a miracle could she ever bear her king a child. And then he would tell them about the ivory casket upon the altar, and how it held the finest gems in all the world—those holy and miraculous diamond earrings which the Queen of England, to her infinite discomfort, would be forced to wear through her first marital night.

That was Pétya's story. A month ago, in actual fact, Philip had sent the Marquis de las Nevas to England, that he might lay before Mary the finest diamond in Spain—a table diamond—together with a necklace of brilliants and much else besides. These gifts, however, as the Marquis made clear, were no more than a consolation for Philip's defects as a correspondent. Philip wrote with difficulty, and to his future wife, ten years older than himself, he had been hardly able to write at all. He could never bring himself to the point. The Marquis de las Nevas had therefore hinted that the greatest gift of all, the gift which would redeem all, the King would bring himself to England—the gift of the Holy Earrings.

Cut from the finest stones from the New World, these earrings, these flashing twelve-pointed stars, two inches across, were doubly unique, both materially and spiritually. Materially because, in spite of the fabulous nature of each separate diamond, they were quite perfectly matched. No man could tell the left earring from the right. Spiritually they were unique because, it was devoutly believed, each earring, beneath its central diamond, concealed a tiny fragment of the Virgin Mary's robe—the robe she wore at Bethlehem. Each night at his *prie-dieu*, Philip could therefore clutch the earrings to his lips in an ecstatic kiss. Mary Tudor, it was true, was now nearly forty, but that hardly mattered; Philip had decreed that, not only at their wedding feast, but in their moment of marital consummation, she would wear the Holy Earrings. The wearer of such miraculous jewels could hardly remain barren. There would be a miracle and assuredly the Queen would bear Philip a son—a son who would one day bring England back to the Faith; a daughter was unthinkable.

On July 11, 1554, *The Holy Ghost* slipped slowly out of La Coruña harbor, the sound of the *Veni Creator* being carried across the water from ship to shore and shore to ship. On the sixth day they sighted Ushant and three days later passed the Needles. The King had not been sick—a good omen. God was with them. As the galleon moved gently up Southampton Water against the wind, these Mediterranean people, who had never seen a tide, cried out that there had been a miracle, a belief that lingered long in remote Spanish valleys.

As *The Holy Ghost* dropped anchor, the carved and gilded barge of England was rowed out to meet her. The oars flashed in the sun but already there were dark rain clouds over Hampshire. Beneath the silken canopy there sat, very stiffly, Arundel, Derby and Shrewsbury, also Renard, the Imperial Ambassador of Spain. The oarsmen and the lackeys wore the green and white of the Tudor livery. In the scarlet of the Hapsburgs, the Spanish lined the taffrail. They looked down upon these English —such strange creatures—with a little curiosity and much contempt. The Spaniards had been wondering for weeks what could have possessed His Catholic Majesty that he should have come to this outlandish island. The Spanish contempt was the greater because their curiosity was to remain unsatisfied. A Tudor Parliament had forbidden them to land. The King was to be allowed four hundred unarmed servants and—since nobody really wanted him poisoned—his own cook, his priest and nobility. Everyone else, week after week, must remain on board *The Holy Ghost.* This royal visit must on no account become a Spanish bridgehead.

The gray walls of Southampton looked out upon a scene of maritime activity such as they would never see again. The great galleon, its banners flying, dominated all. In serried ranks the Lord Howard's fleet showed line upon line of flags, one ship behind the other, until over The Solent they faded into the mist.

The Holy Ghost lay isolated in her glory; around her on the waters, like buzzing flies around a lion, innumerable barges, wherries and rafts were carrying the baggage and bullion to quays and beaches where, beneath the flash of naked swords, they passed from Spanish hands to English.

The story of jealousy and hate had begun, but in the gilded Tudor barge, as it returned from the galleon, all was smiles. It was on the barge that Arundel invested Philip with the Garter. His banner would not hang in the Chapel at Windsor until he went there in the autumn, but it was on the barge that Philip placed his foot upon a golden faldstool that he might land on English soil a Knight of the Garter. A smile was frozen upon every face, and as these gentlemen stepped ashore there were even more smiles—smiles from all the Catholic peerage of England and Ireland.

The quay had become, quite suddenly, like a great parterre in the month of June. The English tailors and their French broiderers had excelled themselves. Of the English lords, Pembroke had ridden down from Wilton with a troop of gentlemen, some in black velvet and some in crimson, while Montague had jingled over from Beaulieu that morning, with a large retinue, to offer himself as the King's English equerry, and when Philip mounted, kissed his golden stirrup.

They all knelt on the cobbles to pray, using their gauntlets as little mats, while the Hieronymite monk sprinkled them with Holy Water. And then, with their feathered hats at their sides, they stood awkwardly in a great circle. Beyond the circle the grooms held the horses. Philip, for all his pietistic cruelty, had much worldly wisdom. Toward the English he displayed his charms—great charms—but to his own nobility he was more circumspect. With the excuse that poniards or poison might be hidden in their baggage he had been given a long list of every single thing that they had brought with them to England. Only Alba, the greatest of them all, was to be left alone by the spies and the guards. There was a good reason. Already, on the barge, an English officer had noticed that Alba clutched something beneath his saffron cloak. Thereafter he was watched. It was unnecessary. It was only the ivory casket that he carried for his sovereign. Those Holy Earrings, those fragments of Our Blessed Lady's robe, could after all scarcely be entrusted to porters or soldiers. They were, very nearly, a sacrament.

But, apart from that, as Alba and Feria and Medina, Celi-Pescara, Egmont and Hoorn, and even Ruy Gómez, Philip's special friend, stood behind their King, he knew to a button, to the last pearl, what each was wearing—silver breastplate, jeweled aiguillettes, cloth of gold embroidered and powdered with devices, white satin slashed with emeralds or trimmed with miniver, garters of pearls . . . and all the rest.

Philip knew that these men were tall—chosen for their height like so many guardsmen—and that he himself, although neat, was short. Without a single jewel, therefore, he had clothed himself from head to foot in black. It was a stroke of genius, in more ways than one. Nobody except Pétya, the valet, need know that beneath that tight doublet and trunks and elegant codpiece there was a fine coat of mail. The folds of that black suit gave perfect concealment; they also made every man on the quayside—Spanish grandees and English lords—look bizarre and even tawdry. For Philip, however, the black was a foil both to his honey-colored skin and to that fair beard which hid the Hapsburg jaw. He knew too that while these other men's beards would be heavily perfumed, such crudities were not for him. He had, of course, kissed Arundel and Shrewsbury very warmly upon both cheeks, but from now on he would kiss only the Queen, and for her a perfumed beard was unnecessary; he would make sure his breath was sweet.

The Queen was now lodged in the Bishop's Palace at Winchester. She, pathetic creature, had long been passionately in love with Titian's portrait of Philip, praying before it hour after hour as if it were some icon, her eyes within inches of it, so short was her sight; praying always that this man might give her a son. Every day, too, on board the galleon, Philip had prayed before the Queen's portrait, prayed that she might not have changed too much since Holbein had painted her twenty years ago, prayed that her mother's Spanish blood might give her a little beauty.

For months this man and woman had wondered about each other, and now at last between them there lay nothing but the gentle water meadows of the Itchen and the great tower of Romsey. It would have been unseemly for Philip to rush to his bride. For five days he lived in state at Southampton, the road to Winchester, meanwhile, being filled with wagons carrying baggage and gifts. During those five days the English summer had broken. On the fifth day Philip saw something to which he was not accustomed—a very green landscape beneath a very heavy rain. The Spaniards were taken by surprise . . . but the show had to go on.

The huge cavalcade, three thousand horsemen and scores of coaches, set out from Southampton on a dark, wet afternoon. The Spanish cloaks of velvet or satin, even Philip's improvised cloak of felt, became soaked and saturated within an hour. The English, under their oily sheepskins, laughed and enjoyed themselves greatly. The whole sodden crowd stopped at the Hospital of St. Cross, just outside Winchester, where Philip at last managed to change his clothes. He entered the city upon a white horse, his black suit now abandoned for a rich cream coat embroidered with gold, and with a heron feather in his hat.

The Deanery had been furbished and furnished for him, but after once again changing his clothes, and the rain having abated a little, he crossed the lawns to the Bishop's Palace. At the door of the Long Gallery Philip was seized with panic and with nausea. Excitement and pleasure, it was true, had transformed Mary's sour face; torchlight had also perhaps disguised her age. But, as Philip whispered to Ruy Gómez, "Is she not very red and white?" The nose was broad and, in spite of the dropsy which was to start so many rumors of pregnancy, she was very thin. She had but few teeth, bad sight and a perpetual headache. As she came forward to embrace him it was with difficulty that he managed to kiss her on the lips in the English fashion.

And then, an endless business—many courtiers on both sides had to be presented, also Gardiner, Bishop of Winchester, and those other bishops who would aid him in the marriage ceremony. All this meant a plethora of ring kissing and benedictions, so that it was almost midnight before the King of Spain and the Queen of England could talk together by candlelight. They talked long rather than easily, she understanding his Spanish, he understanding her French—with a little Latin and Italian to help them out. She sang him a madrigal in Gaelic and he read her a sonnet from Petrarch. It was all marvelously false but, for all the disease and the dirt, the cruelty and the credulity of those days, these two had had a Renaissance education—and that at least was something.

After exhausting the language of endearment, they spoke of what was most in their minds—the fruit of their marriage. And so, after she had shown him her wedding ring—a plain hoop of gold "because maidens were so married in old times"—he told her of the diamond earrings. In the cathedral tomorrow, at the right moment, Alba would produce them and they would be laid upon the altar. He told her how the diamonds had been brought from the New World, and of how those fragments of the Virgin's robe had been brought to Madrid from a lonely monastery on Athos, and of how they would, for certitude, bring about her conception of a male child. Her eyes brimmed over with tears of joy. Not for one moment did she doubt the certainty of the miracle. Clearly, it was all a great dispensation from God whereby she might become an instrument for the redemption of her father's sins. She would not be barren. Not only was Philip here in Winchester but, by this single act, he had answered all her prayers. He would be the father of her son —which, as all Europe knew, was what he had come for.

"Ah, *mon cher Philippe,* our son is now assured. My belly will be forward by Michaelmas, my travail will be in Lent, our son will be born at Eastertide, and the people will rejoice at Maypole time. It is certain. The ways of God himself are often very strange, but God's Mother at least will not desert us. . . . Oh, Blessed Virgin, Mother of the Lord Jesus, through the mediation of these most Holy Jewels and relics, grant us also a son."

He murmured the prayer after her and then they crossed themselves again and again.

"Oh, she will, Philippe, she will! Just think, a Catholic king for England and for half Christendom."

Philip's mouth hardened a little at this rush into *Realpolitik*. Half Christendom indeed! However, there was no point in discussing it now. First there must be a son. So he hurried on to tell her of his plans. He told her how he had arranged for the betrothal gift of the Holy Earrings to be entwined, as it were, into the ritual of the marriage sacrament. This might be unusual, but there was precedent for these things, especially among the Byzantine emperors. She would see when the time came, and with joy, exactly what he had planned. The earrings would be upon a golden salver so that Alba could give them to the Bishop; he, in his turn, would place them upon the altar to be blessed with the Bread and the Wine. Then, at the last moment, the Lady Margaret Clifford would fix them in the Queen's ears. After all, these glorious diamond stars were adornments of the flesh only in a very secondary way; primarily they were precious relics—a sacramental thing. Mary would wear them at the wedding feast but also through her first wedding night. That was necessary to secure a miracle, a son.

"Ah, yes, Philippe, that will be wonderful"—she was ready to agree to almost anything—"and after that we will lay them upon the altar of St. George's."

"St. George's—why St. George's?"

"The Holy Chapel of St. George at Windsor. You are now a Knight of the Garter, my lord, and it is now *your* chapel. When we go there together as Knights of that Holy Order, we will place your banner and your crested helm over your stall, and then to the sound of a great *Te Deum* we will lay the Holy Earrings upon the altar . . . in a golden reliquary."

"But you will wear them, Marie—at least sometimes. . . ."

"Tomorrow, Your Grace, and of course tomorrow night in our marriage bed . . . I will wear them then. I will wear them to conceive a son since I, too, am to be blessed among women. But after that, surely, the whole world must be allowed to kneel before them, to worship these holy and miraculous diamonds. Perhaps they will work miracles for other poor and barren women."

Philip's mouth had hardened for a second time. This pietistic emotion was all very well, but now his eyes were steely. His plans were being thwarted and that was a very novel experience. Half-a-million ducats' worth of diamonds locked up in an English chapel. Why, with a miracle to their credit, they might be worth twice that in the European market. He was deeply pious, but he saw no sense in the Queen's plan. She saw his displeasure; she tried to explain.

"You see, my lord, St. George's has more marvelous relics than any church in England. Even Westminster and Canterbury have not so many. It is like your church of St. James at Santiago da Compostella. The pilgrims come from all the world. Yes, St. George's is like that. Oh, Philippe, cannot you see how fitting it would be? Once our son has been born, a son born to redeem the world from heresy, then those Holy Earrings must surely be placed in some glorious reliquary to stand forever on the altar at Windsor . . . surely, Philippe, surely?"

The King of Spain remained silent. This was not the time to argue. He must talk to Renard, his excellent ambassador. He turned, therefore, from the subject of earrings to the far more painful business of making love. He gritted his teeth. It was too late to turn back: he was fully committed. It was weeks now since Mary Tudor, as was usual among the far-flung courts of Europe, had been married by proxy. She and Renard had together partaken of the Sacrament; they had placed rings on each other's fingers; they had been ceremonially unrobed in each other's presence, and then together chastely bedded—all in Philip's name. Indubitably, in God's sight, he was already married to this woman. So, very dutifully, he forced himself into making gestures of love—an art in which he was not without experience. A single candelabra was now burning. The log fire, on this summer evening, showed only a spark; the only sound was that of torrential rain beyond the thick walls. Very gently but awkwardly, because unwillingly, he took her in his arms.

The sun had risen into a stormy sky but for the moment it could still send a few shafts of light across the Hampshire hills—long shadows across wet grass. Philip had dressed early and now, with some kind of cloak over his white wedding suit, was pacing the terrace of the Deanery, his ambassador beside him.

"I am quite sure, Renard, that this miracle will happen. The Blessed Virgin, after all, could hardly desert the King of Spain—her own Catholic Majesty."

"Certainly not, Your Grace"—and Renard crossed himself—"but I can see that Your Grace is unhappy."

"Yes. The miracle will work, Renard. There is no doubt of that. Those little fragments of the Virgin's robe are vouched for by the most learned doctors of the Church, both in Byzantium and in Rome. They are an absolute assurance, especially just now, when the moon is waning, that the Queen's Majesty will not be barren."

"Then what troubles Your Grace?"

"The diamonds, Renard, the diamonds! We went too far. Any decent gold snuff box would have done for the fragments of robe . . . but half-a-million ducats of diamonds! Oh, Renard, what waste, what waste!"

"But, Your Grace, I do not understand. The diamonds are still there. . . ."

"No, Renard. They are lost to us—lost to Spain. Once the Queen is pregnant, once the diamonds have turned the trick, she will place them upon the altar of St. George's at Windsor

—and forever, as a holy relic. We shall never see them again. What terrible waste!"

"But, Your Grace, it need never happen. The diamonds can be made to vanish. . . . She would never dare to tell you."

"Vanish—but how?"

"You know quite well, sir, that we have our ways and means. You know that this realm is riddled with our friends, our spies and our agents."

"Naturally, but this is the one case, Renard, where spies and agents are useless. You must know that the Queen, although ugly, is passionate. She is in love with me, but even more is she in love with her unborn son. That means that she is also very much in love with the Holy Earrings, her assurance of a miraculous pregnancy. She will dote upon them day and night."

"Listen to me, sire. The whole Court will move to Richmond in time for Advent. By then the Queen should be with child and the Holy Earrings no longer needed."

"But how will you know, Renard, that she is pregnant? It may not be obvious so soon . . . with these new farthingales."

"I am not so naïve as Your Majesty seems to think. I imagine that the Queen will proclaim her pregnancy from the housetops. All the church bells in England will be rung—and possibly those in Spain too. But in any case, as Your Grace must know, I have only to lift my little finger to get daily reports upon every movement of the Queen's bowels, upon every sneeze. The Queen will be pregnant well before Advent and the Court as always will move to Richmond. When the English Court travels, Your Grace, the noise and the confusion are indescribable—a score of wagons piled high with bundles, two or three hundred horsemen in the courtyard and as many squabbling women in the Queen's apartments. For the diamonds to vanish at such a moment will be the easiest thing in the world."

"But how, Renard, how? She will never let them out of her sight."

"She will, my lord, she will. Even the Queen of England sometimes sleeps and goes to her stool. . . . That will be enough."

"But again I ask how."

"The Lady Margaret Clifford, Your Grace, is reliable, and is also very close to Her Majesty. She will be the first of the Queen's attendants at the wedding this morning. . . ."

"I know that, Renard, but she is a very devout Catholic. Not only would she be loyal to her mistress but she would never, never defile the Holy Earrings. She would fear a curse."

"When will Your Grace learn that all the people here, in their own obtuse minds, are what you and I would call Catholics. The Princess Elizabeth herself, now gaoled at Woodstock, meticulously observes every feast and fast of the Church, and makes her confession. They are all Catholics . . . but, terrible as it may seem, they are English first and Catholics second."

"That, my dear Renard, is why the whole nation is in heresy; that is why we are here—to rescue them."

"They are not in heresy according to an Englishman, only in schism. The only issue—a very big 'only' I admit, my lord—is their allegiance to His Holiness. They actually call him a 'foreigner' as they call you a 'foreigner.' "

"Indeed!"

"Oh, dear me, yes. They even talk of 'reforming' *their* Church, if you please. Their stupidity is abysmal—even the flames of Smithfield cannot cure it—but it is, one must try to believe, stupidity rather than wickedness. It is all very terrible but I suppose that God may forgive them on the Last Day."

"I trust not. But what of it? You were speaking of the Lady Clifford and of the diamonds—*my* diamonds, Renard."

"The Lady Clifford, Your Grace, may be, as you say, a good Catholic, but for that very reason she is not beyond our powers. She is already our agent in small matters, and may be corrupted further."

"How so?"

"Doubly so. First, she nurses a resentment against the Queen. In childhood she had an illicit and lesbian passion for the Lady Jane Grey. She was at a window looking onto Tower Green when the Lady Jane was led out to die, and, well . . ."—Renard gave a significant shrug—"well, she remembers the day. That would be enough but there is something else. . . ."

"Yes, you said you had a double hold over her."

"Yes, indeed. We know, my lord, what the Queen does not know, that the Lady Clifford has a deformed toe on her left foot."

"My dear Renard . . . really!"

"It pleases Your Grace to laugh, but it is a curious fact that these English heretics are far more credulous than we Catholics. Naturally we are more sophisticated, more capable of using our reason, but sometimes I think these people have more faith."

"Perhaps you have been too long in England, Renard."

"Not at all, Your Grace. It is simply that the Lady Clifford has this deformed toe; indubitably, therefore, she is a witch—yes, a witch, my lord. Not only can we hold the terror of fire over her but, quite frankly, I would not like to be there if she were handed over to the London mob."

"You exaggerate, Renard."

"No, Your Grace. You may remember that the Lady Anne Boleyn had a sixth finger on her left hand. His late Majesty King Henry could, it is true, have had her burnt alive for incest, but, incest being the national vice, the sympathy of the common people would have been with the lady rather than the King. Once, however, it was known that she was a witch, the King was able to appear merciful by using the axe—or, strictly speaking, the sword—rather than the stake. He thus endeared himself to his subjects as being tender-hearted. Your new bride, Your Majesty, will recall the episode; she will not forget that her stepmother was a witch."

"The Princess Elizabeth, then, is not only a bastard but was born of a witch."

"Precisely so, Your Grace—something to note for future use."

"Maybe, but let us get on. What do you propose in this affair of my diamonds, Renard?"

"Only, sire, that the Lady Clifford will do whatever we want.

I suggest that when the Court moves to Richmond, the Lady Clifford, choosing her moment—when the Queen is at her stool—will simply put the Holy Earrings in a cloth and drop them out the window—in the dark. I shall have an agent stationed there all through the night. Two minutes later she will make sure that the Queen actually sees her packing the ivory casket, now empty, of course. And then, my lord, when the earrings do not arrive at Richmond, it will be a certain Mary Finch—Keeper of the Queen's Jewels but otherwise a hunchbacked wench of no importance—who will be blamed and doubtless whipped, or even manacled. . . . That is neither here nor there.

"And after that, Renard. What then?"

"My agent will pass the earrings to the first link in a chain of loyal Catholics—real Catholics—until eventually they reach my house in the Strand, where, I need hardly say, Your Grace, they will be as safe as if they were in the Treasury at the Escorial."

"Have it your own way, Renard . . . as long as they never get into St. George's at Windsor to work miracles for barren peasant women—that is all that matters."

"Then Your Grace is satisfied with my efforts?"

The King did no more than shrug his shoulders. He looked up at the windows of the old Deanery. Someone had opened a casement, emptied a chamber pot and put out a mattress to rid it of lice. The King drew his cloak about his shoulders.

"Come, Renard, the world is awake. Let us brave this horrible rain. It is my wedding day—my second. Oh, Renard, Renard . . . never be a king!"

Renard had no desire to be a king, but he wondered—he had often wondered—whether it was even worthwhile being an ambassador. There were, of course, the glories of office and the joys of delicious intrigue. Most precious of all was to be at the springs of power, to be the recipient of royal but whispered confidences. He adored his office and all its trappings, and yet so often, so very often, he had measured the rewards against the burdens and found them paltry. One got blamed when one was blameless, and always, always, there was the chance of the dagger in the back, of the poison in the cup.

Above all, while Philip's governesses and tutors might have taught him many languages and much music, they had never told him the meaning of gratitude. Philip was not, Renard felt, a master whom one could like. First in Paris, and now in London, Renard had had to console himself with large bribes and beautiful women. True, there were also the shadier transactions which could not be revealed even under the seal of the confessional—but fortunately God was merciful and would understand. Renard was loyal to the Church, to Spain and to his office; it was only Philip whom he positively disliked.

So, as Philip gave that shrug of indifference and of ingratitude, Renard suddenly glimpsed something bigger—bigger for himself. He had served his master well and owed him nothing. He owed Mary Tudor even less. Had not Renard negotiated this match, this day's wedding, in order to lead a whole nation out of heresy, into the bosom of the Church and into the power of Spain? He had scarcely been thanked. Half-a-million ducats' worth of diamonds would really be a very small reward for his work. Surely he deserved something. Those diamonds, when on their way from the English Court to his house in the Strand, could so very, very easily get lost, could they not? Again and again he thrust the thought from him. But again, later in the day, as he knelt in the cathedral, with the organ reverberating round the vault and the boys' voices rising to Heaven, the thought came back to him with renewed vigor. That night he told his confessor of the temptation racking his soul. Hardly had he been absolved than the thought was again burning within him. He deserved something, and God, surely, would not grudge him this one thing. He had served God as well as Philip. When the Holy Earrings had done their work, when Mary Tudor had miraculously conceived a son, then neither she nor Philip could have any further use for them. Their palaces were stuffed with such things.

Only little Mary Finch—the hunchbacked Keeper of the

Queen's Jewels—was likely to suffer; she could be recompensed and was, in any case, of no account. Again and again Renard told himself that on one of his great estates, far away in the hills above Cordoba, he would build himself a wonderful house. He had always wanted it—a fairy château such as the King of France had been building by the Loire. It would be a dream come true. The diamonds would easily pay for it, and when it was finished it would be among the wonders of the world. God would approve this thing. He had served God well, and when the diamonds had been sold one by one in the Netherlands, those fragments of the Virgin's robe would be kept very secretly upon the altar of his own chapel. God could not mind that. Yes, Renard deserved this thing and, above all, it would be so very easy.

While Renard and his king were in the Deanery garden a horseman, forty miles away, was galloping over the bridge at Abingdon. He was almost at the end of his night's ride. Until long after midnight this man had been waiting in Winchester, waiting in the stables of The White Dog. At last, in the small hours, some lad had brought him a carefully-sewn packet. The man knew what to do. By three o'clock he was past Newbury, where at a certain house there were dry clothes and a fresh horse. And now, in the clear, rain-washed dawn, he could look across miles of cornland to where the towers and spires of Magdalen, Merton and St. Mary's were catching the first sunlight. Clattering over the Oxford cobbles, assailed by the morning smell of cesspools, he could again feel the rain on his face. And then he was out of the town, into the mire of wet lanes.

In the old manor of Woodstock the Princess Elizabeth was at her table in the window, as restless as she was sullen. Earlier that year, from Palm Sunday until the end of May—long enough—she had been lodged in the Tower. And sometimes still in the night she would wake and feel her little neck; then often she would light her candle, open the amethyst locket so that she might look upon the miniature of her mother—whose name must never be mentioned. But now she was "free"—free to have a few of her own servants, free to move between Woodstock and Hatfield and Ashridge, free to be a prisoner. At that moment—and she could set her clock by it—two mounted men were patrolling the lane beyond the orchards. She could see their wet capes and their shining lances.

The Princess Elizabeth was twenty-one. Two months ago, when she had been rowed from the Tower to Richmond, and then taken on by road to Woodstock, the people of England had beheld her strange beauty for the first time: the high cheekbones, the aquiline nose, the ice-blue eyes, the auburn hair—as well as the great dignity with which she bore herself. The journey had been a triumphant progress. From the sides of the roads, which were gay with spring flowers, the people had showered gifts upon her. Her face had glowed with the glory of it.

She knew that it was all terribly dangerous. When flames from green logs had consumed poor Bishop Hooper the people had wept. For Mary's prisoner, as she passed through the little towns, they had stood in the gutter and sung old songs. Elizabeth knew very well that her own head was not secure upon her shoulders but thought it more likely that they would marry her off to some lecherous old prince in Savoy or Hungary; she would sooner die. All she asked was the fulfillment of her destiny—to govern. Very faintly, across the fields, she could now hear the bells of Woodstock. She knew that those bells, as those of every village in her sister's realm, were echoing the peals of Winchester.

It was Edward Courtenay, last sprig of the White Rose, who came first into the room. He laid a small sewn packet upon the table.

"May it please Your Highness—from Winchester. It has just come into the house under the baker's loaves."

Elizabeth cut the stitches and spread out the sheets with their crabbed Tudor handwriting.

"From the Lady Clifford . . . Is she reliable, Edward?"

"She is a double agent, Your Highness, of a curious kind. We have a check on her through the Spanish King's Russian valet, a man called Pétya, also our spy. But the Lady Clifford is very cautious; she serves both you and Spain."

"How so?"

"It seems strange but it is true, and as long as one knows it, then all is well. Her whole hatred is reserved for the Queen—she much loved the Lady Jane Grey. To the Queen she dissembles with skill, but she is to be trusted."

"All the same the silly woman has been wasting her time, while risking our messenger's life. This is hardly worth reading; it tells us only what we might have known."

The Princess read the sheets one by one and passed them to Courtenay, remarking upon them as she did so.

"Well, Edward, it would seem that Philip has arrived. . . . Of course: those bells would hardly be ringing had he been drowned at sea. He was not sick—more's the pity. He claimed a miracle as his ship sailed up The Solent—does His Grace think God is a Spaniard? And here the Lady Clifford tells us what we might have guessed, that Philip brought with him a vast retinue, but that no soldiers were allowed to land. . . ."

"That confirms what Your Highness knew, that Parliament is not too papistical."

"From the moment the King stepped ashore at Southampton it was smiles, smiles all the way, kisses and embraces for Arundel and Montague, and then the Garter. Well, well, what does this Lady Clifford expect? After all, the man is a Christian sovereign. Ah, ah! He was wearing mail under his shirt. Good, good! And between Southampton and Winchester he got soaked. God must be an Englishman after all, Edward!"

"The Lady Clifford, madam, may have a trivial mind, but obviously she learns much from Pétya, the King's valet. She misses nothing and she passes it on; on the whole she serves you well."

"True, and this must have been written very late last night.

Listen, Edward: Philip and my sister were together until after midnight; he unlaced her bodice and fondled her, fondled her breasts . . . old and withered, my lord, old and withered . . . or very soon will be."

"One would have thought, madam, that he could have waited until tonight, but in any case she can hardly bear him a child now. She is old beyond her years as well as dropsical."

"If the babe does not leap in her belly by Advent, my lord, then this poor prisoner at Woodstock will be in peril of her life. I shall begin to matter, Edward, I shall begin to matter."

"If the Queen were barren beyond all doubt, and Your Highness were to become the heir apparent instead of merely the heir presumptive, then frankly, Your Highness, I would not give a fig for your safety."

"We will make plans for that, Edward, sure enough. But here, look, on the last sheet, is a different handwriting. A note from the crippled Finch, the girl who keeps the jewels. Is she too our spy then?"

"Assuredly, madam. Finch has a sweet nature but she is despised and ridiculed for her humped back, and may have become bitter. Also, she is of Puritan stock and cannot abide the Mass—that is enough."

'Well, listen to this. Philip has given the Queen's Majesty some diamond earrings—Finch calls them 'the Holy Earrings' —and they are to be used at the wedding this morning."

"Indeed, and what of it, madam? A pair of earrings is neither here nor there."

"Maybe, but listen! These 'Holy Earrings,' it seems, are not only priceless diamonds—that is nothing—but each contains a tiny fragment of the Blessed Virgin's robe, the robe of Bethlehem. What do you say to that, my lord?"

As Edward Courtenay paced the room he looked grave. His whole tone had changed. He was frightened.

"I do not like it at all, Your Highness. I gather, from what Finch tells you, these are not just earrings. They are very holy relics. The King of Spain, madam, has been very clever. I do not for one moment doubt the authenticity of these relics. The Spanish pilgrim routes are marvelously organized and policed, and that, no doubt, was how the sacred fragments came to Madrid. But, in addition to that, the astrologers of Valladolid are the best in the world. Philip and Mary will know each other's nakedness this night. The moon is waning, while Venus, Saturn and Mars are all in the ascendant. The timing is perfect. These Holy Earrings—and who can doubt but that the Queen will wear them in the hour that the marriage is consummated—will give her the babe she wants. I do not like it, madam. A miracle would seem to be almost inescapable. We must expect the worst: a Catholic prince before Eastertide. Mary may yet be blessed among women!"

Elizabeth would one day be famous for many things, not least her outbursts of rage. As yet, however, this trait was hardly known. The Lord Courtenay, therefore, was more than startled to see, first, the color drain from her cheeks, and then the papers and ink swept onto the floor. She spat three times. She tore in two the necklace she was wearing, scattering the pearls over the parquet. Only the old nurse, eavesdropping in the next room, lacked surprise. She shrugged a shoulder. She had known for years that these tantrums were not just childish rages—that they were purely Tudor.

In the end the storm subsided. The Princess turned upon Courtenay, white and trembling.

"How far back to Winchester?"

"Sixty miles, more or less, madam."

"The time?"

"Nearly noon."

"Can the horseman still be found?"

"At The Bear, madam."

"And this Pétya, the King's Russian valet, the Lady Clifford and the crippled Finch—they are all in our pockets? They will practice for us?"

Courtenay bowed assent.

"And Renard. Is Renard corruptible?"

"All Spaniards are corruptible, Your Highness, at a price."

"Then it is all quite simple, Edward. The horseman goes back to Winchester, and with plenty of money. You will draft our instructions and he will see to it that they reach the Lady Clifford. But you must hurry."

"I fail to understand Your Highness."

"Then you are a fool, Edward. There is only one thing that matters, man. The Queen must not wear those Holy Earrings this night and with this moon. She must be barren, Edward, barren—at all costs."

"That is clear enough, madam, but it will not be easy now. It is already the eleventh hour."

"Nothing which matters is easy. But somehow, between this day's wedding and this night's bedding, the Holy Earrings must vanish. Presumably there will be a banquet. Presumably the Queen will unrobe more than once before nightfall. A few moments will be enough—while she goes to her stool. The earrings can be dropped from the window."

Courtenay was silent.

"Can they not, Edward, can they not?"

"Winchester will be transformed into hell, Your Highness, when it is discovered. That is neither here nor there. But, may I ask, what would Your Highness do with these diamonds if you had them?"

"You are an idiot, Edward. Do you think I care what happens to them? Are not my own coffers stuffed with jewels and would I not give them all to be a queen with a son—a Tudor boy. All that matters is that Mary should be denied this miracle."

"I did not think that Your Highness wanted the diamonds for their value—that would be vulgar. I only wondered . . ."

"No, Edward, nor would I be such a fool as to put them on the altar at Windsor to work fertility miracles for other women. Might I not need them myself one day, and for that very purpose? No, you had not thought of that, had you? Meanwhile they shall be hidden away until they can be placed forever among the Crown Jewels of my Realm. And now, my good lord, you know what to do. For Jesus's sake, hurry!"

At last the bells of Winchester were dumb. William of Wykeham's great nave was empty and silent. The whole space of the stone-flagged floor was swept and deserted. Painted effigies and chantries of dead bishops echoed the richness of the roof. But for all the color and the carving it was the austerity that was overwhelming. The place was dark and empty. Then came the gleam of a distant taper. Two cowled monks were lighting candles before every shrine. Far away in Choir and Transept and Lady Chapel these little candles were almost lost in the gloom until, one by one, like stars at dusk, their number grew. Then, finally, came the tremendous blaze of light around the high altar. The cathedral was ready.

And now, every few minutes, the big western door creaked on its hinges. A few men would come in and close the heavy door behind them. First came English soldiers with drawn swords and daggers, stationing themselves at the foot of every pier. They were joined by a hundred torchbearers, the light from the torches making strange patterns upon the stone vault above their heads.

After that, in tens and scores, came men and women. Some flung down their cloaks to make a sodden pile just inside the door, while others spread them upon the paving to form kneeling places. If the candles, one by one, had been like the beginning of a starlit night, so the cathedral floor was now like a garden in April—it was, almost suddenly, crammed with flowers. As the grandees and the nobles arrived, their women knelt on the floor and crossed themselves; the men stood proudly, almost every one of them with a pole bearing a stiffened banner. Like armies arrayed, the English took up positions on one side of the nave, the Spaniards on the other, until the whole flickering torchlit nave was full of people and of heraldry, the people existing more as symbols of the living heraldry than the heraldry as symbols of men.

Peering down from the dark triforium gallery white faces now and again became visible. It was to this gallery that the small fry had been relegated: servants, secretaries, barbers and the like. Little Mary Finch, for instance, had been made to climb the winding newel, not because her rank was low (on the contrary she was the bastard of a Brandon), but because she was unsightly. And Ivan Pétya—ostensibly a nobody—had spent the last hour in that gallery, elbowing himself into a strategic position just above the Crossing; from there he could look down upon all the ritual and the ceremony.

It was immediately below Pétya that the two canopied thrones had been built. By midday Philip, with Alba at his side, was there with a mantle of cloth of gold, thrown back to show his collar of the Garter. As the bells stopped and the first *Te Deum* seemed to fill the vault, the Queen's procession moved down the cathedral. When William of Wykeham built this place he could not, even in his wildest dreams, have conceived of this moment. Mary Tudor wore white satin encrusted with jewels. She wore scarlet shoes. She wore a golden veil. The maids of honor and courtiers were innumerable. What was more unusual was the accompanying circus: prancing dwarfs, unkempt hermits, infant boys swinging censers until the incense hung in the air like the black clouds outside . . . and then the long line of priests, abbots, friars and nuns, so that the last in the line had to remain outside in the rain still chanting. Even at the height of the Middle Ages such a procession would have caused comment. It was excessive.

Gardiner held out his illuminated book. Alba placed upon it the ring, the plain hoop of gold. Philip, as was the custom, placed upon it a little pile of money. Then Alba, with a flourish, added the Holy Earrings. The Lady Clifford quickly and deftly fixed them to the Queen's ears. First a gasp and then a most curious shudder ran through the cathedral. What was this? What was going on? These diamonds had picked up the light from all the torches and candles so that even those at the back of the crowd had seen a prismatic flash of rainbow colors pass across the walls and across the choirboys' faces. In the night there had been many rumors about the miraculous nature of the earrings. There were some who now crossed themselves, a few who even prostrated themselves upon the pavement; most were merely curious.

Philip and Mary moved to the altar. Philip's heart was like ice. Mary was at the gates of paradise—the chosen of the Lord.

In the silence that follows upon the ringing of a sacramental bell any man may commune with himself in secret. High in the gallery Ivan Pétya, the valet, thought his thoughts in Russian; he licked his lips and his eyes bulged at the glint of the diamonds. Behind him, little Mary Finch wept silently because she had been sent up here with the common servants on account of her crooked back and crooked legs. As the ceremony dragged on, her bitterness turned to hatred and then to cunning. The Queen must never be allowed to bear a child; there must be no miracle of the Holy Earrings. She leant forward and found herself shoulder to shoulder with Pétya. Their hands touched.

The Lady Clifford, kneeling one pace to the rear of the Queen, presented to the world nothing except a tight-lipped impassivity, hoping only, as she too took the chalice, that her thoughts might be hidden from her Saviour. Renard, the Imperial Ambassador, kneeling in his canopied stall, kept his dark eyes rigidly to the front. He gazed between the dark heads of Spanish choristers to the English boys across the Chancel. He saw nothing. He was dreaming of a fairy castle on the hills above Cordoba—and, as always, calculating and calculating.

As Philip raised his head from the Sacrament no shred of his sensual and sexual body stirred toward the woman at his side. He allowed his shifty eyes to slide sideways toward his wife's profile, to her ears, but this served only to concentrate his mind upon the coffers, the iron chests and the great cupboards in the Treasury of the Escorial, where surely the Holy Earrings must ultimately rest. As for Mary, she was carried away into a golden paradise; in the music of the organ and the choir she could hear only the harps of angels; she spared a thought, nevertheless, for the jeweled reliquary within which she would place the Holy Earrings upon the altar at Windsor.

The last long *Amen* had ceased to echo around the stone vaults of Winchester. All of Spain and England, seeking their banquet, had drifted across the wet grass, like fallen petals in the breeze. In the cathedral porch there still remained two figures, talking and talking. In some chaotic mixture of French and Spanish and Church Latin, little Mary Finch, Keeper of the Queen's Jewels, and Ivan Pétya, the King's valet, made themselves very clear to each other, each pouring greed and bitterness, cunning and hate, into the other's soul.

In the crumbling manor of Woodstock the Princess Elizabeth stood by her window. Almost unseeing she watched the rain pouring down upon the garden and orchards. Every few minutes she would glance at her clock, timing the events in Winchester, but thinking always with that clever, determined and courageous mind, that avaricious, cruel and acute mind, thinking always her own thoughts, thoughts of her own destiny, and of the destiny of the Crown Jewels of England.

VICTORIAN EPISODE

1

The Bonnet Jubilee

A hot June day, one of the hottest of that broiling Jubilee summer of 1887. The press of traffic between Tower Hill and the Mansion House was tremendous. Wagons, drays, pantechnicons, omnibuses and cabs formed a solid block. The horses steamed. As the flies tormented them they shook their heads, jingling their harness. They struck sparks from the granite blocks with their great hooves. The sweating drivers and cabbies had long since passed from caustic cockney wit to resigned gloom. The tops of the hansoms bore their gay and tasseled linen covers, their summer clothing made by the cabbies' wives, while on the buses men had put up their umbrellas to ward off the blazing sun. The big bearded policeman at the corner of King William Street waved his white-gloved hand in vain. Nothing moved. This was a real traffic jam. The noise, the stink of dung and the heat were all terrible.

The little chocolate-colored brougham, picked out in scarlet, with the royal emblem on the panels and a Windsor gray between the shafts, was like an orchid in a cabbage patch. The coachman and the footman, buff-coated and with crepe bands on their arms, remained aloof above the hammercloth. To such remarks as "'Ow's the ole girl?" they merely turned up their noses or curled their lips. Inside the brougham, perspiring in his morning clothes, Sir Henry Ponsonby, Private Secretary to Her Majesty the Queen, pursed his mouth. His fine patent-leather boot, an inch of cloth top and pearl button showing below the striped trouser, tapped the floor in irritation. The City was no place for him, still less for Her Majesty's livery. He glanced uneasily at the plain white hat box on the opposite seat. He stopped pursing his mouth and closed it tightly in annoyance. He disliked these trips to the Jewel Tower. He disliked them very much. They were, thank God, few enough, not more than half a dozen since the death of the Prince Consort a quarter of a century ago. All the same there had been more than he liked. They were so melodramatic and unnerving, breaking the placid rhythm of family life and Palace routine. Besides, he reflected, while it was all very well to let the public see the Regalia itself, all those other jewels would be so much safer in the Strong Room at Windsor.

The glamour of his errand meant nothing to him. He had lived in high places too long. It was nothing to him that inside that plain hat box was yet another box: a casket of shagreen leather with golden clasps, three locks and a lining of cream velvet. It was nothing to him that embedded in that velvet was a galaxy of flashing stones—pearls, sapphires, emeralds and diamonds—stones that had come long ago from the treasure ships of the Spanish Main, to gleam around little white Tudor necks, on white bosoms, in shell-like ears, as gorgeous combs or to be sewn into wimples. It was nothing to him that, after three centuries, these stones had been brought together in one setting, that single tasteless piece of Victorian headgear known as the Tudor Tiara. It was nothing to him that in the Crystal Palace, all through the summer of 1851, the Tudor Tiara had been shown to the people, ostentatiously guarded by guardsmen—only in the end to be part of that priceless junk known as the Crown Jewels. He knew only that all this drama had made people think that the Tiara must be worth millions. In actual fact, Messrs. Garrard of Regent Street and Messrs. Ascher of Hatton Garden and Antwerp had fixed its value at about a million, but had admitted that if the Tiara were ever broken up the single stones might fetch quite surprising sums. Why the

Tudor Tiara should be worth less than the sum total of the individual gems was a most peculiar fact—surely the opposite should be true?—so peculiar indeed that it was the one thing that had interested Sir Henry's precise mind. It puzzled him. Messrs. Garrard had never explained it to him. They were oddly reluctant to talk about it—even to the Queen.

But, so far as Sir Henry was concerned, that was all. He was not a romantic man. He knew just enough about art to enjoy the Prince Consort's Italian Primitives, and to realize that the Tudor Tiara, like most things from the Crystal Palace, was grotesque. That was all; he knew nothing about gems and did not want to. His life was wholly taken up with his family, with politics, with the papierasserie of a great Court and with the mechanism of government. For him, therefore, this was not only a very hot day, it was a wasted day. He was also annoyed that such responsibility should have been thrust upon him. He had quite enough on his hands at the moment with the Jubilee only a few days ahead, and this sort of jaunt was not what he was paid for. It was all most unfair and also, in his view, dangerous.

Sir Henry Ponsonby leaned forward a little in the carriage, not enough to be seen but enough to see. He looked distastefully at the traffic. Two naked urchins were frolicking under the spray of a water cart. They were quite nude. Someone should tell a policeman—the boys should be birched. What a mercy there were no ladies in the City. Sir Henry wrinkled his nose at the smell of the cart horses alongside and then, peering a little further, reassured himself as to his guard. Yes, his outrider was there, at a discreet distance such as would prevent him from being spotted as a detective but still allow him to keep the brougham well within sight. Inspector Hughes, mounted on his own roan mare, was tastefully disguised in broad-checked trousers tightly strapped under his boots, a black hacking jacket and a buff bowler—but with a holster under the jacket.

Sir Henry Ponsonby let his mind run on, wondering indeed why he should be there at all. Last year, when the Queen had opened Parliament herself (and would she never let the Prince of Wales—dear Bertie—do anything?), she had worn the little Coburg diadem—discreet and appropriate. He had hoped, when returning the diadem, that that might be his last ride to the Tower. But, oh no! He had not foreseen what a fuss she would make over this damned Jubilee. A plain thanksgiving service would have been ample. One moment she insisted upon being the stricken widow and the next upon being the Queen-Empress—it made life very difficult. That the Constable of the Tower, old Field Marshal Lord Wilson, should have given him such an excellent luncheon was scarcely a compensation. True, before he finally signed the receipt for the contents of the hat box, he had savored a most excellent brandy. It had been a very good brandy indeed. Its warming, delightful and soporific effect upon Sir Henry had been almost instantaneous—and was still with him. He was tired, he was worried and he was sticky—but he was also sleepy.

It was only his annoyance that was keeping him awake. He was making this trip for the second time in a week: six times in twenty-five years and now twice in a week. It was intolerable, but then, as he so often reflected, the life of Queen Victoria's Private Secretary was likely to be both intolerable and thankless. Nevertheless, like most men of position, he loved it all; that is one way in which men differ from women. Sir Henry put his hand in his trouser pocket; he felt very lovingly the single key on its thin gold chain, that little gold key which opened the red dispatch boxes. All down Whitehall there were at that moment Ministers of the Crown and Permanent Secretaries all handling with affection their little gold keys—symbols of power, position and prestige. Sir Henry was a man without vanity, and yet he found the little golden key a great comfort. It was something other men hadn't got. It made an intolerable life more bearable —even glorious.

The second trip to the Tower in one week. Four days ago he had fetched the Kohinoor. That the Queen, for the service in the Abbey, should wear an ordinary bonnet with the Kohinoor simply mounted as a brooch was reasonable—the suggestion of that reasonable woman, the Princess Beatrice of Battenberg. True, bringing the Kohinoor to Windsor had been a nuisance, and getting it mounted, all in a week, had been a damned nuisance. Telegrams and messages had flown between Windsor and Regent Street. But the idea had been sound. But that the Queen should now, in a life of unending funereal gloom, suddenly decide to wear this atrocious Tiara not for the Jubilee itself but for a purely family dinner of a couple of hundred royals was really going to the other extreme. It was pretentious and self-indulgent. It was worse: it was out of character. The Abbey would have been different; and for that her children, one by one, had begged her to wear the Crown itself. They had been snubbed—was she not still in mourning? It was to be "the Bonnet Jubilee"—ladies in the Abbey to "wear bonnets and long dresses without mantles"—and yet, on the Jubilee eve, just for the family, there was to be this Tiara with its ghastly 1851 setting. It was perverse, stupid and unaccountable.

It was also one of those occasional throwbacks to Hanoverian vulgarity which Sir Henry loathed. True, the Hapsburg, the Greek, the Bourbon, Bonapartist and Romanov jewels would all be worn by somebody or other. The Waterloo Chamber would glitter with jewels. But the Queen knew, and had always known, that she could never compete with all that. That was one of the facts of history, one of the facts about little England in a great Europe, one of the facts about, say, the Czar's Byzantine inheritance, or France's Bourbon loot. It was a fact with which, until now, the Queen had dealt in her own way. Like Napoleon, who wore his corporal's coat when surrounded by the gaudy Marshals of France, so the Queen, with a shabby black dress and a scrap of lace, had always made everyone in the room look third rate. This dumpy little middle-class Frau, thought Sir Henry, was the only woman in the world who had ever made dowdiness smart. That was her trump card and, so far as he was concerned, she had better go on playing it. It saved such a lot of trouble. Moreover, there was just the possibility that with the Tudor Tiara on her head the Queen might be making herself ridiculous, and, to be fair to Sir Henry Ponsonby, he did not really want that.

And what was all this nonsense he had heard from dear Lady Ely? She had come twittering to him, whispering in his ear, her eyes shut with excitement: Jays were making the Queen a new black satin dress, trimmed with miniver and covered with gold thread; also, presumably there would be a jeweled corsage, the Garter sash, at least one German and one Russian order, the Saxe-Meiningen pearls, the old Nemours lace veil "borrowed" years ago from the Empress Eugénie and never returned, the inevitable Albert locket, a tartan bow somewhere or other; and now, literally surmounting all, this absurd and irrelevant Tudor Tiara at that moment lying in its casket and in its cardboard hat box on the other seat of the carriage.

Still the traffic did not move. Sir Henry Ponsonby, usually an equable man, snorted with annoyance, both at the traffic and at the Queen. Why, he said to himself, the woman will be positively overdressed. Could it possibly mean, after twenty-five long years of gloom, that she was using the Jubilee to mark the end of mourning? Impossible . . . but if it was, God knows what might happen. He began to wonder. He had already been twice dragooned into some ghastly amateur theatricals. And apart from the usual gillies' ball at Balmoral, when she had danced Scottish reels till two in the morning—a deathly secret south of the Border—only last Christmas at Osborne she had danced a quadrille with Prince Alfred—with "Affie." She could never, naturally, approve of the *valse*—that was for the "fashionables" at Marlborough House—but (it all came back to him now) there had been other signs of life in recent months. The De Reskes, Jenny Lind, Grossmith, Irving and Ellen Terry had all performed in the Waterloo Chamber, and had been presented afterward as though they were ladies and gentlemen. Windsor was becoming almost gay.

Sir Henry shuddered. It might mean changing his habits. Later hours, more parties, more visitors to the Castle, a more frequent use of Buckingham Palace. It would all mean more work. He even began to see the Tudor Tiara as a harbinger of change, and of change for the worse. Of course, what the Queen wore was her own business. The most he could do would be to have a word with the Princess, or perhaps dear Lady Ely would speak to the head dresser. Yes, the dresser, old Fräulein Skerret, would be the one. Queen Victoria, after all, had always preferred the advice of her servants—that long line of nurses, governesses, footmen, gillies, dressers, and now this sinister Indian servant, the Munshi—had always preferred their advice to that of her own children.

Sir Henry had begun to nod. He now gave a violent movement. Through his Jaeger combinations and his trousers his perspiring buttocks had stuck to the tooled Spanish leather of the carriage seat. He winced as he freed himself. The traffic had begun to crawl, but to the heat and the stink was now added the noise of a thousand iron-shod wheels on granite blocks. Sir Henry again closed his eyes and reflected upon his wasted day. There were masses of jewels at Windsor, and to insist upon a Crown Jewel for a dinner party was unfair to everyone—to the detectives, the police, the overworked footmen and, above all, to him. . . . Five miles across London, from Paddington to the Tower and back again, on the hottest day of the century, and then again next week to return the damned thing, plus the Kohinoor. It was altogether too bad.

When he took office General Gray had warned him about these idiotic trips, assuring him that they were outside a Private Secretary's duties—a matter solely for the Home Office. A Black Maria was clearly the proper vehicle for the purpose. Sir Henry had written to Sir Frederick Rogers, the Commissioner of Police; but he could hardly have chosen a worse moment. The Queen had been making it quite clear—recently and publicly—that Sir Frederick hadn't been fulfilling his duties to her utmost satisfaction. The Commissioner and the Home Secretary were piqued, they were hurt, and short of a direct command, disinclined to oblige the Palace. In George IV's time the Crown of England had been conveyed through London in a coach, with a puffing Beefeater walking on each side. The other day, when he fetched the Kohinoor, Sir Henry had been given an escort of Horse Guards. He disapproved of this since it served only to advertise his whereabouts. For the Tudor Tiara, therefore, he had suggested the decent anonymity of a hansom cab. This had been instantly vetoed as being "quite impossible . . . and must never be referred to again"—hence the Palace brougham and the Windsor gray.

So here he was in the blazing sun, both sleepy and bad-tempered, in the middle of King William Street, with a coachman, a footman, an outrider and a hat box. Sir Henry pulled the silken cord and the footman opened the trap in the carriage roof.

"Sir."

"Fulleylove, this traffic is quite intolerable. Tell Macdonald, as soon as he can, to turn down one of these lanes to Lower Thames Street and then along the Embankment. It is simply terrible here."

"Yes, sir, most unpleasing. But you remember, sir, that it's Paddington we want, not the Palace."

"Of course, of course. Do as you're told, man, it will save time in the end."

"Sir." Sir Henry Ponsonby would have been surprised to see the coachman and the footman exchange a wink; royal servants do not usually wink in public.

Really, they could have come along the river all the way from Tower Hill. It might be a little further, but with the traffic at Ludgate Circus and Charing Cross getting worse every day, it was a great saving. Sure enough in a few minutes (and thanks of course entirely to him) they were passing Printing House Square and the end of Blackfriars Bridge. He remembered as if it were yesterday the opening of the bridge by the Queen. It had been her first emergence from the seclusion of grief and he had had to arrange the whole thing as if it were a second funeral. The bridge was soon behind them and they were clip-clopping along the Embankment, outpacing cabs and trams all the way. There was not a horse in the Royal Mews, Sir Henry said, who could hold her head so well or lift her feet so high as little Primelbund. He had specially asked for her. Inspector Hughes cantered bravely in the rear.

With a tiny breeze off the river the carriage seemed cooler. Sir Henry looked wistfully at the sailing barges and was reminded pleasurably of Cowes, rather less pleasurably of those infuriating journeys to Osborne. Of course he knew—he and Mary Ponsonby both knew—that they were fortunate. Had they not got Osborne Cottage as their home, just as they had the Norman Tower at Windsor? It was only at Balmoral that he "lived in"—that cold attic with the iron bedstead—and was parted from his family. But of course, even from Osborne he often had to travel to town, perhaps two or three times a week, and once (during the Greek crisis) it had been seven times. This always made him feel more like a messenger than a Private Secretary, so that he was sometimes resentful. He felt taken for granted. The year's round, for instance, had to go on at all costs. The dates were fixed and were sacred. The Queen's doctors had been dragooned into saying that her nerves would stand no change of routine. She had been exploiting this edict for a quarter of a century, refusing ever to return from, say, Osborne or Balmoral one day sooner than had been planned. The convenience of emperors, kings, czars, shahs, ministers of the Crown—not to mention the families of private secretaries—was neither here nor there. It did not exist. Windsor, Biarritz, Osborne, Balmoral, Osborne again for Christmas, and so back to Windsor—nobody mattered. There were only the most fleeting visits to town—Buckingham Palace, fully staffed, was virtually uninhabited. Sandringham she never visited—symbol of a world that she disliked. Sir Henry had become an intermediary for an absentee sovereign. It was too ridiculous!

And now, in the carriage, he was tired and he was nervous. He was no longer alert and he knew it. That Tower of London brandy, combined with the heat, was having its effect. He kept closing his eyes and then jerking them open again. He knew that even within the security of the brougham he must watch that million-pound hat box. . . . The path of duty might be hard but it was clear.

At a spanking pace the carriage passed under the grim black arch of Waterloo Bridge. He recalled nostalgically how, only a few years ago, the rusticated bastions of Somerset House used to rise straight out of the mud and the tide—a magnificent sight. He glanced up at the Adelphi, that shabby haunt of artists, and found himself thinking of it as building land—a large hotel so near to the Strand would surely be a fine investment for some innkeeper. London was becoming so cosmopolitan: only last week he had seen two Japanese at the Royal Academy.

He must have dozed a little for quite suddenly he realized that they were in Parliament Square. He was back at last on his home ground—the world he knew, the familiar world of Westminster and St. James's, of clubs, embassies and even palaces. There was a flurry of saluting policemen. He had been recognized—how nice! All round him there was a great hammering: only two days now before the Jubilee. The masts were up everywhere, ready for the banners—the heraldic banners of other empires and of royal houses, banners bearing the emblems of colonies and far-flung possessions. It was only the stands that had to be finished—all heavy planks and huge balks of timber —hundreds of navvies sweating in the sun. Sir Henry, in his dry way, thrilled a little; his blood ran faster at the sight of the busy scene, and even more at the thought of Empire.

They bowled along Birdcage Walk, one or two men raising their hats to the livery. How brightly the lake glittered in the sun as one saw it through the rich tapestry of foliage, and how trim were the lawns; the Office of Works should be congratulated; Sir Henry would draft a letter for the Queen's approval.

Between the trees he could just see the flagstaff on Marlborough House; it was without its banner. The Prince of Wales must be out of town—already at Windsor. Sir Henry's mouth set a little grimly. The Prince would want to talk—to talk about those perennial problems, debts and Eddy. All the world knew about the debts, but for the great British public, dear, unspeakable Eddy, Duke of Clarence, second in line to the throne, was little more than a mild joke—"Collar and Cuffs." What a pity, mused Sir Henry for the thousandth time, that little Georgie—not clever but good—had not been the elder boy. Primogeniture was all very well but Nature played her tricks. . . .

At the corner of Buckingham Palace Road the coachman had a little trouble with Primelbund; she knew better than anyone the whereabouts of the Royal Mews and was thinking only of cool hay. The coachman had to use his whip to make her turn right in front of the Palace en route for Paddington. A few moments later, however, and the brougham, with Inspector Hughes alongside, had Constitution Hill to itself. What a pity, mused Sir Henry, if the Queen ever threw open this fine avenue to the public. She was being pressed to do so, at least when the Court was out of town—which was almost always.

The police had opened the gates of the Wellington Arch and were holding up the Knightsbridge traffic; how much more thoughtful were these Westminster police than those in the City, so much more sense of what was fitting. In no time at all the brougham was in Hyde Park. The grass was more parched here, surprisingly so for early June, and there were too many bits of paper and orange peel about. Perhaps congratulations to the Office of Works should be left until the crocuses were out next spring, and then Princess Beatrice might like to write in her own hand—always a good thing.

Beyond the Marble Arch, all up the Edgware Road and along Praed Street, Sir Henry was once more in an alien world, a proletarian world which he neither understood nor liked. All these rough and probably dirty people jostling each other on the pavement . . . they were animals from a different jungle. Sir Henry could think of them only in terms of whether or not they might be "loyal." It was all most distasteful. He sat well back so as to shut it out, only, once again, to succumb to drowsiness. When the brougham finally stopped alongside the departure platforms at Paddington, Sir Henry Ponsonby was sound asleep.

Had he been awake he might have noticed a number of things. Although the Queen's Secretary did not quite qualify for a red carpet or a handshake from a GWR Director, everything was strictly according to protocol. A space had been railed off where the carriage could pull up, and where the Station Master, in frock coat and topper, and a stout Inspector of Police with a waxed mustache had long been waiting. They were flanked by four rather more ordinary bobbies, while a few yards away, trying to look nonchalant, was a plain-clothes detective with Dundreary whiskers, a meerschaum pipe and a straw boater. There were only a couple of onlookers—a youth in a ginger suit with a pair of carpet bags, and a golden-haired girl. It was a quiet time at Paddington. There were no porters; it was the Inspector of Police who would carry the hat box to the train; porters do not carry Crown Jewels.

As the carriage stopped, the coachman leaped down on the off side in order, as the detective duly noted, to adjust Primelbund's bit, quite unnecessarily. The footman had already jumped from the box and, running alongside the carriage, had opened the door, awakening Sir Henry with a light touch on the knee. He now stood deferentially, his left hand on the embossed silver knob, his right hand at his side clutching his cockaded hat. Inspector Hughes, having obeyed his instructions—"to escort Sir Henry Ponsonby's carriage as inconspicuously as possible from the Residence of the Constable of the Tower of London to the Paddington Station"—gave a valedictory salute and walked his steaming mare up the slope in search of water for her and whisky for himself. Inside the carriage Sir Henry pulled himself together with a jerk, realized where he was and stepped out. He looked in blank amazement at the footman.

"What's this, what's this? I thought Fulleylove was on duty. I was most clearly told that it would be Fulleylove."

"I was ordered to replace him, sir. I regret to say, Sir 'Enery, that Mr. Fulleylove 'as been attacked by the mumps—most unfortunate, sir."

"Dear me, dear me. Mumps indeed! I trust this won't mean an epidemic in the stables, and just at Jubilee time. Really, this is too bad of Fulleylove . . . usually such a reliable man. Dear me! How very vexing!"

"As you say, sir."

"And your name, my man? I don't think I've seen you before."

"Smith, sir."

"You're new to the service then?"

"Yes, sir. I was with Lord Iddsleigh, sir—first as groom and then as footman, until 'Is Lordship's sudden death, sir . . . on the staircase at No. 10 . . . dyin' in the Prime Minister's arms, I understand, sir. So I decided to better myself, sir."

Good heavens, thought Sir Henry, how the lower orders did exaggerate—sensation at all cost. Poor Iddsleigh, he felt sure, had been carried into the Cabinet Room some minutes prior to death, and had actually died on a sofa. Anyway, it was certainly not the footman's business.

"Well, Smith, I trust you will give the Household good service. If you do, you will have no cause to regret it. . . . But the first rule, my man—remember—is no gossip, no tittle-tattle."

"Sir."

The Station Master had been showing signs of impatience. He coughed and stepped forward.

"Excuse me, Sir Henry, but I have been holding the Windsor train for you. It should have left twenty minutes ago."

"Dear me, Mr. Station Master! I had not observed the clock. The press of traffic in the City was terrible. We were much delayed, and now . . ."

"Quite, sir. And now, since I shall have to lock you into your compartment, and since you *have* been delayed, I am wondering whether you might not care for, er, a wash . . . if you will pardon my mentioning it, sir."

"Thank you, Mr. Station Master, thank you. Yes, indeed . . . most timely, most necessary . . . especially as one gets older."

"Not at all, sir. Come to my office—rather pleasanter than, er, the public urinals, if I may say so, sir. The Chief Inspector will take your, er, hat box to the train and will guard it until you rejoin him. There are four constables here to escort him. You will find a tea basket in the compartment, sir, and your coach has been routed right through to Windsor—no need to change at the Slough Station. . . . Everything in apple-pie order, sir . . . trust the Great Western, sir."

"Thank you, thank you . . . all most convenient. Fulleylove—Smith, I mean—give the Inspector the hat box. Handle it carefully, my man, and you, Inspector, pray do not let it out of your sight."

"Certainly not, sir. The Metropolitan Force knows its duty, Sir Henry."

Smith, as the detective again duly noted, now went round to the far side of the carriage, since it was from that door that the coachman had removed the hat box after adjusting Primelbund's bit. The onlookers had now drifted away. Sir Henry gave his last orders.

"Thank you, Fulleylove—er, I mean Smith. You and Macdonald will return to the Royal Mews and will report that your duty for the day has been completed. Now, Mr. Station Master, pray lead the way to your office . . . most timely, most timely."

The brougham went off at a smart pace but once in the Edgware Road slackened to a trot. Hardly turning their heads, for they knew only too well that they were being admired, the coachman and the footman once again gave each other a big wink—the second of the day. Then, playing their role to the end, they looked stiffly and silently ahead. Only a close observer would have noticed that the two men, like so many who have lived under the rule of silence, could talk to each other without moving their lips. In the Buckingham Palace Road, fifty yards from the Royal Mews, they abandoned the carriage. An hour later, when Primelbund began to whinny for her oats, it was found there by a policeman. For the two men, as for Primelbund and for Sir Henry Ponsonby, it had been a long hot day, longer than anyone knew.

Meanwhile, at Paddington, the vast space beneath Brunel's iron roof was a splendid and magical sight. Shafts of June sunlight thrust down between the girders to illuminate clouds of steam—all steam, smoke and sun, orchestrated by the thud and whistle of big locomotives. The two glossy toppers, almost lost in the crowd, sometimes hidden by piles of trunks, mailbags or milk cans, bustled off to the Station Master's office. The stout Chief Inspector, holding the hat box as gingerly as a birdcage and as self-consciously as a sacrament, made his way to the Windsor train, now half an hour behind time. The four constables followed, well aware that they were part of a royal occasion. The detective, having no instructions about what to do if Sir Henry and the hat box were separated, was thrown into confusion. He remained in an agony of apprehension until the Right Honorable Sir Henry Ponsonby, K.C.B., P.C., G.C.B., having duly relieved himself, at last reappeared.

One other passenger—the jaunty youth in the ginger suit, with his two carpet bags—had followed the Chief Inspector, his hat box and his four bobbies onto the platform. He must surely have been aiming at the next train, and was now in luck with this one. Hard on his heels came the two toppers.

Sir Henry was now securely locked in his compartment. The hat box and the tea basket were beside him. It was cool here and he could gaze at the hat box more calmly than in the brougham. He had no great sense of history, but with his feet up he could now relax and could recall some of those Tudor sovereigns whose portraits he had seen a hundred times in the royal galleries. He thought of their jewel-encrusted garments, their necklaces, pendants and earrings, their buckles and belts, and how much of that jewelry was now with him in that railway carriage, all embedded in that one Tiara. He thought first, naturally enough, of the great Elizabeth, then of Henry and his wives, of "Bloody" Mary and even of some of their subjects—Bacon, Essex and Raleigh . . . and so on.

Sir Henry's troubles and his long, hot day were now over—or so he thought. In the Windsor train, after all, he was nearly home. Without dereliction of duty and with a clear conscience he could now finish his nap. History faded from his mind. By the time the train had rattled over the points, and before it had even begun to glide through Berkshire meadows, he was snoring heavily.

2

Bertie

The Windsor railroad station is accustomed to royalty and such other oddities as visit the Castle. It even has a bleak courtyard with a glass roof where, through the long years, most of the kings, queens and presidents of the world have—strictly according to protocol—been ushered into their carriages for the two-hundred-yard drive to the Castle. The station is still peopled by the ghosts of wedding guests and mourners, by the ghosts of coaches and hearses.

The Station Master, therefore, did not overrate Sir Henry Ponsonby. He knew he was only a secretary, if an exalted one. Sir Henry had to wait five minutes before being released from his compartment, and then had only his coachman to greet him. The Ponsonbys did not run to an outdoor footman.

"Good evening, Philpotts . . . a most fatiguing day."

"Good evening, sir. The heat in London must have been most trying, but you have escaped a good deal of coming and going at the Castle, sir . . . this Jubilee, I suppose. Allow me to carry the hat box, sir."

The two men, master and coachman, went out into the station yard. The little dark green carriage was waiting for them, but Black Beauty—usually a staid old beast—was rearing up on her hind legs and foaming at the mouth. Fortunately the youth in the ginger suit—so conspicuous at Paddington—had already come to the rescue and was having his work cut out to hold the horse's head. His two large carpet bags were beside him on the pavement.

"I'm doing my best for yer, guvnor! Thought as 'ow a train whistle might 'ave started 'er off like, but no—it was this 'ere bearin' rein. I'm blowed if it ain't drawn blood."

"Thank you, my man. My coachman can see to it now. I'm obliged to you."

Black Beauty was still trembling when Sir Henry got into the carriage. Philpotts had put the hat box on the pavement and in a few moments had calmed Black Beauty, patting her on the nose. Sir Henry leaned out of the window to tip the young man in the ginger suit. He gave him half-a-sovereign and instantly regretted it—a crown would have been ample. Then they were off, up the hill to the Castle, the hat box once more safely on the carriage seat.

As he clattered through Henry VIII's Gate and across the Lower Ward, Sir Henry sighed with relief. Very soon now he would be back in his own home, the Norman Tower, with Mary and the children. First, however, he must look in on his office in the Private Apartments to see such letters and telegrams as had come in during the day. He must also, and above all, put this Tudor Tiara in the strong room. He was not going to have it in his office all night—that would mean turning out his own little safe. And certainly he and Mary were not going to have this one-million-pound monstrosity in their own bedroom. The Castle strong room—somewhere down among the dungeons—was the proper place.

Back in his own office, Sir Henry Ponsonby put the hat box on his desk. He poured himself a hock and seltzer. He lit a Corona Corona. He gazed out the Gothic window. Really, you know, life in this place had its compensations—the Avenue and the Long Walk, the distant policies of the Great Park and of Ascot, the long afternoon shadows across the turf—all so much fresher and greener than in London. And then, through the other window, shimmering in the sun, the pinnacles of Eton College Chapel and the great curves of the Thames—a perfect

Cotman. And then, above all, there was the whole aura of Majesty—the feeling that one was near to Divinity, actually in the next room but one—the assurance that, after all, one was not quite as other men.

There were no letters of importance—they could all wait—and only one telegram, that the Emperor Frederick would be bringing a suite of thirty-five to the Jubilee instead of twenty. That was a routine matter, and Sir Henry turned gratefully to a folded note in the handwriting of the Princess Beatrice:

Mama and I trust that in spite of the heat your visit to the Tower of London was successful and that that precious Tiara is now safely at Windsor. Mama asks me to say that she would be pleased if you and Lady Ponsonby would dine tonight—quite informal. It seems hard after your exhausting day but, as you know, what must be must be.

The Maharajah and the Maharani of Kashgar arrived at the Castle this afternoon, their P and O liner being one day early. I suspect that he was annoyed because Mama was not with me on the doorstep when he arrived. And now I am afraid that Mama will insist upon trying out her Hindustani on him—oh dear! The Maharajah's aide-de-camp is a seedy and dubious-looking English colonel called Pinkerton; the Maharani's lady-in-waiting, a Miss Nummuggar, speaks only Urdu. How helpful.

Also dining will be the Denmarks, the Waleses with Eddy (again, oh dear!) and Georgie. The Salisburys will be with us if the P.M. can get away from the House in time. Not a very tactful moment to ask Ld and Ldy Randolph—not with the P.M. here—but as they are in attendance upon Bertie there was no help for it. My Henry is still laying foundation stones in Yorkshire. Mr. Arthur Balfour, as Minister in Attendance, will make the numbers right, plus, of course, the Dean and Mrs. Randall Davidson. Mama will see to it that Mr. Balfour is not put next to anyone clever—he must not have a chance to show off.

This afternoon—I knew you wouldn't mind—I sat in your office for an hour. It was deliciously cool and the only place where I could smoke undetected. By the way, the Maharajah, having masses of jewels himself, is supposed to be an expert—has already been to Garrard's and Cartier's and doesn't think much of them! Mama thinks, therefore, that we might have the Tudor Tiara on show this evening and also for the luncheon guests tomorrow as they will not be at all the same people as those who will see the Tiara on Mama's head at the dinner. Also, if we show the Tiara tonight, presumably in the Great Corridor, it may help to break the ice when the Household and Family meet for coffee, specially as you, I gather, are expected to hold forth on its history. You don't know this yet; I am warning you. Papa's 1851 sketches for the design have been dug out of the Library to pin up on an easel alongside. I am warning you of this too as a slightly funereal note might be in order. By the way, I suppose the Tiara you brought from London today is the real thing. Pss B.

Sir Henry Ponsonby gave this note a moment's thought. Then he read it again. Then, from sheer habit, he noticed the names of the dinner guests—one must have the right kind of small talk ready for them. Then he read the last phrase—"I suppose the Tiara you brought from London today is the real thing." He read it four times. Had he gone mad, or had the Princess . . . ? He liked the woman very much—she was the best of the bunch and the sanest—but really . . .

He took three sheets of the black-bordered Windsor notepaper and dashed off three letters of his own. The first was to his wife.

Darling. A terrible day—hot, tiring and irritating—all details later. To cap all we have to "dine" tonight. I was so looking forward to a quiet evening—perhaps coffee on the lawn and then a game of backgammon . . . but now! There is no help for it. She wants to show off this hideous Tiara, with me as cicerone. So, alas, my love, our salmon must go back on ice. I will be over about 7:00 to dress—no gongs or ribbons, thank heaven! H.

And another note to General Sparling, the Master of the Royal Mews at Buckingham Palace:

My dear Sparling. I was rather expecting to be served today, on my visit to the Tower, by Fulleylove and Macdonald. I must admit I never really noticed the coachman, but the footman—a callow youth called Smith—told me that he had been ordered to replace Fulleylove, who had mumps. He had been given his orders by Mr. Thomas, the head groom, but I presume that you know all about this change in my arrangements. I am only surprised that I was not informed. Also, my dear Sparling, a private secretary—if I may say so—should not be fobbed off with a newcomer to the service; novices should be tried out on the messengers' little berlins or the servants' wagonettes. Much more alarming is this intelligence about the mumps. Mumps indeed! This is really too bad. With the Jubilee in two days' time an epidemic just now would be disastrous. Every servant and carriage will be needed. The disease, moreover—or so I have been told—is particularly virulent and painful in the adult male. Kindly keep the Duke of Norfolk informed as to the condition of your men, and let me have a full report immediately. What a splendid horse you have in little Primelbund. Yrs Ponsonby.

And then one to the Queen:

Sir Henry Ponsonby, with humble duty, has received Your Majesty's gracious command to dine tonight, which he and Lady Ponsonby will be most pleased to obey. Sir Henry had a successful visit to town. He took luncheon with Field Marshal and Lady Wilson at the Tower—all very pleasant. The royal parks were in all their summer glory. Your Majesty will be relieved to know that the very beautiful Tudor Tiara—and what a triumph of design—is now safely within the walls of the Castle. Sir Henry suggests placing it on the onyx table in the Corridor this evening, and also tomorrow morning for the benefit of Your Majesty's luncheon guests. He forgot to mention that at the Tower today Sir Henry inspected a detachment of the Yeomen of the Guard—acting as Your Majesty's representative. A splendid body of men. Sir Henry trusts that Your Majesty's headache has quite vanished. He much looks forward to meeting the Maharajah and Maharani of Kashgar this evening.

After all these years the Queen's Private Secretary was still amazed at his royal mistress. Outside her own curious experiences—a cloistered childhood and then, very suddenly, the big world—she was abysmally ignorant. She had read very little once the schoolroom days were over—the *Times*, specially printed for her on art paper, the *Berliner Tageblatt*, and an occasional dip into Marie Corelli were about her limit. She was often rude, selfish and thoughtless, and yet, somehow, Sir Henry seldom felt uncharitable toward her. The key to her character, as he had long since discovered, was her directness, her unalloyed simplicity—what was good was good and what was bad was bad; the good must be rewarded and the bad punished. Life was as simple as that. He realized that, given her impossible mother, those ghastly German forebears and her governesses, it was a miracle that she should be even presentable—after all, one might have been landed with another Queen Caroline! At least Victoria washed. He also knew that her simple shrewdness often came near to genius. Her dinner lists, for instance—Sir Henry knew exactly how she would arrange her table tonight. Arthur Balfour must be given no chance to dazzle anyone with his dazzling intellect, and indeed no two people who had anything in common must be next to each other— they might talk too much. Long ago there had been a disastrous evening when Uncle Cumberland and old Lord Lyndhurst had compared notes on the haunts of St. James's, and that other occasion when, from the soup to the savory, Macaulay and Carlyle had discussed the origins of Whiggery. Things were different now. The Queen had learned her lesson. Politics, religion and expectant motherhood were altogether banned, naturally, but the arrangement of the guests was also a very clever trick to make sure that table talk should remain small and general; on no account must the conversation ever rise above Her Majesty's head—that would never do, and so it never did.

Sir Henry Ponsonby came back to earth. A tinkle of his bell and the silent and liveried automaton was at his side, immaculate and pomaded, but with brandy on his breath.

"Ah, Wainwright. This note is for my wife. You must get it sent over to the Norman Tower immediately."

"Sir."

"This one is for General Sparling, the Master of the Mews at the Palace. If anyone is going back to town they must take it. Otherwise get it franked and taken down to the station."

"Sir."

"And this one is for Her Majesty; ask Her Royal Highness kindly to hand it to her."

"Sir."

"And then, Wainwright, I would like to see one of Her Majesty's dressers. I suppose there will be six on duty as usual—but preferably Fräulein Skerret."

"Sir. May I have permission to speak, sir?"

"Well, what is it?"

"Your own coachman, sir, Mr. Philpotts, is outside and would like to see you, sir."

As Wainwright silently vanished, Philpotts came in. As the two men passed each other it would have been improper for them to speak, but, somehow, Sir Henry sensed that either would have been glad to have murdered the other. Philpotts was now in gaiters, ratcatcher and white stock.

"What is it, Philpotts?"

"Black Beauty, sir. I'm worried about her."

"I don't wonder. Most unlike her to prance about like that. You must watch that bit and bearing rein, Philpotts."

"That, sir, with respect, was not the cause."

"But that ferrety youth, Philpotts—in the ginger suit—who was holding her head, he said the bit had drawn blood."

"Sir, that was not so. The bit and rein were perfectly adjusted. The blood was not from the mouth at all."

"Come, come, Philpotts, something had startled her."

"Yes, indeed, sir. She had been cut in the right foreleg, just above the hock. Quite a bit of blood there, sir. A clean cut about an inch long, made with a sharp blade—perhaps a razor. We can ask the vet, sir, but there is no doubt about it. Two of the Castle grooms can vouch for it, sir."

"Very well, Philpotts, you were quite right to tell me. All very strange, very strange indeed. Of course it will have to be looked into, but that will do for now, Philpotts. Good night."

"Good night, sir."

Sir Henry Ponsonby, with a puzzled frown, finished his hock and seltzer. He was worried and, worse still, he did not know why he was worried. The feeling had been coming on all day; it had been started by the fumbling ineptitude of that foolish nonagenarian, Field Marshal Lord Wilson, the Constable of the Tower of London; it had been increased by the unaccountable absence of his favorite footman, Fulleylove, and now it had been capped by Philpotts.

With his cigar still in his mouth, the frown still on his face, Sir Henry placed the hat box on a chair, opened it and lifted out the shagreen leather case. This he placed on his desk. He then pulled from the pocket of his coat skirts a tiny box of gold filigree. It held three keys, one topped by a sapphire, one by an emerald and one by a pearl. Each of the three escutcheons on the case bore a corresponding stone. Sir Henry now removed the Tiara from its bed of cream velvet and placed it upon his blotting pad. The whole Tiara—there was no doubt about it—was quite repulsive. It summoned up all the ghastliest memories of the Crystal Palace. On the other hand, the gems were unrivaled—probably unrivaled in the whole world. Sir Henry, knowing nothing of jewels, was fascinated mainly by the sheer ugliness of the thing.

"Ach, mein Gott! It is too beautiful!"

Fräulein Skerret, the Queen's senior dresser, had come into the room. She was a privileged being who never knocked on doors. She wore a tight dress of black bombazine with tiny steel ornaments; also a curious little starched cap. She was said to be over ninety but was unchanging and ageless. Trained in the Palace at Darmstadt, she had come to the Queen at her accession. If Sir Henry Ponsonby sometimes believed in the myth of royalty, Fräulein Skerret believed in its divinity. For her, to her dying day, there would be only one Prince—Albert—not least in matters of art. She was now holding up her hands in ecstasy at the marvelous Tiara which "he" had designed.

"Ach, mein Gott! It is too beautiful!"

"Ah, good evening, Skerret. This is the famous Tudor Tiara, which Her Majesty will be wearing for the great Jubilee Dinner in the Waterloo Chamber. It will have to go in the strong room, but I thought you should see it and measure it now—I see you have a tape on your reticule. This Tiara, Skerret . . ." as if she didn't know "... has been in the Tower of London for thirty-six years, and although the separate gems are all some three or four hundred years old it has never, so far as I know, been worn by anyone. It may need altering to suit Her Majesty's present—er—coiffure, and there is also the problem of the veil . . . we don't want a disaster like the one we had at the last levee."

"Ach, no, sir. That was too frightful . . . everything came away . . . everything, diadem, veil, coiffure, absolutely everything . . ."

"Quite, Skerret, quite . . . best forgotten. Meanwhile, this Tudor Tiara is being shown to the guests this evening, on the onyx table in the Corridor."

"Ach! It will look too marvelous. . . ."

"Quite. But I was wondering, Skerret, whether you could, very quickly, get a suitable cushion covered with black velvet. Her Majesty might not like to use one of the Garter cushions, and in any case they are probably all locked up in the Chapel."

"It shall be done, sir."

"Thank you. I am now going over to the Norman Tower to dress. Examine and measure the Tiara, then lock this door—here is my key—and return the key to me before dinner through one of the footmen. Have the velvet cushion put ready on the onyx table and I will see to the rest. Good night, Skerret."

Outside Sir Henry's office the long passage—red carpet, white paint, gilded mirrors, lacquered Marie Thérèse cabinets and Albertine gaseliers—all combined to frame in an almost endless perspective. Sir Henry had been ready to slip through a little side door leading by way of a newel to the courtyard and so to the Norman Tower. This was not to be. From the far end of that rich perspective a portly gentleman was hurrying toward him—a figure not unknown throughout Europe.

Edward, Prince of Wales—dear Bertie—wreathed in blue cigar smoke and with the Star of India at his throat, was dressed for dinner, except that he still had to discard his smoking jacket.

The guttural, bronchial and Teutonic voice hailed Sir Henry down the length of the passage. There was no escape. The Prince was almost in the room.

"Hello, Ponsonby, you're the very man I wanted to see. Ah, ah, so you have Mama's gewgaw. Handsome object, I must say. Good evening, Skerret."

Skerret bobbed her curtsy and stood aside. The two men now had the Tiara between them.

"Hm, as I say, very handsome. Of course taste and fashion change. I was brought up, so to speak, on the Crystal Palace. I know nothing about art—never did—but I know what I like. Now frankly, Ponsonby, between ourselves, wouldn't you say that this was a bit gaudy for Mama?"

"I very much fear so, sir. I can't understand it—so unlike Her Majesty to make such a mistake. Perhaps the Tiara's close association with your father clouded her judgment. You know he designed it himself—we have his drawings. But what can we do, sir? The Princess Beatrice just won't interfere in matters of dress—she says she's been snubbed too often. A word from you, sir, to Lady Ely . . . or possibly Fräulein here could say a word to the Queen. . . ."

"No good, Ponsonby. Mama will have her own way. I know exactly what her idea is. With all these relations, all those Germans, Russians and Danes coming over for the Jubilee—not to mention the Orléans clan with their marvelous Bourbon jewels—Mama just wants to fly the flag—it's as simple as that."

"You know, I never thought of it like that, sir."

"Oh, dear me, yes. After all, whatever they may say about us Coburgs, the Tudors are English enough for anyone—I know they were actually Welsh, but that doesn't matter—and all these superb gems really are Tudor, I gather, and really are superb—eh, Ponsonby?"

"There's no doubt about that, sir. And I think you're right about the Queen—a gesture to show that even in jewelry the Old Country can hold her own. Well, she always seems to have her own reasons for what she does. And the jewels themselves, as you say, sir, really are Tudor—the equivalent in jewelry of, say, St. George's Chapel in architecture—the finest gems of the sixteenth century, at any rate outside Spain. . . . If only they weren't in such a ghastly setting; but that is the one thing that is impossible to mention."

"Quite. And the actual gems—you can identify them all, Ponsonby?"

Sir Henry took a very large envelope from his desk.

"Almost all. Here is the file, sir. Here you see engravings from Holbein's paintings, Nicholas Hillyarde's and Isaac Oliver's miniatures, as well as photographs of effigies and so on. It's a regular parlor game of 'spot the jewel.' This enormous pearl, for instance, in the very center of the Tiara, may be identified quite easily in the Hatfield portrait of Elizabeth, where it lies like a fine plover's egg in the middle of the royal bosom, only to crop up again in James II's scepter . . . quite a fascinating story. And then again, sir, these twelve-pointed stars—said to be worth all the other stones put together—are almost certainly Mary Tudor's wedding earrings, a gift from Philip of Spain."

"Really, poor old Bloody Mary, eh?"

"Yes, sir, and there are many other romantic tales hidden in this Tiara. . . . But I understand that I am expected to dilate upon it all this evening after dinner."

"Poor old Ponsonby, eh?"

"Oh, I survive these things, sir."

"I am sure you do; I admire your resilience. However, we'll come back to the Tiara later. Skerret, you may leave us—give me Sir Henry's key."

Skerret duly bobbed, to vanish in search of black velvet and a cushion.

"Now, Ponsonby, a word with you. With all these Jubilee guests in the Castle I must help Mama as much as I can; I shall be kicking my heels here for a couple of days. Can you spare me an hour sometime?"

"So far as duty permits I am at your service, sir."

The reply was cool, but Sir Henry knew only too well what

was coming, and the Prince knew that he knew. Sir Henry's mouth had tightened.

"Yes, Ponsonby, you're right . . . it's the old story. Parliament still thinks that Mama should pay my debts from her Civil List —Gladstone started that hare. Mama thinks that Parliament should pay them from Revenue—Dizzy started that one. Dizzy, of course, was right, but he's dead. Now, as you know, ever since Papa died I have performed more and more of Mama's social duties, in town and abroad—what Gladdy called 'the visible attributes of Monarchy.' Clearly these are public duties and the public should pay for them, in other words Parliament. Now you, Ponsonby, know Parliament better than I do. Talking to ministers is your daily job. Anything you say will be much better received than if it came from me or from any of my friends, all of whom are supposed to connive at my extravagances. Cust, Hirsch, Esher or Dickie Fisher, let alone the Rothschilds—no member of the Cabinet would listen to them. So, it's up to you, Ponsonby, for Mama's sake as well as mine. I thought that perhaps you might have a word with the P.M. tonight."

"I might, sir, if I thought that it would be of the slightest use. But I must remind you that this is a liberal administration, almost radical—intent upon soaking the classes for the sake of the masses. No, I am not hopeful; but may I at least know, sir, whether your finances are worse today than they were, say, a year ago."

"Well, there's still that old debt of £80,000 on Sandringham. It still stands."

"Dear me, dear me, I had hoped that that was paid off long ago."

"It's no good saying 'dear me, dear me' like that. On Sandringham my conscience is absolutely clear. It was a capital expenditure on property reverting, in effect, to the Crown. Whether or not Eddy ever marries and lives there—or Georgie, since I can't see Eddy ever marrying—the place will be an asset to the nation—the finest game bag in England—and yet I'm supposed to actually restore the capital. It's not only unfair, it's rotten finance."

"Maybe, sir; but whether the Treasury would ever take that view is another matter. After all Sandringham is not a palace—of which you have too many. It's your own house and you bought it yourself, sir, in preference to living in one of the houses on Crown Land, of which several were available."

"Rubbish, my dear Ponsonby! How could a gentleman nowadays live in a place like Bushey or Claremont—no sport for his guests, and much too near London or Windsor. Anyway I wouldn't want to be on Mama's doorstep, and I had as much right to buy Sandringham as Papa had to buy Balmoral."

"Your father had some Coburg money, Your Highness. In any case, I am merely stating the view of the Treasury. A Select Committee of Parliament would probably be even more critical. The time is not propitious. What else, sir?"

"Oh, well, there's always Poole of course, but then I suppose that Savile Row expects to wait for its money—it's a tradition of English life. Anyway it's less than £10,000 and Poole can always borrow on what I owe him."

"Ten thousand, sir, for clothes!"

"You know nothing about it, Ponsonby. With my ample—er—girth I really can't wear a suit more than twice. You don't understand. There are all the uniforms. Kilts are expensive and Poole has just had to send his head cutter to Berlin to check the details for my Death's Head Hussar uniform. These colonelcies, Ponsonby, are damned expensive . . . harness and accouterments as well as just clothes . . . swords, hats, decorations and God knows what else."

"And your wine merchant?"

"Really, Ponsonby, perhaps you would like to see the butcher's bills. Oh, well, if you must know—about the same as Poole. I had to lay down a cellar at Sandringham, you know."

"But, Your Royal Highness, I can't possibly put debts like these in front of either the P.M. or the Queen. Such debts are far more shocking than the really big things such as the Household. They would be horrified."

"What you must make them realize, Ponsonby, is that I live as I do solely for the sake of the nation. As long as Mama sticks to her shabby weeds, and won't be seen in public, then I have to deputize for her—without her income. I don't even get an allowance for entertaining foreign sovereigns—a big item."

"Can't you raise money, sir? After all, there must be assets—the Duchy of Cornwall, for instance."

"I can't touch it—all entailed for the next P. of W. But of course you are right. Naturally I *can* raise money, although not so easily as you might think. Don't you see, my dear Ponsonby, that while my tradesmen can borrow on my debts to them, I can't go around borrowing money from my friends as other men can—and do. Nobody is ever going to dun the Prince of Wales, but in return, don't you see, there is a certain *noblesse oblige*. I can't behave like a cad; therefore I can't exploit my rank. You must know that."

"But isn't there one single extravagance of which Your Royal Highness could divest yourself—at least as a start."

"It's all very difficult. There's the *Britannia* for instance. They make me Commandant of the Royal Yacht Squadron and won't pay me enough to keep a boat at Cowes."

"You could consider a smaller yacht, sir, and sell the *Britannia.*"

"I can't afford to keep her, but I can't sell her either. Boni de Castellane, with all those Jay Gould millions in his pocket, offered me £10,000 for her—just what I owe Poole—but now he's backed out, almost bankrupted himself on his pink marble palace in the Avenue de Bois—bloody fool! That was a blow. To be frank, Ponsonby, that was one of the things that brought me here today. That . . . and other things."

"Other things . . . gambling debts, sir?"

"Peccadilloes, my dear man, peccadilloes! People think I gamble and so I do, but always in strict moderation. Oh, I know that my Tattersall account is a running sore, but, like Poole,

Tattersall's can borrow on it. As for the card debts—the Jockey Club and White's—they have never exceeded three figures in one evening."

"And in Paris . . . ?"

"Oh well, naturally the Faubourg St. Germain stakes are rather higher, but even so—my God—just compare it with Regency times when whole estates used to pass over the card table."

"Those times have gone, sir. Few remember them and none would tolerate them, least of all from a man in your position. They are as obsolete as dueling."

"A man in my position! Exactly. You've hit the nail on the head. My position! It's so damned unfair. I have to be all things to all men—never myself. Half the nation cheer themselves hoarse—here or in Ireland—if I back a winner, and the other half wink or shake their heads if I so much as cross the Channel. And why on earth, Ponsonby, should it be all right to lose a fiver at whist and a mortal sin to lose it at baccarat? Tell me that. Besides, damn it all, I win as well as lose, don't I?"

"No one doubts that, sir. You are lucky on the turf and skillful at the card table. But don't forget that ever since the Reform Bill governments have been very sensitive about the Nonconformist conscience or—which is much the same thing—the middle-class vote. That is a fact of political life. But to go on to other things, sir. What about the cost of all these cozy establishments which you provide for your—er—friends? . . . if I may be allowed to ask."

"Don't be such a fool. Of course you may ask—we're both men of the world, aren't we? Besides, you know better than anyone that I adore Alix, but you also know that her heart is always in the nursery or in Copenhagen—when she isn't there herself. You also know, or you damn well should know by now, that I am a virile man. I am a man who cannot sleep alone. And that, my dear Ponsonby, is that—one of the physiological facts about His Royal Highness the Prince of Wales. After all, what do people expect? I'm a Hanoverian on both sides; I'm damned lucky not to be riddled with disease. Thank God I'm not even a hemophiliac like half my miserable cousins. But I *am* fond of women—and women are expensive."

"I must accept your own estimation of yourself, sir. I am concerned only with the financial consequences."

"Well, I have a streak of loyalty in me. I may get tired of people—even of beautiful women—but I don't drop them."

"We all know that, Your Royal Highness."

"Well, then, I haven't the slightest objection to you knowing everything. Nellie Clifden—not so young now, bless her—still has chambers in Dover Street, and Hortense Schneider in the Rue Royale—with a modest settlement for both ladies. That for a start."

"And the Villa Olga at Dieppe, sir?"

"What?"

"The Villa Olga, sir. At Dieppe. Is it still there? Little Olga must be growing up. . . ."

"Good God, Ponsonby, you know about that. And neither Alix nor Mama suspect a thing."

"You are naïve, sir. In any case, it's my business to know if I am to be of any use to you."

"Well, you can forget it. Olga Alberta is the dearest child in the world. She is very, very beautiful, Ponsonby, with marvelous hair below her waist. In Dieppe the people are kind; they call me her 'godfather,' *le parrain royal de la petite.* But you can forget her; she and her mother are provided for forever, and the capital written off. She is my most precious secret."

"Very well, sir, but with the French Government putting twenty detectives in Dieppe every time you see the child, secrecy is relative."

"I don't care a damn. In two years Olga Alberta will be here —her first London season. She can never be presented at Court but when she dances in the great London houses she shall wear the finest diamonds in the world—I swear that."

There was a palpable silence between the two men. Both had

dropped their eyes to the Tiara on the desk between them. It was Ponsonby who, rather sharply, changed the subject.

"Let us get back to business, Your Highness. There was a Miss Walters, if I remember rightly."

"Skittles? Oh, she's Hartingdon's friend now. No trouble there, Ponsonby. I must tell you a joke about her one day."

"And this Parisienne, Your Highness, known, I believe, as—er—La Goulue?"

"I do wish, Ponsonby, that a man with your responsibilities would stick to the facts instead of reading the newspapers. True, I paid for champagne all round that night at the Moulin Rouge—my own affair, I think. But I am not in the habit of sleeping with cabaret girls."

"I stand corrected, sir. And Miss Le Breton?"

"Miss Le Breton, Ponsonby, as you would know if you would only read the newspapers, is now married to a Mr. Langtry and has become a wealthy woman as well as being a good actress. People may stand on chairs in the park to look at her, or so I am told, but Langtry doesn't mind, and it costs me not a farthing . . . so really, my dear Ponsonby, she is quite irrelevant."

"I suppose you give her presents, sir. It all mounts up."

"Of course it mounts up. Knollys is selling capital all the time as well as borrowing on my expectations. Those expectations, I need hardly remind you, Ponsonby, are stupendous. I am the most gilt-edged thing in Europe. But I can never, never take advantage of it. I cannot exploit my rank. Prinny did, you know, both with Barings and with Coutts, and the prestige of the Crown dropped to rock bottom. That did far more harm than all his blowzy mistresses."

"Oh, I see all that clearly enough, sir. Have you yourself any solution to offer?"

"The obvious one and the correct one. Dizzy told Parliament years ago that my expenditure was bound to exceed my income by £20,000 a year. Dizzy was the only Prime Minister who realized what it meant—financially—to live in Society—the first man with less than a hundred thousand acres ever to hold the job. What he said is still true. The point is, Ponsonby, and Dizzy saw it—the point is that I do so much for Mama—twenty of her guests filling Marlborough House this week—that that £20,000 should come from her Civil List. In any case, what on earth does Mama do with all her money? If she handed over to me officially, if I were Regent, there would be no question . . ."

"No, Your Highness, but that has not happened and won't—not until pigs fly. Moreover, with this Cabinet I am, frankly, not at all sanguine about your affairs. It would be madness to speak to Salisbury at the moment—there's always that puritanical streak in the Cecils—and in any case the government is far too busy with Ireland and Egypt to pay attention to anyone's mistresses or gambling debts—even yours, sir."

"I must say, Ponsonby, I thought better of you."

"I am speaking for the Cabinet, not for myself, sir."

"Well, well, let's go through it all tomorrow morning. Knollys has it all down in black and white. After all, it's his job, not yours. But sooner or later Mama has got to be tackled and that, my dear man, brings it back to you. If I went to Mama myself she would only give me one of her jobations, as if I were still a naughty boy. It is for you to reason with her, Ponsonby; but do remember that she has a very warm spot in her heart for me—if only she can be made to forget what Papa would have said. You convince Mama and she will convince Salisbury."

"I'll do my best, sir, when this Jubilee is out of the way."

"Good, but don't wait too long. And for heaven's sake, Ponsonby, keep my wife out of this. Alix has no extravagances. In Paris last month two of her ladies each ordered a dozen dresses from Worth, and God knows how many hats. Alix ordered only three. Mama likes Alix well enough but is always looking for faults—she loathes the whole Danish connection of course—and Bismarck writes a poisoned letter every week or so. If Mama can blame Alix she will. . . ."

"The Princess of Wales's name shall not be mentioned, sir."

"All right then, but don't wait too long, Ponsonby. The Paris couturiers seem to have less faith in my credit than have the London tailors."

"Very well, Your Highness; but frankly I am not at all optimistic, not at all."

"Then what is your own suggestion—damn it."

"Your Highness can always go to the Jews."

The two men were still standing with the Tudor Tiara between them. The Prince threw away his cigar end, savagely cut and lit another, and then walked across to the Gothic bay. He stood there, gazing at a landscape still basking in the sun. For fully five minutes there was silence except for the Prince's heavy breathing. At last he turned back to the desk.

"May I ring your bell, Ponsonby?"

In less than twenty seconds—he must have been almost by the door—Wainwright, salver at his side, was making his obeisance.

"Ah, Wainwright, please ask one of the princesses to tell Her Majesty that I would like to see her in her own room—I suppose she will be in the Gold Room—in about a quarter of an hour—better say seven o'clock."

"Sir."

"And to add my apologies for appearing before the Queen in a smoking jacket, but the matter is urgent."

"Sir." And Wainwright vanished.

"And now, Ponsonby, the Jews! What the hell do you mean, go to the Jews! Really, you know, I am most unwilling to remind you of our stations in life, but I do resent your remark. It has, to start with, a very nasty anti-Semitic twist. Secondly, as you well know, some of my best friends are Jewish—not to mention several of the Queen's most loyal subjects."

"Your Highness has completely misunderstood me."

"I hope so; but really, Ponsonby, it did rather sound as though you were advising a visit to the nearest pawnbroker."

"Oh, no, sir . . . really!"

"Or, alternatively, that some of my Jewish friends might be more amenable to a financial deal than my gentile ones."

"Allow me to explain, sir. Anti-Semitism was far from my mind. On the contrary I was thinking of the great qualities of Judaism. It pleases Your Highness to be humorous about pawnbrokers. May I remind you, sir, that a merchant banker is but a glorified pawnbroker. Your Highness will doubtless remember that the three golden balls which hang in our streets were the arms of the Medici family—worthy predecessors, sir, of the Rothschilds, and incidentally not Jews."

"Ah, so that's it, is it? Go on, Ponsonby, go on."

"Well, you will remember, sir, that eight years ago, when Lord Beaconsfield bought the Khedive's Suez Canal shares, he needed an enormous loan at three hours' notice. You will also remember that he got it—in two hours—from Baron Nathan Rothschild—his security, the British Empire."

"Yes, yes, Ponsonby, of course—one of Monty Corry's more romantic Dizzy stories. Unfortunately I am not the British Empire."

"The whole Rothschild tribe, to put it mildly, sir, is well disposed toward Your Highness."

"Maybe, Ponsonby, but, as I say, I am not the British Empire. I am an officer and a gentleman. It would be caddish—possibly even unconstitutional—to offer my rank, my person, let alone my prospects, as some kind of security . . . it would be pawning the Throne! If Mama died the whole thing might become a public scandal—half the new King's Civil List in pawn to the Rothschilds! And then, if I died, just think of poor Eddy's position. Pawning the Throne . . . and for Eddy of all people, or if he died, for good little Georgie. Yes, Ponsonby, pawning the Throne!"

"Not quite, sir. Some of your gentile friends might think like that—Esher, Beresford, Fisher—although others, such as Lord Randolph, might think it rather a clever wheeze. The Rothschilds, however, would think very differently. Their discretion would be absolute; money is in their blood. Remember, sir, that there is more money in the Vale of Aylesbury than anywhere else in the world outside the City of London. A few minutes' chat with the Baron Nathan in the library at Tring, and your troubles are over. A million-pound loan, with His Royal Highness the Prince of Wales as security . . . why, sir, it would be one more battle honor for the House of Rothschild, and also a secret that would be kept forever. I beg you, sir, I beg you. A million pounds—take it, Your Highness, and then hand it to Maurice Hirsh and watch him play with it on the Stock Exchange. I beg you, sir."

"No, Ponsonby, no. I will not and cannot offer myself as security. One day the Treasury might have to redeem me. Another generation of Rothschilds might foreclose. The scandal could be the end of the monarchy. Nobody believes it, you know, but unlike other men I really own very little. Now if I was one of the great dukes—a rent roll from a hundred thousand Irish acres and half-a-dozen London squares—life would be simple. Or, Ponsonby, if I had great possessions in tangible form—a few Rembrandts or Raphaels or even, say, the Kohinoor—something Natty or Ferdy could put in their strong room in exchange for the check—I should at least feel like a gentleman. But I have nothing like that. Sandringham is not paid for, the pictures all belong to Mama, the Kohinoor and the Cullinan belong to the nation, and the Duchy of Cornwall is entailed. Now if only I had one single thing of my own—a single object worth, say, the odd million, something which I could just hand across the table to Natty, any evening over the brandy—that would be different, Ponsonby. That would be how I like things. Yes, yes, that would be quite different. . . ."

There was another long and rather terrible silence. The two men were not looking at each other. They both had their eyes fixed upon the bizarre object on the desk. Very gently the Prince of Wales put out his fat hand and turned the Tudor Tiara round and round, examining the jewels one by one.

"Very well, Ponsonby, until tomorrow then. But something must be done soon. I'm pretty desperate, you know. Now let us forget money. Let us look at this pretty object." He held the Tiara aloft.

"All Tudor gems, Your Highness, from many sources. Spain was particularly generous, as were our own great Catholic families. But of course the work of assembling the gems and of designing the setting was entirely your father's. The librarian, Herr Mütter, has all his meticulous drawings."

"He was a meticulous man, Ponsonby. My God, he was! And so this pretty thing is our own property—Mama's and then mine in due course. Our own personal property to do what we like with, eh, Ponsonby?"

"Strictly speaking, sir, I should want to refer that question to the Solicitor-General. Crown Jewels, surely, are held by the Crown on trust, not by the Sovereign personally."

"Nonsense, Ponsonby. They're ours. In George IV's time, for instance, in the Pavilion at Brighton, Lady Conyngham often wore the Great Sapphire—and it has never been seen again. One of her bastards, Mountcharles probably, must have pawned it, but no questions were ever asked."

"Those days have gone, sir. The Queen would never agree. . . ."

"Never mind the Queen. Remember, jewels don't become Crown Jewels merely by being put in the Tower for safety . . . there's a lot of rubbish in that place anyway."

"True, sir, but the matter is legally very complicated . . . and I have not yet dressed for dinner. Your Royal Highness will excuse me."

"I'll keep your key then. A quiet smoke here, with a go at your decanter, will soothe my nerves very nicely, ready for my chat with Mama. Now, be off with you."

Sir Henry Ponsonby walked across the little courtyard deep in thought. What a hopeless creature the Prince was. Popular of course, but not always with the right people . . . more at home in Paris or Dublin than in London. Sir Henry had heard the whole story of the debts many times and always with the same excuses. He would have to tackle the Queen sooner or later. Fortunately she really did have a warm place in her heart for Bertie—"Bertie is a dear, good boy"—and did not disapprove of his antics nearly as much as people supposed. After all, she had been brought up in the shadow of the Regency . . . men will be men, and it was not for a daughter of the House of Hanover to cast the first stone. "Society," as she often said, was "heartless" and "showy" but she never blamed it for being "wicked"; it was the function of Society to be wicked, just as it was the function of the Court to be moral. If her affection for Bertie was sometimes muffled, that was only when Albert's ghost, redolent with all the tight-lipped prudery of Stockmar or Uncle Leopold, had triumphed over her better and more worldly nature. Privately she might scold her son; publicly she kept a loyal silence, and within reason—or even beyond reason—would do anything for him.

Sir Henry Ponsonby was far more critical than the Queen. The Prince of Wales was a damned nuisance—a spanner in a well-oiled machine. Sir Henry disliked his personal habits. Why on earth, for instance, had the man dressed so early for dinner? It was this disgusting habit of drinking before dining—an American custom which Jennie Churchill had imported from the Jockey Club on Long Island. The Prince had probably already been boozing for an hour with the Denmarks and Randolphs—both sexes. And these smoking jackets—they might be all right in Virginia or even at Marienbad, but now they were being worn every night at Marlborough House and even in the clubs. Horrible! And why the Star of India? The Maharajah would be officially honored tomorrow—the Princess had said so —and now Sir Henry would have to go to his bureau and get his own precious Order of the Bath. Then he would have to summon Mary to his dressing room to clip the ribbon behind his collar. Then the damned thing would have to lie flat on his chest, which meant a hard shirt front instead of the frilly one which was probably already laid out for him. Sir Henry snorted with annoyance, but could at least thank God that *he* did not yet have a smoking jacket and did not consume spirits just before breathing in the Queen's face. . . . There were limits!

The courtyard was now in shadow and quite cool. These long

June nights . . . the children would hardly be in bed yet; there might just be time for a game with them while Suzanne was doing his wife's hair. He looked up at the Norman Tower—yes, he could see nanny's shadow on the blind. The story of his day's work, with all its worries, would keep until he and Mary were in bed, peaceful and secure. He looked back at the blaze of gaseliers, just lit in the passage outside his office, noticing how they picked out the pattern of Wyatville's lacelike plaster vaulting. Wainwright had not yet pulled the curtains and Sir Henry could see the massive head of Albert Edward, Prince of Wales, as he bent over the desk.

Up there in Sir Henry Ponsonby's office, the Prince was alone, with the door locked on the inside. He was fat, he was florid, he was immaculate. His eyes were bloodshot. The cigar was set at an angle as the lip curled. He had swallowed two brandies. He had taken a magnifying glass from the desk. He was examining the diamonds with great care—those diamonds which, long ago in the Choir at Winchester, had flashed with all the colors of the rainbow. The Prince bit hard on his cigar. He was swearing quietly in German. He glanced at the clock. It was time to see Mama.

3

Mama

She sat in the little Gold Room. Was she a mummified puppet or was she some kind of Buddha—rigid, almost immobile among her possessions? She had been walking on the South Terrace with Beatrice and with dear Lady Ely, and now, with two hours to go before dinner, was still wearing her curious hat, that little pouf with its hint of crepe. She still wore her mantle with its sparkles of jet.

Her stature was negligible. Only years later, when they saw her coffin, did Englishmen realize how little was their Queen. But now, at this moment, on June 19, 1887, she completely dominated this private temple in which, for this hour, she had enshrined herself. It was a small room, not so much furnished as redolent with the somber gold of the embossed walls and heavy picture frames, also somber with the browns and whites of sepia photographs and creamy statuary—and the yellow sunlight filtering through drawn blinds.

The Gold Room, in this golden light, might well be a shrine, but it was also the royal counterpart of a thousand parlors of a thousand British matrons. Nothing here for use or for beauty—every inch a memento, a gift, a souvenir, a relic, a votive offering. For more ordinary widows there would be the texts, the Berlin woolwork, the waxed flowers, the "present from Broadstairs" and the photos of nephews who had long since ceased to write. The Gold Room at Windsor was no more than an apotheosis of all such sanctums—the parlor of just one more selfish, bourgeois old woman. Two hundred photographs, each in its repoussé silver frame, some with sprigs of white heather, some with black bows—all these kings and emperors and czars, and over a hundred royal or serene highnesses. Here, however, in this room they were transmuted from their royal status into the long list which she carried in her heart—Vicky and Fritz in Potsdam, Nicky and Alicky far away in Petersburg, and Eugénie, so handy at Chislehurst . . . and then there were the rest: Liko and Drino and Tino and Sandro, Affie and Louischen and Lenchen and Ena, and Georgie and Eddy and May—four generations, all long-nosed and long-mouthed, and all at that moment, in their hot uniforms and hot corsets, moving in their hot wagons-lits, from ghastly palaces all over Europe, toward Windsor, or toward that no less ghastly palace at the end of the Mall, moving, all of them, toward this Buddha squatting in her shrine.

And there too, among the photographs, were all the other relics, christening mugs and mourning rings, the glass case for funeral cards, the locket, with his mother's hair, that Albert had given her in the woods at Rosenau, the children on their ponies at Laeken, the shells they had glued onto boxes, the miniature of Aunt Adelaide—so kind in '37—and the Barbary dagger from Hughenden, the one Monty Corry gave her in '81 when they opened Dizzy's tomb that she might put china roses on the coffin. Quite the largest photograph was of dear Lehzen, with its memories of the schoolroom at Kensington. There was Stockmar's gold turnip watch, and the last Valentine from Lord Melbourne—so amusing. And there, next to her chair, was Boehm's statuette of John Brown, and the picture of Grant, who, next to Brown, was the nicest of all the gillies. But it was the family that one came back to. The poor Empress of Germany and the Prince of Wales were at either end of the mantelpiece—busts of blood-red marble. And there, over the mantelpiece, was Landseer's "Last Shoot"—Albert by Loch Muick with a dead stag . . . idyllic days! But the altar of the shrine—also Albert—

was in white Carrara marble, silhouetted against the drawn blind, the wreath of immortelles around his brow.

In this last hour before dinner, she was working, reading and signing. Reading and signing—it was her whole life now. There was a knock on the door. She put away her spectacles—spectacles were not allowed at Windsor. The corners of the mouth remained down, but the whites of the hooded eyes just showed as she looked up at her eldest son. He clicked his heels. He kissed her hand. She pecked his cheek.

"Good evening, Mama. How well you look."

"You know that I am never well. . . . My dearest boy, what a stranger you are."

He waited ten ticks of the clock before he was told that he might sit.

"Well, Bertie, I am bound to say that it is pleasant to have you at Windsor . . . for a change. I suppose you still recognize the old place."

"It is always delightful to be here, Mama; but you know how busy I have been in London and in Dublin. By the way, that was a successful affair . . . a few black flags hung out in Cork, but cheering crowds everywhere . . . or—er—almost everywhere."

"Yes, Bertie, strange as it may seem, I do read the newspapers. I also noted that your visit to the Viceregal Lodge coincided very happily with the Punchestown Races."

"Now, Mama, really . . ."

"And that Alix was not with you. She's a sweet child, Bertie, but all these months at the Amalienborg . . ."

"Three weeks, Mama . . ."

"Don't argue with me, Bertie. It was quite long enough to leave you open to temptation. And when Alix is in Denmark, as I suppose she must be sometimes, it would be kind of you to visit your poor old mother. I can't imagine what you do with yourself in London, or why you live in Norfolk—a most outlandish county."

"Not more outlandish than Aberdeenshire, Mama."

"Bertie!"

"You never will realize how much I do for you, Mama, both in London and Norfolk. It was at Sandringham, only the other day, that Willy and the Blue Monkey . . ."

"Really, Bertie, you're impossible. The Blue Monkey—I suppose you are referring to the Portuguese ambassador, the Marquis de Soveral."

"Yes, we all call him 'the Blue Monkey.' Anyway, he and Willy initialed the Mozambique treaty in my library at Sandringham—a diplomatic coup for England. And now, tomorrow night, there will be twenty highnesses at Marlborough House. The suites will have to go to places like Claridge's, but even so, God knows where everyone will sleep. . . . And I don't get a penny for it, Mama."

"Now don't start all that, Bertie. We've been over it a hundred times. You're a very wealthy man and should be glad to show gratitude for your wonderful upbringing and for having had such a wonderful father."

"Yes, Mama, I am not ungrateful; but there are lots of calls upon my money. . . ."

"You've plenty of money, Bertie, if only you wouldn't squander it . . . all this entertaining Society—useless, selfish creatures. I see that you and Alix have had the Duchess of Manchester to dinner again. . . . I told you not to."

"We must choose our own guests. . . ."

"But you had her on a Sunday, Bertie. You've no sense of what is fitting."

"We were talking about money, Mama. That is why I have come to see you. I take on all the—er—pageantry, so to speak, all your London obligations and all the visits to foreign capitals, and never get a penny for it."

"Nonsense. You got several thousands for the Czar's funeral."

"Pooh, Mama. It hardly paid for the cravat pins I had to hand round. Anyway, if my efforts were recognized by Parliament, then you could easily suggest that I should be paid for them. As it is, you shut yourself up here or in the Isle of Wight—or vanish to Balmoral—while I do all the work and get nothing. It's most unfair."

"You just don't know what you're saying, Bertie. You are being cruel and unkind to a very lonely old woman. I have nothing to live for, and you know perfectly well that both Sir John Reid and Sir William Jenner have laid it down, once and for all, that my nerves cannot stand more than a few hours of London. God knows how I am going to get through Wednesday; I shall be an utter wreck. Besides, there is my grief."

"Very well, Mama. As always, when you take that line, there is nothing more to be said. But I have just been talking with Sir Henry and that is what I wanted to see you about."

"Sir Henry! Why on earth should you talk to him? You never asked me if you could. Sir Henry Ponsonby is my secretary, Sir Francis Knollys is yours. You should have asked permission."

"No, Mama. There is a certain point where your Civil List and my Parliamentary Grant are on common ground. Should not something, now and again, be transferred from one to the other? After all, you must have far more money than you need, while clearly I have not got enough. The solution is obvious."

"How often, Bertie, must I ask you not to talk nonsense?"

"Oh, well, that wasn't really quite what Sir Henry and I were chatting about."

"Now come, dear boy, what is it? You know I cannot bear uncertainty. It makes me ill. Say what you have to say, for heaven's sake."

"Well, Sir Henry and I were just running over some of my commitments, my expenditure and so on, and . . . er . . ."

"Oh, do get on, Bertie. You make me quite nervous—and don't fidget with your cuffs like that."

"No, Mama. Well, Sir Henry and I discussed the possibility of a loan."

"A loan—have you gone mad?"

"Not at all. The Hanoverian sovereigns almost lived on loans. The Hoares, Childs and Burdett-Coutts all made fortunes out of them."

"That was quite different. That was history, Bertie. Keep to the present."

"Well, as I told Sir Henry, I wasn't prepared to exploit my rank, to pawn my expectations, so to speak."

"I should think not, indeed."

"Well, we thought—Sir Henry and I, that is—we thought that perhaps in exchange for some real security, some intrinsic but valuable object that really belongs to us, not to the nation, that somebody—Sir Henry mentioned the Rothschilds—might fork out the cash."

"Might what?"

"Might lend the money, Mama."

"Oh, indeed; and where, pray, will you find such security? You've already sold half your stocks. You'll be borrowing the Crown itself next."

"No, Mama, but while Sir Henry and I were talking, we were looking all the time at this Tudor Tiara. He's brought it from the Tower this afternoon. It's in his room now."

"Bertie, you must have gone stark, staring mad—and Sir Henry too. I would expect it of you, but not of him—always such a nice man. Now, no more nonsense. It will soon be time for me to dress for dinner, and for you to remove that revolting American jacket. Do try to dress like a gentleman, Bertie."

"Yes, Mama; but about the Tudor Tiara—do tell me more."

"Very well, my boy. It's a wonderful story. That Tiara was one of the finest works of art in the Crystal Palace. Papa spent many hours upon the beautiful design. Presumably Sir Henry now has the original—not a mere replica."

"A replica, Mama! What on earth are you talking about? A replica, and in the Tower of London!"

"Oh, yes. There were two or three. Your Papa, Bertie, although nobody appreciated it, was a very fine Christian. He was not, thank God, a radical or a Liberal but he followed his Saviour in his belief that 'blessed are the poor'—provided of course that they are hardworking and respectable. He even built model dwellings alongside the Crystal Palace, well ventilated and with taps, just to show what might be done for the deserving masses. And so, when he created such a supreme work of art as this Tiara, he felt most strongly that the laboring people should see it—if only to bring a little beauty to those grimy streets where God had cast their lot. At least three replicas of the Tiara were made, one for Liverpool, one for Glasgow and one for somewhere else—I forget where."

"I never knew that, Mama."

"You never know *anything;* and don't interrupt. Yes, three replicas—not valuable, of course, but almost indistinguishable from the original. They were shown in the Industrial North in '51 and '52, and then one of them was shown in Manchester at the great Art Treasures Exhibition in '57. After that they were stored somewhere or other—probably at the Art College in South Kensington which Papa founded. But of course after '61 I was too crushed, too utterly bowed down, even to think of such earthly things."

"What an extraordinary story, Mama."

"Oh, yes, it has always been assumed that the real Tiara went to the Tower; but I believe that there may have been some sort of muddle at South Kensington—these Bohemian types, you know, so clever but so careless."

The Prince of Wales was now gazing at a picture near the ceiling. He was forty-six. He had spent most of those years learning how to get his own way. He had met defeat at the hands of his father. His mother was different; her affection, her selfishness and her arrogance could be exploited if one knew how. The stream of wrath could not be dammed; it might be diverted. It might, for instance, be diverted in the direction of Sir Henry Ponsonby. The Prince glanced at the clock. There was still time.

"Yes, a curious story, Mama, but of course Garrard's could tell us immediately whether the Tiara on Sir Henry's desk is the real article or not. If it is a replica I am surprised the people at the Tower have never said anything. . . . But there, perhaps it's not worth bothering about."

"Not worth bothering about! But, Bertie, the separate stones may be worth millions. . . . Mary Tudor's earrings alone. Of course it's worth bothering about."

"Possibly, although Ponsonby says it's not yours anyway."

"Not mine! Not mine!" The royal pallor had flushed crimson. "Not mine! Sir Henry must have gone off his head. Of course it's mine. There is no question of it. It was my own Angel's work, my own Angel's idea. And nearly all the gems were our own, or else gifts—gifts to Papa personally. Of course it's mine! What on earth can Sir Henry mean? Disgraceful!"

The stream had been diverted. Bertie could now sit back and let it happen.

"I don't know what he was driving at, Mama. He said that the Tiara must belong to the nation, otherwise it wouldn't be in the Tower at all. He said that the Solicitor-General might object if we used it as security for a loan. I said that I was sure it was yours to do what you liked with. . . ."

The Queen's hand was hardly raised from the table—only the pudgy fingers. It was the command for silence.

"That will do. The matter must not be discussed. Sir Henry must be taught to mind his own business. Dear General Gray would never have behaved like this—not as long as my dear one was alive. And the Tiara too, with all its sad memories! It is too bad. Sir Henry should have kept quiet until I consulted him. The Tiara is ours, yours and mine, Bertie, to use as we like; the matter must never be referred to again. Speak to Sir Henry, Bertie, suavely, of course, but let him see that he has blundered. And now, Bertie, about this loan from Rothschilds."

"Yes, Mama. I know that I am a very imperfect son, but I really do have great responsibilities. Alix and I do our very best to uphold the dignity of the Throne, you know, just as Papa would have wished."

"You are a dear, good boy, Bertie, if only people would try to understand your difficulties."

"I do my best, Mama, but it is all terribly expensive . . . all this keeping up appearances."

"Of course it is. Now about the Tiara. In view of Sir Henry's unaccountable and indeed outrageous behavior, say no more to him about the loan. You understand that."

"Not a word, Mama. I quite agree."

"No, nor to your own Sir Francis Knollys. He also might have some absurd legalistic notions. I am sure he and Sir Henry talk us over. No, after the Jubilee I shall simply announce that I am keeping the Tiara at Windsor—that is all anybody need know. And then, Bertie, in due course, and with my permission, you may make use of it in a way which will have my approval."

"Oh, thank you, Mama. That will be simply wonderful!"

"Don't be foolish. It will be no more than good business. A great stroke for the House of Coburg. Papa would have approved and, what's more, so would Baron Stockmar. It will enable you to leave your affairs in apple-pie order for dear Eddy and for Georgie."

"That will be splendid, Mama. Parliament is always so mean to the younger generation. And Georgie is already so good and confiding. I wish I could say the same of Eddy. I am paying his debts, you know, as well as my own."

"Eddy is unspeakable. That is the cross you and Alix have to bear. Keep it secret at all costs—from the public, I mean—that is all that matters. It is Uncle Cumberland all over again. But still Eddy is your heir, and he and Georgie must both be provided for one day. But what were we talking about?"

"The Tudor Tiara, Mama. I shall take it to Natty or Ferdy at Tring, and then . . ."

"You will do no such thing. Baron Ferdinand would twist you round his little finger. I hope you don't think that *you* have any Jewish flair."

"Really, Mama, why should I?"

"Why shouldn't you—if you listen to gossip."

"Oh, you mean the old story about Grandma Coburg and the Jewish riding master at Rosenau . . . the year before Papa was born."

"That, Bertie, is the kind of cruel nonsense that people in our position have to put up with—and in silence. Mind you, I'm not saying that Lieutenant von Hanstein wasn't very elegant and handsome—he was. But the Duchess Louise was a dear, sweet, faithful creature. It was all wicked lies. But who, may I ask, was so monstrous as to tell you this story?"

"Papa, Mama."

"Never. Never. He never spoke of it. When?"

"Oh, I was about fifteen, I think. Walking up Glen Gairn. We'd gone on ahead leaving the gillies and ponies behind. Papa tried to tell me how babies were born, as if I didn't know, and then he told me about his own birth, how everybody said horrible things about his mother so that she had to go and live in Paris. But tell me, Mama, have I any Jewish blood?"

"Certainly not, Bertie. What an idea! And that is why you must on no account deal with the Rothschilds yourself; they would get the better of you."

"Then what do you suggest, Mama?"

"Give the Tiara to Baron Hirsch."

"To Maurice . . . I didn't know that you had ever heard of him."

"Certainly I have. First, get Knollys or Esher to take the Tiara straight from here to Hirsch at Bath House. On no account, at any time, must you have it in your own possession. And none of this nonsense of house parties at Tring or Waddesdon, where you spend the night knocking on each other's bedroom doors. Hirsch must do the thing properly, negotiating with the House of Rothschild in their City offices, in a decent manner."

"You are very shrewd, Mama."

"I have had to be. Set Jew against Jew. The Rothschilds may be part of history but none of them is quite like Hirsch. Pure flair! It is difficult to invite him here—he's been blackballed at the Jockey Club—but he writes to me regularly."

"Writes to you—great heavens!"

"Don't exclaim like that, Bertie. Why shouldn't he write to me? He sends me a list every week, a list of your holdings on the Stock Exchange, and I check the prices in the *Times*. Hirsch has done very well for you, Bertie—copper, sugar and foreign railways."

"Oh, yes, Mama; but I had no idea you knew anything about such things."

"They interest me, and I have to keep an eye on everything. It was Hirsch, for instance, who, on my advice, told the French police to keep the moneylenders out of your hotel in Paris. You are a dear boy, Bertie, but you are not the man of the world you think you are. How could you be, brought up as you were?"

The Prince of Wales was silent. After nearly half a century Mama still left him dumb with amazement. Whenever he had one of these tête-à-tête talks with her she always began as his mother and ended up as the Queen. First he had thought he was in for a scolding, then she had turned right round and given him what he wanted—the Tiara—and in the process had assumed entire control of everything.

"And if the Tiara is only a replica, Mama?"

"It won't be—I know that—but if it is then the real thing will be safely locked up in a cellar in South Kensington, so that can soon be put right. But remember one thing, Bertie."

"Yes, Mama."

"Remember that the Tiara may not be worth a million—it sounds quite absurd to me—but remember that the twelve-pointed diamond stars, one on either side, are more than half its value."

"So Sir Henry tells me."

"Yes, they were Mary Tudor's wedding earrings—'Bloody Mary,' as they will call her. She was a most unsatisfactory woman. She had no babies and she was a Roman Catholic. However, she was firm with her bishops and her husband gave her some magnificent jewels. So remember, Bertie."

"Yes, Mama."

"And now I just have time to dress for dinner, while you have time to take off that jacket."

"Yes, Mama."

In the labyrinth of Windsor are many corridors. The Great Corridor, or "the Corridor" as they call it, is a grander affair. Looking onto the quadrangle of the Upper Ward, it is often gloomy, but on this particular evening the tall mullion windows threw bars of sunlight across the carpet. The sunlight also gilded the rosettes of Wyatville's ceiling, causing them to sparkle like little suns in their dark coffering. The whole length of the Corridor was punctuated by white marble busts, each on its malachite pedestal—busts of those who had once strutted there—while in every embrasure was some object, curious, grotesque or sentimental. The total effect was majestic, rich and middle-class.

Across the Corridor, opposite these tall windows and these *objets d'art*, a long line of varnished doors, each in its crenelated frame, opened onto the whole suite of Private Apartments. Tomorrow the Queen would use the State Apartments, their grandeur more attuned to the Houses of Hanover and Coburg. Tonight, however, all was intimate and informal—or at least as informal as was ever possible. Except for the Maharajah and Maharani, everyone would know each other.

At nine o'clock two dinners would be served. At one of these, night after night, whenever guests could be fended off, the Queen would dine alone with the Princess Beatrice. This was known as the "Family Dinner." Its setting was the Green Drawing Room (with the smaller Winterhalters) and the Green Dining Room (with the smaller Landseers).

The second dinner—the "Household Dinner"—was much jollier. It was for the ladies and gentlemen in attendance, for secretaries and equerries, for physicians and clergy, for the suites of visiting sovereigns and for such guests—actors and actresses, for instance—as could hardly expect to dine with the Queen herself. There were two rules. The first: no laughter must be heard in the Green Dining Room next door—hence the suppressed giggles. The second: the two dinners must end at the same moment. As the Queen gobbled this was barely possible. When the major-domo tipped off the Household that the moment had come, the *bombe surprise* had to be left a ruin upon the plates, the pineapples and nectarines untouched, while the gentlemen, having gulped down their sweet sherry, sprinted to the distant water closet, only to queue behind the Prime Minister or Mr. Balfour. Only thereafter could the "Family" and the "Household" meet democratically for coffee in the Corridor.

Tonight, her Jubilee so near, the Queen was in a hospitable and, indeed, expansive mood. There were twenty-four covers at her table; there were to be ten courses instead of the usual eight. She would be entertaining one of her own tributary princes, a reminder to others that she was Empress as well as Queen.

Half an hour to go before dinner, a quarter of an hour before they would all assemble in the two drawing rooms. Since everyone at Windsor must always be where they were supposed to be, the Corridor and drawing rooms were still completely deserted. The Caroline plate, the Ming porcelain, the Nemours napery, the Albertine epergnes, the Palatine candelabra, the Yorkist salt cellars, the smilax and roses, the fruit from the glass houses, had long since been set out with precision, but in all that vast expanse of carpet, where the sun was now striking almost horizontally through Venetian blinds, there was no human soul. Not a soul except a single footman guarding the Tiara, and he, since footmen have no souls, hardly counted. An hour earlier and he would have worn tight trousers and pomaded hair; now it was officially evening and so his hair was powdered, his calves padded, his stockings of silk.

He was alone. The silence was absolute. Then far away at the end of the Corridor, there was the rustle of a satin dress. This was unprecedented. It was barely half past eight. It was against the rules. The soft step came nearer until, ever so slightly, the man dared to slide his eyes sideways. It was a black dress—black with a silver thread. There was the brilliant white of the starched widow's cap. The man stopped breathing. She lifted one eyebrow—the Windsor signal of dismissal. He vanished.

Just ahead of her the Queen could see the onyx table. She walked past her own Crimean medal—"Blessed Are the Merciful" in diamonds; she walked past the assegai that had killed the Prince Imperial; she walked past General Gordon's Bible, eternally open at the 23rd Psalm. And then, at last, she was in front of the Tudor Tiara. Skerret had found the black velvet; Sir Henry had placed the thing to advantage. He had set up two gilded easels, one for the Holbein engravings, one for the Prince Consort's own drawings.

She looked at the Tiara very closely. It was thirty-six years since she had seen it in the Crystal Palace . . . how clearly she remembered it in its handsome glass case railed off and guarded by guardsmen. On that day, May 1, 1851, the Crystal Palace had been so packed with marvels, all, in a way, her precious Angel's doing, although for this one exhibit he was so particularly responsible. She had stood there, thirty-six years ago, on Albert's arm, with the sunshine pouring through the great glass roof. The old Duke of Wellington had been with them, and Sir Henry Cole and, for some reason, Mr. George Stephenson and, of course, Mr. Paxton, who had once been a common gardener's boy. And there, at her side, had been dear Vicky and poor, dear Alice, both in their sprigged muslin and their little pantalettes, with Bertie in a sailor suit (H.M.S. *Bellerophon*) and behind them little Arthur in his nurse's arms.

She had been so happy. Nobody ever understood how wonderful life had been . . . then. And now, more alone than ever in this vast, empty Corridor, she dabbed her old eyes. She put out her hand, her pudgy fingers, and touched the Tiara, caressing Mary Tudor's diamonds. She looked up to Heaven. . . . Albert was surely with her, watching her as he must always do. The tears were streaming down her furrowed cheeks. One might have heard her murmur—"Oh, Bertie, my dear, dearest son." She looked left and right—a carpeted desert of emptiness. She put both hands upon the Tiara. Ye Gods! What is Majesty going to do? In her long life she had faced many difficult moments, but none like this. The doors of all the drawing rooms and dining rooms were closed. There was nobody. She did what she had to do. Five minutes later, with a trembling hand but a firm step, she walked back to her little Gold Room.

A dowdy party with a little brilliance . . . The Maharajah's coat of black watered silk—made by Poole—was buttoned to the throat; his turban was of dazzling white, making the untidy complexities of English shirt fronts and ties look foolish. The Maharani wore a sari of deep and mysterious black-green with little constellations of amethysts—like a starlit night seen in the dark waters of an Indian river, the current swirling as her body moved.

For all the other ladies, had they but known it, this was a fortunate year. The old crinoline had quite gone; there was now the sweeping tulip skirt, while neither the bustle nor the full sleeve had quite arrived. The bodice was cut to reveal so beautifully a good bust, the hair drawn up from the nape of the neck —lovely necks above lovely busts. Alas, however, this had been fully realized only by the Princess of Wales, her dress having been created by Worth, and by Lady Randolph Churchill, her dress created in a cottage at Blenheim. All the others, in deference to the Queen, wore untidy coiffures and perpetual mourning.

The presentations and hand kissings were smartly disposed of in the Green Drawing Room—or as smartly as possible. True, the Queen was disappointed to find that the Maharajah's equerry, so far from being a handsome oriental who might have said a word to the Munshi, her own dear Indian servant, was merely a rather dubious English officer called Pinkerton. True, the Maharajah had knelt on both knees, and when welcomed in Hindustani had replied, in an Etonian drawl, that he spoke no German. True, Lord Randolph had asked dear Eddy (known to the family as Eddy but to the world as the Duke of Clarence, or "Collar and Cuffs") when he would get his first command at sea. Eddy, who would never know port from starboard, only giggled. But at last all these strange creatures were got to table, a gold-and-scarlet footman behind each chair, and with the Munshi, in white-and-yellow satin, behind the Queen. The Queen knew perfectly well that at, say, Woburn or Hatfield, there would be two footmen behind each chair; Bertie and Alix could ape such aristocratic nonsense if they chose—she knew better.

Gloom and apprehension hung over both dinners. It had been rumored that there was to be a "treat." At its very worst this meant amateur theatricals, with the Munshi piqued at being put in the back row with the dressers, and the footmen piqued at his being there at all. At its dubious best a treat might be a brief lecture from a distinguished guest—a disastrous magic lantern was still remembered. This evening the lecture was to be by old Ponsonby himself. Nobody knew why.

If the Household Dinner was subdued, the Family Dinner was more so. Only those who enjoyed hearing the Queen squash all attempts to make small talk bigger got any fun. The Maharajah's comparison of the Irish Question with the Buddhist-Hindu problem was strangled at birth: "If only the people of India, Maharajah, would join the Church of England, like everybody else, life would be simpler." Bertie, in return for his riposte that since Mama was an Anglican at Windsor and a Presbyterian at Balmoral, she should be a Catholic in Dublin, was told not to talk such wicked nonsense. When Arthur Balfour quietly asked his uncle, the Prime Minister, about an appointment to the See of Durham, he was told down the length of the table that "Durham Cathedral always looks so well from the railway—one of the joys of our journey to Deeside." The real difficulty, however—what to do about the Duke of Clarence—had been neatly solved in advance; Eddy was placed between Lady Esher, who didn't matter, and the Maharani's lady in attendance, Miss Nummuggar, who spoke no English. Bertie, to his fury, had been placed between two ladies who, palpably, offered no temptation to flirtation.

People's thoughts, however, are more fascinating than their words—the thoughts of these twenty-four peculiar minds. His

DINNER AT WINDSOR, JUNE 19, 1887

H.M. the Queen

H.R.H. the Maharajah of Kashgar		H.M. King Christian of Denmark
H.R.H. the Princess of Wales		H.R.H. the Maharani of Kashgar
The Very Rev. Randall Davidson		The Marquis of Salisbury
Lady Jane Ely		Lady Ponsonby
Colonel Pinkerton		H.R.H. the Prince of Wales
Lady Randolph Churchill		Mrs. Randall Davidson
Mr. Arthur Balfour		H.R.H. Prince George
Lady Esher		H.M. Queen Louise of Denmark
H.R.H. the Duke of Clarence (Eddy)		Lord Randolph Churchill
Miss Nummuggar		The Marchioness of Salisbury
Lord Esher		Sir Henry Ponsonby

H.R.H. the Princess
Beatrice of Battenberg

Royal Highness the Maharajah of Kashgar, on the Queen's right, was wondering whether there were any jewels in this ghastly place better than his own—and how to get hold of them. Her Royal Highness the Princess of Wales, next to him, wondered who would be the real hostess at Marlborough House on Thursday, and then began to dream about the magnolias in Copenhagen. . . . The Very Reverend Randall Davidson, Dean of Windsor, was wondering why he had not been asked to say grace; he had found a charming one in an old Book of Hours, and was now feeling hurt. Lady Jane Ely was wondering whether the Queen might not make a fool of herself by wearing this idiotic Tiara, and rather hoping she would—she had been so snappy lately. Colonel Pinkerton was wondering what he was going to get out of all this, and whether or not he could double-cross the Maharajah in the matter of jewels. Lady Randolph Churchill, apart from wondering, as always, how on earth she had ever landed herself with this gang, was jealous of the Maharani; Alix being, after all, no more than pretty, Jennie Churchill expected as of right to be the only beautiful woman at Windsor. Mr. Arthur Balfour, while looking clever, was wondering how to improve his forehand drive at tennis. Lady Esher, four months gone, was wondering whether the Queen would notice—the crinoline had had its advantages. Eddy, with his mouth open, was wondering how to pay his bills at Willis's—all those private rooms for entertaining naval cadets; if only he had something to borrow on. Miss Nummuggar was wondering whether this mixing of the sexes at dinner, which she had so dreaded, was after all so dangerous—the men were so ugly; and whether or not the Munshi might be an untouchable in disguise—which he was. Lord Esher was wondering whether he might not still be the Prince of Wales's executor when the Prince died—he would hardly make old bones—and if so whether he should not then burn all the papers. Her Royal Highness the Princess Beatrice was wondering why Mama was in one of her moods: it was not her bowels and so at the moment it must be Bertie; later, after red beef and ice cream washed down with iced water, it would be indigestion. Sir Henry Ponsonby was wondering for the tenth time what had happened to Black Beauty that afternoon at the station. The Marchioness of Salisbury was wondering whether to accept Mr. Oscar Wilde's invitation to write for a Society magazine. Lord Randolph Churchill was wondering why they did not give medical certificates to prostitutes in London as they did in Paris. Her Majesty Queen Louise of Denmark was wondering whether dear Alix was really past childbearing or whether it was all Bertie's fault, and why dear Alix had never had her share of the Family jewelry. His Royal Highness Prince George was not wondering anything very much—and never would. Mrs. Randall Davidson was wondering whether to have gas put into the Deanery or whether the vacancy at Canterbury might not come soon—cancer was so unpredictable. His Royal Highness the Prince of Wales was wondering why he should have to eat his mother's beef and mutton when he might have been at home enjoying grilled oysters followed by ortolans in brandy or quails *à la Greque*, or both. Lady Ponsonby was wondering why on earth the Queen should send Henry all the way to the Tower of London for the Tudor Tiara, when all the time it was upstairs, locked up in Albert's bedroom, the famous Blue Room. The Marquis of Salisbury was wondering whether he could ever get new blood into this awful family—all so unmentionable, so difficult. Her Royal Highness the Maharani of Kashgar was wondering whether the Queen knew that one could see the cleft at the top of the Princess of Wales's bosom, and would be as shocked as she was. His Majesty King Christian of Denmark was wondering why his spies were so useless; he had learned more about the Queen and Bismarck in three days at Windsor than anyone had told him in a year; they must all be corrupt—corrupted by the Queen's Prussian relations.

And her Majesty the Queen . . . the Queen was just wondering and wondering; she hardly noticed what was going on round her; crouched over her plate she might now and again show the whites of her eyes, or even speak, but she knew the whole business by heart, and had for years and years. So she just went on wondering and plotting . . . wondering, and thinking about dear, dear Bertie and the Tiara, and Dizzy and John Brown and the dear Munshi . . . whom everybody seemed to dislike.

Only when coffee was served, only when the Household and the Family had assembled in the Corridor, could Windsor enjoy its brief democracy. In the Dining Room the Queen had taken a peach; she would not eat it, but the signal had been given. Everyone knew that no matter what remained on their plates or in their glasses they had just ten minutes. At the end of ten minutes they must be flattened against the walls of the Corridor while large baroque chairs were set for majesties and highnesses. A few more presentations might be made, a few more words said about the weather or the horses . . . and then it was time for coffee and for the "treat."

It was all very odd, set in all that delicate and spiky Gothic —twenty-four people from the Queen's dinner, thirty-eight from the Household, including six tall and sinister gentlemen from the Maharajah's suite, all in zebra-striped turbans, together with "the Maharani's Secretary," a twittering little eunuch in pince-nez. The scene was animated, bejeweled, bourgeois and ridiculous.

The Prince of Wales, who had had the courage to bring his brandy glass from the Dining Room, still stood in the doorway, looking with fascinated cynicism at all these orientals—his mother's subjects—who could so easily buy him out. He looked also upon these giggling, gossiping English ladies—rusty black, ill-fitting corsets and ill-used curling tongs—only to feel a vast yearning for a slaughter of birds at Sandringham, an afternoon at Newmarket, a breezy day at Cowes or, best of all, a great ball at Marlborough House, with the carriages lining the Mall, a summer night heavy with the scent of banked orchids, the scarlet marquee on the lawn, gorgeous uniforms, ribbons and stars, rich Jews and beautiful women, all chic, opulent, subtly perfumed, wicked and delectable . . . and all turning and turning slowly in the Mandela Waltz. And even that, he said to himself, was nothing to what he might do one day. . . . One day he would take back Hampton Court as a palace: an English Versailles. He would need the diamonds and he would need the Rothschilds.

Why, here at Windsor the only smart women in the whole room were his own Alix and Lady Randolph; the only seductive one, the Maharani. Alix wore an astonishing confection—coffee-colored satin, no gems or bows—with a great swirling skirt below a tight bust, and a coiffure that was an André masterpiece. Could it really be that only a couple of hours ago he had told Ponsonby that she had no extravagances? Oh, well, Ponsonby probably hadn't believed him anyway, and it didn't matter now that Mama was giving him the Tiara.

He turned his bloodshot eyes from his own wife to Lady Randolph. He could only just believe that Jeanette Jerome had been the loveliest girl on Long Island. She had given Randolph two sons, but then Randolph was easily pleased; she was not the Prince's type, not at this stage of his life, not in this mood. Now the Maharani was quite a different matter. She was not only beautiful and serene; in her oriental way she was chic. If the toilette of the Princess of Wales could be outshone anywhere in England that night, it might well be by that particular sari. At dinner he had thought of the sari as being like stars reflected in a dark river; now he saw it as the starry sky itself, so that as the Maharani walked it was as if clouds were blowing across the constellations. Also it was very subtly and surprisingly made, so that just now and again one glimpsed an emerald corsage—no more than glimpsed. And yet, only a few moments ago—oh, God!—he had heard his mother call it "native costume"!

He sipped his brandy from his big balloon glass. Over the rim he could watch the Maharani almost unnoticed. She was not only beautiful and serene. She was dark, mysterious and indefinable. Oddly enough, in all his forty-six years he had never, not even in India, considered an oriental woman; not seriously, that is, not as a proposition for the bedroom. Such a thing, he now reflected, would surely have panache, piquancy, novelty, daring, cachet . . . or wouldn't it? Probably it just "wouldn't do." There was the Indian army to think of, there was Mama, the position of the Viceroy and of the Empire. Oh, God, no, it would never do! In any case the wives of a Maharajah (there were three more at Claridge's in the guise of "aunts") were surely closely guarded day and night. Perhaps they sold their wives in Kashgar, sold them for diamonds, for instance. What nonsense! He was hot with desire but managed to shrug his shoulders, dismissing a dream to turn his gaze upon the Prime Minister.

The Marquis of Salisbury had failed to bring his brandy from the Dining Room: "You won't need your glass, Prime Minister; we're having coffee now." He was content, however, to dominate the whole scene with his great domelike head—portentous insignia of the Cecils. His head made him look wise when he was not even thinking. His nephew, on the other hand, was exercising his vivid charms upon the Princess of Wales. She was not wasted upon him—Mr. Balfour had written a treatise upon beauty; it was only that he was wasted upon her.

Once again the Prince's eyes moved above the rim of his glass—to the Tiara. He frowned. Ponsonby had set it well upon its black cushion. The purple curtains had now been pulled behind it, the gaseliers had been lit; and yet somehow the Tiara seemed to lack a little of the luster it had had in Ponsonby's office two hours ago. It didn't matter . . . Garrard's would give a valuation and then the Prince would be able to buy all the things he loved, able to buy them for years to come—as long as Mama was alive; after that the Rothschilds would be unnecessary.

Was it true, he wondered, that the Maharajah was really a connoisseur of gems? All these Indian princes had masses of gems but that didn't mean that they understood them. The Maharajah, handsome devil, was now looking very sulky but also smug. He was sulking because at dinner he had three times—oh, so casually—mentioned the Order of the Garter, and three times—oh, so diplomatically—it had been explained to him that it was a religious order given only to Christian sovereigns . . . tomorrow he might like to see the Chapel. That was nonsense. He knew perfectly well, everyone knew, that after the Crimea the Garter had been given to the Sultan; he was therefore enraged. The veins stood out upon his forehead, his eyes bulged. He had been insulted. He craved revenge. The Prince of Wales was much amused.

Sulkiness and smugness, however, always possessed the Maharajah when he was in England. They had possessed him at Eton where he had been baited by snotty little boys. His loathing of the West had been ingrained in him at the age of twelve. He was, therefore, eaten up with desire for revenge. He was smug because he knew that the single ruby in his turban was worth more than that absurd Tiara. Not that he was contemptuous of the Tiara; he was merely realistic. The setting was an outrage; he would melt it down to make rings for his retainers. But the gems . . . ah, yes, the gems; some of them, the diamond stars for instance, he would be glad to add to his collection.

The Maharajah beckoned to his aide-de-camp, Colonel Pinkerton. The Prince lowered his brandy glass. He was no longer amused. He was alert. Only yesterday he had had a note from the India Office—"Very Secret." While not wishing to alarm the Queen, the Permanent Secretary thought that His Royal Highness should know that Colonel Pinkerton had been cashiered in '84; he had almost certainly robbed the mess at Darjeeling, and by the standards becoming to an officer and a gentleman should long ago have blown out his brains. Pinkerton now leaped to his master's side. The Maharajah whispered fiercely:

"Pinkerton."

"Your Highness."

"I would like that Tiara in my baggage—see to it."

"Your Highness, I understand perfectly."

The Maharajah now elbowed his way to the onyx table. He looked more closely at the fountain of jewels upon the velvet cushion, and then closer still until his bulging eyes almost touched the diamonds. His expression changed. He held up his hands in amazement. Surprise, shock and puzzlement chased themselves across his saturnine face. He glanced behind him.

They were busy chattering, had hardly noticed him. The Queen's sight was appalling. The Prince's eyes seemed to be upon him—only to be hurriedly withdrawn. Again he beckoned to his aide-de-camp.

"Pinkerton."

"Your Highness."

"I do not want the Tiara—trash!"

"Your Highness, I understand perfectly."

The Prince was now devoured by curiosity. What was all this whispering? He must know. The detectives must be warned that something was in the wind, Heaven knows what. There was a voice at his elbow, that of his difficult and unspeakable heir.

"P-papa."

"Eddy—how very nice of you to address me. I wasn't sure that we were on speaking terms."

"Now, P-papa, p-please. That is how your father used to scold you . . . p-please, P-papa."

"Very well, Eddy; but when you do dine here with Grandmama—and we none of us enjoy it—do try to behave like a gentleman; try to say something to those next to you at dinner."

"That Indian woman spoke no English."

"There were others around you. But what is it?"

"This T-tiara, P-papa."

The Prince glanced sharply at his son.

"The Tiara—what has that got to do with you?"

"Whose is it?"

"Really, Eddy, what an extraordinary question! What put that into your head?"

"I only wondered. Well, P-papa, who d-does it b-belong to?"

"If you must know, it belongs to the Family, but why?"

"To G-grandmama, then to you, then m-me."

"What are you driving at, Eddy? Speak up for heaven's sake."

"I'm in a fix, P-papa."

"We all know that. It's entirely your own fault and you know that you have to be punished for it. Frankly, Eddy, we just don't know how to deal with you. A world tour might not be so bad, my boy. At least it would get you away from your ghastly friends into the more wholesome atmosphere of a naval wardroom."

"That's all you know about the Navy, P-papa. But this T-tiara, P-papa, couldn't we make use of it somehow? We're b-both in the same b-boat. I need c-cash and you need c-cash. We could p-pawn it and split the takings . . . and live happy ever after. G-grandmama need never know."

"That is quite enough of your impertinence, Eddy. You forget yourself! You are breaking your mother's heart as it is . . . don't make things worse. That is enough!"

"Very well, P-papa, then I must l-look after myself."

The footmen were serving coffee. The Queen refused it; it was easier to control a situation when not encumbered by a cup and saucer. Everyone else was allowed exactly five minutes to gulp down the tepid liquid in the golden cups from Portugal. Normally the company would disperse to other rooms—to whist or backgammon or to turn idly the pages of albums until, terrified to yawn, they could no longer keep their eyes open. This, however, was not a normal evening. There was the "treat." It had to be gone through. The Queen liked "treats."

Her Majesty spoke to Lady Ely.

"Jane dear, will you please tell someone to ask Bandmaster Fane to silence his men, and to thank him. The excerpts from the Savoy operettas were most entertaining."

The Queen turned to Lady Cadogan.

"Sarah dear, will you please ask Princess Beatrice to tell someone to tell the major-domo that we want silence."

These messages having been duly passed up and down the ranks, the Coldstream Guards laid down their instruments in the middle of a bar, the major-domo tapped the floor with his staff . . . and there was silence.

"Now, Beatrice, say your piece, dear."

"Yes, Mama. Majesties, highnesses, may it please you; lords, ladies and gentlemen: you may know that tomorrow night, at a great family dinner party in the Waterloo Chamber, on the eve of her Jubilee, Her Majesty will wear this famous Tiara, created by my beloved papa, but never worn before. Here it is on the onyx table. Sir Henry Ponsonby has kindly undertaken to tell us its curious history."

Nobody was sure whether or not to clap; "Papa" having been mentioned, better not. The Prince of Wales, still aloof at the back of the crowd, emptied his glass. He was still watching the Maharajah—now a most extraordinary sight, walking to and fro in a frenzy, beating his breast and wringing his hands. He kept whispering to Pinkerton until a cough from the Queen told him that he was making himself conspicuous. The Prince made a sudden decision. Quietly, through the dining rooms, he slipped away. His absence might not be noticed for half an hour. . . . Ponsonby could be long-winded.

Sir Henry knew what was expected of him—or so he thought. He began solemnly with a few words about the Prince Consort. He explained how Albert, when he first came to England in 1840, had begun to catalogue the royal possessions, and had then gradually brought together the scattered jewels of the Tudor and Stuart epochs. He explained how, ten years later, for the Great Exhibition of 1851, the Prince had had the finest of the gems set in this marvelous Tiara, made to his own design. And here, on the easel, were the Prince's very own drawings, masterpieces of meticulous draftsmanship. There was, at this point, a dab of the royal handkerchief, also a suspicion of a wink from Arthur Balfour to Randolph Churchill.

Sir Henry now got down to business. He actually touched the great pearl, hanging, so to speak, on the forehead of the Tiara. Then he pointed to it on the Hatfield portrait of Elizabeth. "The reality is here on the Tiara; its simulation by Holbein's brush is something that you, Mr. Prime Minister, may see every day upon the wall of your home." The Marquis of Salisbury woke up in order to nod.

As for the jewels of Mary Queen of Scots, went on Sir Henry, they had been a great problem. When she came to England as a prisoner, this wanton creature left a vast quantity of French jewelry behind her at Holyrood, and all this, in due course, came to us with the accession of her son, James I. This big ruby, however—and here Sir Henry placed his finger upon the apex of the Tiara—was more romantic. It had been the lid of the locket within which Mary of Scotland had kept the sacramental wafer smuggled to her by the Pope; probably, therefore, it was secreted in her bosom when the axe fell. It was found in the Vatican Treasury in 1850 and, thanks to Cardinal Wiseman, restored to the English Crown.

"And now," went on Sir Henry, "I turn to the *pièce de résistance,* the *bonne bouche* of the Tiara, to those gems which are said to be half its value. You will all have noticed these two magnificent clusters of diamonds . . ." heads were craned forward ". . . these twelve-pointed stars, one on each side so as to flank the face of the wearer. You will all remember that Mary Tudor, who bears such an unfortunate sobriquet, also contracted an unfortunate marriage. On the eve of that marriage —it was in Winchester Cathedral—the bridegroom, destined to be our foe at the time of the Armada, gave his bride these superb diamonds in the form of earrings. They had come to Europe in a Spanish treasure ship, one of those Drake missed . . ." slight laughter ". . . and after Mary's death disappeared completely. It was presumed that they had found their way back to Spain. Anyway, three hundred years later, among the many gifts showered upon the Duke of Wellington after the Peninsular War were the diamond earrings. In 1851 the old Iron Duke gave them to the Prince Consort that they might be the glory of the Tiara. So you see a strange tale will complete itself tomorrow night when Your Majesty, beneath Lawrence's portrait of Wellington in the Waterloo Chamber, will wear this Tiara in which Bloody Mary's Earrings are so magnificently set. I now turn to . . ."

"Thank you, Sir Henry—most instructive. That will be enough."

Sir Henry Ponsonby was startled. He had been interrupted. He had been cut off in full flood. Had he gone on too long? Had he given offense? He still had much to say about Anne of Cleves' emeralds, about the seed pearls from Henry VIII's gloves, about Sir Francis Bacon's shoe buckles, not to mention Lady Jane Gray's stomacher. He was startled. He was also hurt.

"Thank you, Sir Henry; most instructive and—er—romantic."

"I trust, ma'am, that I have not tried your patience."

"Not at all, Sir Henry; most instructive, if not very edifying."

"No, ma'am?"

"No. Maybe I am prejudiced. I always say that I am a Stuart. I have never held with these Tudors . . . a thoroughly bad lot."

"Really, ma'am . . . I don't see . . ."

"No, Sir Henry, there can be no two opinions. A bad lot. Of course things are different now; but they knew perfectly well they were doing wrong. And moreover, Sir Henry, I have never liked this vulgar way of referring to Mary Tudor. I know that she was a Roman Catholic—that would never be allowed now—and that she burnt people alive. That too would not be allowed today—more's the pity. But, after all, she was a queen. . . . Come, Beatrice dear, it is after eleven."

Everyone waited until the Queen and the Princess had disappeared. The other royals followed smartly, knowing exactly where they would find Bertie, baccarat and brandy. Then came the stampede of the Household to such corners of the vast castle as they could each call their own—to gossip and cocoa, or to French yellowbacks. The Corridor, gaseliers still blazing, remained silent and almost deserted—deserted save for one figure. Tall, willowy, gangling, His Royal Highness the Duke of Clarence—dear, unspeakable Eddy—stood by the onyx table. The lower lip was pendulous. He blinked and muttered.

"I must l-look after myself, must I? I'm in a b-bloody fix. They say I'm n-no use, that I m-must be p-punished. I'll show them. I'm a man. I d-damn well will look after myself. I will—so there!"

At the far end of the Corridor, very quietly, someone had opened one of the folding doors—ever so slightly. A head appeared; a black face beneath a white turban. It was the Maharajah. It vanished. Eddy had hardly recovered from the shock when there was a sound behind him. He whirled round. A door had opened—the door to one of the dining rooms. A head appeared; a black face beneath a yellow turban. It was the Munshi. The color drained from Eddy's face. His choker collar almost strangled him. His long cuffs shot out from the gold-laced sleeves. His hands twitched even more than usual. His face twitched. He took a step toward the onyx table and toward the Tiara, which, by some unwonted oversight, Sir Henry Ponsonby had left unguarded.

4

Beatrice

Back in his office, Sir Henry Ponsonby flopped into one armchair, his wife into another.

"Well, Mary, what do you make of that? I had only been talking for five minutes. It was damned rude."

"But, my darling, you've been treated like that for twenty years. What are you fussing about? It's nothing new."

"This is different. Something has upset her. . . ."

"It often does."

"Yes, Mary, she's upset every day of her life; but she always tells me what it is. She tells me before anyone, even before Beatrice. This time she hasn't said a word. What is it? It can't have been the few 'bloodys' that were bandied about—surely?"

"Of course not. That was her excuse. She's not squeamish. The public may think so, but you and I know better. After all, the older generation were the most foul-mouthed gang in Europe. Hasn't it ever struck you, Henry, that although advanced people are now talking so oddly about 'the Victorian Age,' the Queen is not particularly Victorian? No, no, it wasn't the 'bloodys.' As you say, she's upset. She has committed herself to this vulgar Tiara and now, for some reason, wants to get out of it, doesn't want it talked about."

"But she could just change her mind—wear one of her little diadems, and nobody would say a word. No, something has upset her. She hardly spoke to the Maharajah at dinner, except to snub him. And now I—I, of all people—am not in her confidence. I don't like it, Mary."

"Henry, my darling, you may be a model royal secretary, but what a good thing you never went into business."

"No doubt—but why?"

"Can't you see, dear, that the Tiara itself is the thing they are all worried about. Not only the Queen. Bertie has none of what the newspapers call his 'usual bonhomie.' Randolph told him a dirty story and he never even smiled. Beatrice is like a cat on hot bricks, and even poor Eddy seems aware of his surroundings."

"But why, why?"

"You're being a little obtuse, Henry. Don't you see there's a million pounds' worth of hideous jewels lying there on that hideous onyx table. Everything in the place is catalogued and labeled—Albert saw to that—but this is a new-found wonder, a windfall, and all they want to know is to whom it belongs—to the Queen, to Bertie, to Eddy? . . . Even the Denmarks would like it for Alix one day. The Maharajah I wouldn't trust an inch, and even dear Beatrice must be wondering."

"Beatrice . . . really, my love!"

"Why not? If the Tiara belongs to the Crown—the Crown, that is, as an institution—then in due course it goes to Bertie and after that to Eddy. If, on the other hand, it belongs to the Queen personally, under Albert's will, then she can pawn it, sell it, leave it to Beatrice—the comfort of her old age—or anything she damned well likes. It's rather like the palaces: they belong to the Crown, whereas Balmoral is her own private property—all the difference in the world. And when the private property is worth a million pounds and is also in highly portable form . . . well! Anyway, I suppose Bertie is the most interested person —the bankrupt heir. He at least must want to know whether the Tiara will ever be his or not . . . if so he could borrow on it now, you know."

"But, good God, Mary, what has made you think of all that?"

"It's only too obvious, isn't it?"

"But, Mary, Bertie came into this room as soon as I was back from the Tower this afternoon, and asked me that very question. Sometimes I think, my love, that you must be the cleverest woman in the world."

"No, Henry, I'm not clever but I'm always right. Mark my words: Bertie has seen you already; *she* will be after you in the morning."

"But again, why?"

"Why? Because Bertie is head over heels in debt and Parliament won't give him a bean. When Beatrice married last year she got only an extra ten thousand on the grounds that she was still going to live at Windsor, and so, naturally, her Henry blues it, popping over to visit various Battenbergs and so on. He's human; you can't expect him to spend the whole of his life with mother-in-law. I repeat, darling, there's a million pounds, or more, going begging, and they're all buzzing, to say the least, with curiosity."

"But why? Damn it all, they're rich. Oh, I know their incomes aren't what people imagine; but the State—Office of Works, Office of Woods and Forests, Commissioners for Crown Lands and so on—pays for everything. They don't *have* to have places like Balmoral and Sandringham . . . but they do . . . and then grumble."

"But, Henry, they just don't see it like that. What they do see is half a dozen of their subjects—the big dukes, Sutherland, Bedford, Devonshire and the rest—living more royally than themselves and . . ."

"But that is quite different, Mary. The dukes are landed aristocrats, the royals are middle-class—like you and me. You have only to imagine a Cecil or a Cavendish on the throne to realize what a middle-class crowd the royals are . . ."

"Of course; but that's just what hurts. Don't you see, Henry, that poor Bertie goes over to Germany, lives in baroque palaces with his awful relatives, or takes a whole hotel at Marienbad, and then comes home to complain about his tailor's bill? They're all quite absurd, the whole lot of them; but one does see that a million pounds is not to be sneezed at. Hence the burning issue: is the Tiara theirs or not?"

"Of course it's not theirs, Mary; don't be silly."

"Well then, whose is it? It must belong to somebody."

"It's—it's—oh, well, I suppose if it ever came to the point, and I trust it never will, I suppose it's part of the Crown Jewels."

"The Regalia?"

"Well, no, not exactly . . . but it has been kept in the Tower of London, hasn't it? . . . with all the other junk?"

"For less than forty years. Now, come, Henry my darling, you just don't know whose it is, do you? Now I do. I have all the time in the world. I spent the morning in the library with that nice Herr Mütter. Now look: Albert got some of the gems from foreign courts, others he cadged from old Catholic families—Arundels, Talbots, Throckmortons and the rest. The commissioners for the Great Exhibition paid for the setting as a kind of gesture to Albert and his Crystal Palace. They never claimed the Tiara and never can."

"Then that doesn't get us any further. Did you discover anything else from your nice Herr Mütter?"

"Of course. When the Great Exhibition closed Albert had the thing sent to the Tower—a clear implication that it was on trust for the nation . . . yes, an implication; but it was never legally consigned to anyone. The Constable of the Tower, considering the august source from which he received the Tiara, probably never checked either its ownership or its value. If it was really Albert's private property it almost certainly now belongs to the Queen, although his executors never said so; equally it could be argued that he meant it to belong to the nation. So, either way, my dear Henry, for any member of the family to sell it or even pawn it might be illegal and would certainly be scandalous; for the Queen, with all the Albertine associations, it would certainly be blasphemy . . . unless of course . . . unless . . ."

"Well . . . unless what, dear?"

"No. That's unthinkable."

"I said—unless what, dear?"

"Well, you see, Henry, several replicas were made—for the provincial galleries, I suppose—and the Queen kept one of these for herself, or so she said."

"Now what are you driving at, Mary?"

"Well, it's just possible, isn't it, that for her 'Angel's' sake she sent a replica to the Tower, and that the original, the real Tiara, is upstairs in Albert's bedroom, the Blue Room, in mothballs, so to speak, with all his clothes. It would be just like her."

"Good God! But the Tower would know."

"No. As I said, they might not check, and if they did would never dare to say anything."

"All right. But you must be wrong. If the real Tiara, Bloody Mary's Earrings and all, is in the Blue Room, what on earth was the point of my journey to London today? She's got the Tiara and she can wear it tomorrow night."

"My dear Henry, you really are rather simple sometimes. You know perfectly well, even if you haven't been there for years, that the Blue Room is untouchable . . . that the wreath still lies on the pillow, that the clean linen is laid out every morning, the nightdress placed on the bed every evening, that everything must remain exactly as it was on that night of '61. Nothing, nothing must ever be touched—least of all the Tiara, locked up in that huge wardrobe."

"Hm!"

"And pray, my love, what does that mean?"

"Nothing, my dear, nothing . . . only that our Bertie, for one, may have different ideas."

"Well, I hope *you* didn't put them into his head."

"Of course not, my love, of course not."

"If you did, and there was a scandal, he would say it was all your fault—that he only took advice."

"Oh, well, sooner or later the matter will have to be settled. I envisage months of correspondence with Garrard's and with the Solicitor-General. I wish the damned thing could have been left, forgotten, in its glass case in the Tower."

"Henry, my darling, you are not going to be allowed ever to

forget it again. The hunt is up. Whatever the public may think, nobody, you know, has ever really thought of trying to steal the Crown and Scepter; it's just not practical. But this is different. The Tiara is fair game and far too many people know about it —the Royal Family, servants, policemen, Beefeaters, railwaymen, the Maharajah, Colonel Pinkerton, Lord Randolph, the Munshi, Miss Nummuggar, Eddy . . . not to mention the carriage footman called Smith and the young man in the ginger suit—the one with the carpet bags. . . ."

Sir Henry leaped from his chair. He stood looking right down on his wife. He was even trembling a little.

"Ye gods, Mary, what in heaven's name are you getting at?"

"Well, Henry, my experience of human nature tells me that when a strange character says that his name is Smith he is probably lying."

"Oh, don't be so ridiculous. The coachman, Macdonald, must have seen him and known him."

"You said that you never saw the coachman's face, that he never got down from the box. . . . I expect his name was Jones. And all that nonsense about Smith having been in service with Lord Iddsleigh—a man whose death has just been in every newspaper—all a little too obvious, don't you think?"

"My dear Mary, you may be very clever, but this is a bit much. And the boy in the ginger suit, what about him?"

"What indeed? Remember that your train was held thirty minutes for you at Paddington. The next one was not for three-quarters of an hour—I looked it up in Bradshaw while Suzanne was doing my hair for dinner. 'Ginger suit' boarded the train when you did. Why? He was much too late for that train, much too early for the next. Oh, my Henry, do try to think! And then at Windsor he must have nipped out of the train in a flash—run down the platform while you were waiting for the Station Master to let you out. 'Ginger suit' was already holding Black Beauty's head when you and Philpotts came out of the station . . . dear old Black Beauty, steady as a rock."

"But, my love, this may be all very ingenious but it's also great nonsense, and you know it. I never once lost sight of that hat box from the moment when I took it from the table in Field Marshal Wilson's library . . ."

"After a very good brandy . . ."

". . . until I carried it into this room myself."

"Didn't you, Henry, didn't you?. . . Just think, my love, and then think again."

"Oh, well, if you must . . . There was a call of nature, inevitably; but the thing was always in good hands. Anyway, what are we talking about? The Tudor Tiara, real or replica, is here in the Castle safe and sound—and that is all there is to it. Whether Bertie raises money on it or not is an entirely different matter."

"So it would seem."

"Really, my love, I simply don't understand you."

"Well, he can't raise money on a replica, can he? Anyway, we shall see. But now it's time for bed. Be off with you, back to the Corridor, and take that hideous thing to the strong room. I'll wait here, then we can walk home across the courtyard to get some air."

The Corridor was deserted, the Tiara unguarded. Sir Henry felt a twinge of guilt—he and Mary had talked too long. Only one of the big gaseliers was now burning. The curtains had been drawn back so that one could see the terrace bathed in moonlight. Sir Henry Ponsonby's steps echoed strangely in this emptiness. He took the Tiara in both hands, clutching it to his shirt front. He listened. Away in the darkness at the far end two people were talking, whispering. Sir Henry walked back to the great stair. His curiosity, at this point, got the better of him. Still clutching the Tiara, he climbed to an upper landing from where he could look down upon the door from the Corridor. In a few moments he heard steps upon the marble. It was the Maharajah of Kashgar and the Princess Beatrice. They stood leaning on the balustrade.

"Yes, it's gone now, Maharajah. I expect Sir Henry Ponsonby,

Mama's Secretary, has taken it to the strong room. . . . But what you have been telling me is terribly serious—quite too shocking."

"Your Royal Highness must forgive me. I had to speak to someone. Naturally I did not wish to trouble the Queen. The Prince of Wales is now—er—otherwise engaged, I understand. So I ventured . . ."

"You were quite right, Maharajah. Mama must know nothing of this until after the Jubilee. She would be frantic. You see, Maharajah, apart from the value of the Tiara, it is intimately associated with my father, and for Mama that means . . ."

"Your Highness need say no more. I understand perfectly. But of course you will tell her one day."

"I hope not. These things upset her so. If our own detectives or the people at the Tower can solve the problem, then she need never know."

"Quite, quite. I do see that. But, Your Royal Highness, I would like Her Majesty to know that I have done her this small service. Perhaps in return . . . she is so generous, so kind . . . and that lovely blue ribbon . . . the Garter, I mean . . . a little something between fellow sovereigns . . . a memento of my visit to Windsor."

The Princess, so impeccably trained, bowed and changed the subject; the Maharajah was meant to know that he had made a mistake.

"I must not detain you, Maharajah. Mama is now with her dressers, but she likes me to be there, in the Blue Room, when she says her prayers. You are certain you are right about the Tiara?"

"Oh, yes, Highness. Otherwise I would not have spoken. I had no magnifying glass but of the big pearl I am almost certain. Of the diamond stars on each side, the famous earrings, I am absolutely certain. There can be no doubt at all. Wonderful workmanship but mere paste, mere paste—nothing more."

"I see. Then we must speak of it again tomorrow. Meanwhile,

on your honor, Maharajah, not a word to anyone, I beg you. Goodnight, sire."

"Your Royal Highness, goodnight."

Eight o'clock on a June morning, the day before Queen Victoria's Jubilee. The State Apartments both at Buckingham Palace and at Windsor—not to mention the streets of London—had been prepared and garnished. The Office of Works had spared no effort. They had done their worst. Clearly it was to be a sweltering day. There was one oasis. The Ponsonbys' little breakfast room in the Norman Tower, with the Venetian blinds lowered, was cool and pleasant. Sir Henry had disposed of his porridge (every year he brought a sack of oatmeal back from Balmoral) and also of his kedgeree. He was now weighing in upon his bacon, egg and kidney. He had already turned from the outer to the inner page of the *Times* (as he always did) to check his own writing of the Court Circular. Its uninformative brevity was his daily pride.

Windsor Castle. 19th June 1887. Their Majesties the King and Queen of Denmark and Their Royal Highnesses the Maharajah and Maharani of Kashgar have arrived at the Castle. Her Majesty gave a small dinner party.

He nodded in self-satisfaction. His wife replenished his coffee cup. The parlormaid came in with the post. As he took his letters from the salver, throwing two across to his wife, he noticed that one of his was a folded sheet sealed with a wafer—clearly sent across from the Castle. It was not (thank God) from the Queen; that would have been conveyed by more exalted hands. This was a hurried and nearly illegible scrawl from the Princess.

Sir Hy. I am extremely worried, have hardly slept, and must see you without delay. I *do* realize how busy you are, but will be in your office when you come over to the Castle—about nine o'clock. Pss B.

Sir Henry picked up the next letter, a black-edged royal envelope, postmarked in London at 12:20 A.M.

The Royal Mews, Buckingham Palace Road, S. W.
19. 6. 1887

My dear Sir Henry.

Your disturbing letter has just reached me (11:05 P.M.) by the hand of a servant returning here from Windsor. I hasten to reply so that I may catch the midnight post. I can assure you, dear Sir Henry, that there is no epidemic of mumps, or of anything else, in the Royal Mews. One mare had glanders but has quite recovered. On the other hand I am utterly bewildered by the goings-on here—all most unwonted. A few days ago Fulleylove received a telegram from Newcastle summoning him to his mother's deathbed. I gave him leave. He returned this afternoon to say that his mother was in the very best of health. Sir Henry, what is the meaning of this hoax? Fulleylove is a trustworthy fellow—this was no dodge to avoid work. And now, on top of that, I have your information that you were treated to a downright falsehood by your footman this afternoon. We have no footman called Smith. I will keep you informed—also the Master of the Horse.

With my regards to dear Lady Ponsonby,

I am, Sir Henry,

Yours most sincerely,
Roderick Sparling

P.S. I open this letter to give you most terrible news. A constable has just called (11:40 P.M.). It was certainly Macdonald who took out the brougham this morning in order to meet you at Paddington at 10:25 A.M. and then convey you to the Tower. And now, Sir Henry, Macdonald's body, most savagely mutilated and with the throat slit from ear to ear, and stripped of the livery, has been taken from the Paddington Canal at Iron Wharf. It was found by a bargee. So, it would seem that the footman of your carriage was an impostor and that your coachman was murdered. Frankly, dear Sir Henry, in view of the nature of your errand I am thankful that you yourself escaped with your life. And now, with the Jubilee on Wednesday, I must ward off the newspaper hounds at all costs. You will, I know, agree that Her Majesty must know nothing. Tomorrow morning I visit the mortuary—most distasteful—and the police station. I will try to reach Windsor and attend you in the afternoon. Pray telegraph me if this is not convenient. It is now upon the stroke of midnight but I shall send this by runner to the Charing Cross Post Office so that you may have it in the morning. You can imagine my state of mind. R.S.

Very, very calmly Sir Henry Ponsonby spread the Dundee marmalade very, very evenly upon his toast. He then turned to the leading article. Routine must be preserved. If he was not calm he must appear so.

"The nation is sound at heart, Mary, or at any rate the upper classes. I see they are paying as much as a guinea for a seat on the processional route."

"How amazing! But your coffee is quite cold, dear. What can have come over you? I only hope there will not be any traffic in forged tickets."

"What a suspicious mind you have."

"The world is a very wicked place, Henry. I am suspicious because in my experience the worst always happens . . . and those in high places are usually the most wicked of all."

"Really, dear, you shouldn't say things like that."

"I speak from experience. Now, my love, you have a busy day tomorrow—we all have to be in the Abbey by eleven—and you were tired last night. Take it easy today—have you much on?"

"Oh, dear me, no! Nothing at all! Only that the Princess Beatrice is so worried that she has hardly slept; I am seeing her in a few minutes. After that I have to see the Prince of Wales about another hundred thousand or so of his debts, which I suspect he has hidden from Knollys. Tonight there is the family dinner in the Waterloo Chamber, with a couple of hundred royals staying in the Castle. Tomorrow they have all to be got back to London again, in the right trains and carriages, and into their Abbey seats, and all according to protocol, and every one of them touchy. I have every reason to believe that the Tudor Tiara has been tampered with, and at Buckingham Palace they have a very nasty murder on their hands."

"I am not in the least surprised."

"Mary!"

"It's no good saying 'Mary' like that. If you will insist upon positively advertising the existence of a million pounds' worth of jewels in search of an owner, something of the kind was bound to happen. I am the very last person in the world to say 'I told you so'; but if I wasn't I should. I suppose it was Macdonald, the coachman, who was murdered."

"Mary!"

"It's very elementary, Henry, if only you would think. But you know you haven't asked me about *my* letters. . . . Now they're *really* exciting."

"Well, I'm glad there's some excitement in the house—it may prevent us from getting bored."

"Don't be sarcastic, Henry. It doesn't become you. Two letters, one from each sister on the same day—now that's exciting if you like. Sylvia's Dorothy is to have a little stranger before Christmas—I must ask Philpotts to drive me into town to buy some wool. And then Henrietta's Tom has got the Washington Embassy. A pity it's only America, but I suppose you pulled the wires for him and that later on he may get somewhere important like Vienna. Now you must admit that that is more exciting than your squalid murder or that silly Tiara. . . . But all the same you'd better be off to the office. There's salmon for lunch."

"That's something. And now, dear, as you say, off to the office . . . just like other men."

He kissed her. As he left the room she reached for the *Times*. She always liked to see who was dead.

In the red-carpeted passage outside his office the Princess was already pacing up and down, almost in tears.

"Be seated, ma'am, and tell me what it is all about."

"Sir Henry, I am worried to death. After your brilliant little lecture last night—and it was unpardonable of Mama to cut you short like that—the Maharajah asked if he could see me privately."

Sir Henry decided that honesty was the best policy—up to a point.

"Yes, ma'am, I saw you both on the great stair."

"Sir Henry, I don't trust the Maharajah an inch."

"Nor do I, ma'am."

"And Bertie says that that Colonel Pinkerton was a byword in India—an absolute bounder. But still, the Maharajah is an expert, and also, except that the silly man wants the Garter, disinterested. His knowledge of gems is recognized throughout the world—you know that."

"I do, but what is the trouble, Highness?"

"Bloody Mary's Earrings are missing—that's all."

"But, ma'am, they were part and parcel of the Tiara last night, since when it has been in the strong room."

"No, Sir Henry: according to the Maharajah those diamonds are nothing more than paste; very clever imitations, but almost worthless. He seems certain."

There was a long silence. Sir Henry produced a gold box and they each lit an Egyptian cigarette, surveying the gilded ceiling through wreaths of blue smoke.

"Your Royal Highness, you must not let this be one of *your* troubles. The Queen is your care and that, if I may say so, is enough for any woman. The Tiara is *my* responsibility."

"You are so kind; but all the same, where are the earrings? We must know."

"It needs careful thought, ma'am. Offhand I would say, first of all, that the story must be kept from the Queen, at any rate until tomorrow. If she was told now . . . well, I need hardly say what Windsor would be like."

"Precisely, Sir Henry."

"Secondly, but only between ourselves, I would say that the real diamonds may be in the Maharajah's baggage or, of course, Colonel Pinkerton's. The Tiara, or rather the box containing it, never left my sight between the Tower of London and this room, so I would think that it may have been tampered with in the Jewel Tower at almost any time in the last thirty-six years, or possibly en route to the Tower in 1851. After all, cleaners, packers, builders, guards, even one corrupt Beefeater . . . we just don't know, and never will."

"But, Sir Henry, we must know . . . for everyone's sake. All kinds of people may be suspected, not only underlings, but even people like—er—like ourselves . . . someone head over heels in debt for instance, or someone mentally deficient, or . . ."

"My dear Princess, say no more. These are terrible thoughts. Believe me, I too have had them. I too had very little sleep."

"They are thoughts we cannot ignore."

"Quite so, but the police, you may be sure, will consider every possibility, everyone—high or low. The first thing, however, is to clear the matter with the Tower of London. They may have some quite simple explanation. But we must get in touch immediately with Field Marshal Lord Wilson. He's in his dotage—served as an ensign at Waterloo—but we can only do our best—here and now."

Sir Henry tinkled his bell.

"Ah, Wainwright."

"Sir."

"Kindly find me someone reliable who can take a message to town on the next train."

"Sir."

Wainwright vanished.

While they were waiting, Sir Henry spoke to the Princess almost in a whisper.

"Tell me, ma'am, is there something else wrong—I mean apart from the Tiara?"

"Wrong . . . how?"

"Wrong with the Queen . . . and with the Prince of Wales. Curious silences, nerves. The Prince had none of his usual—er—vivacity last night. As for the Queen, I am no longer in her confidence. Why, Your Royal Highness, why?"

"I just don't know, Sir Henry. But you are right. Would it be too fanciful to imagine that this Tiara is upsetting everyone—as if it carried a curse?"

"Fanciful, yes. But it is a feeling shared by my wife."

"Really."

"Oh, dear me, yes. Mary, ma'am, is very matter-of-fact; she

is also very astute. May I suggest a heart-to-heart talk . . . she would be honored."

"Oh, yes, indeed. I will arrange it. Now please write your note to Field Marshal Lord Wilson while I finish my cigarette."

Windsor Castle
20.6.1887

My dear Field Marshal.

May I first of all thank you and dear Lady Wilson for your warm hospitality yesterday. I can assure you that the *Châteauneuf du Pape* and the '07 cognac were worthy of the luncheon—need I say more? Her Majesty was much gratified to hear of the smart appearance of the Yeoman of the Guard.

My dear Wilson, I am most distressed, as I am sure you will be. It is *alleged*—I emphasize the word—that the Tudor Tiara has, at some unknown date, been tampered with, some of the more valuable gems, particularly Mary Tudor's earrings, being replaced with paste replicas. Frankly I do not see how this could have happened since I took receipt of the Tiara yesterday—I never lost sight of it. We have this big family dinner in the Waterloo Chamber tonight, so I cannot ask you to stay in the Castle, but if you and Lady Wilson can take afternoon tea with us in the Norman Tower we may be able to sort out this unpleasant business. I dare not send you a wire; the Tower does not, I think, have the Queen's cipher and a telegram *en clair* might be disastrous. The royal train, for the conveyance of the Emperor and Empress of Germany, the Czar and Czarina, and others, with families and suites, will be leaving Platform No. 1 at Paddington Station at 3:00 P.M. If you and Lady Wilson care to make use of the rear coach, the enclosed card is your authority. My own carriage will await you at this end. I am, Field Marshal, with regards to dear Lady Wilson,

Yours most sincerely,
Henry Ponsonby

By the time Sir Henry had finished a second note a young stable groom—black suit, white stock, horseshoe pin, and billycock in hand—was at Sir Henry's side.

"Your name, my man?"

"Wicklow, sir."

"Very well, Wicklow. You should take the next train to Paddington, then the twopenny tube to Tower Hill—that's probably quicker than hailing a fly. At the Tower of London you must go to the Constable's residence and insist—you may say your orders are as from the Queen—*insist* upon giving this letter personally to the Constable. You will wait for a reply if asked to do so. You understand?"

"Sir."

"You may then take some refreshment, Wicklow, after which you must go to Garrard's, the jewelers' establishment in Regent Street. It is under the colonnade in the Quadrant."

"Sir."

"You will then deliver this second letter to Mr. Friedman, the manager, and again insist upon handing it to him personally."

"Sir."

"You will then return to Windsor and report. And on no account, Wicklow, must you gossip with any strangers on the way. You may go."

"Sir."

As the groom vanished, Sir Henry noted his name, and the time, upon his blotting pad.

The Princess Beatrice was now in tears.

"It's no good, Sir Henry. Those replicas must have been perfect if it took the Maharajah to spot them. Also they were an elaborate arrangement of interlocking stars—almost impossible to copy. How was it done?"

"Careful sketches, ma'am, or possibly photographs in these days, all made in the Tower. What the underworld, I believe, calls an 'inside job.' "

"Surely, Sir Henry, that's most unlikely. There were also Papa's meticulous drawings, every gem exquisitely delineated . . . anyone with access to the Castle library . . ."

"Such people are well known, ma'am."

"There are the genuine students, supervised by Herr Mütter, and there are—er—people like ourselves. *We* can wander in and out as we like."

This raised rather ghastly implications and it was several minutes before either of them spoke again.

"Your Royal Highness, it becomes clearer every moment that our secrecy must be absolute."

"Of course."

"No, ma'am, there is no 'of course' about it. We said that the Queen must not know because it might cast a shadow over the Jubilee. She must never know."

"Never!"

"Let us be frank. You know as well as I do, ma'am, that Her Majesty puts her trust in the most extraordinary people. There is dear old Skerret, for instance, well into her nineties, who, for all we know, is told everything in the privacy of the bathroom. Then there are these new-fangled Indian attendants, as formerly there was John Brown, and long ago Lehzen, whom your father had to get rid of. But above all, of course, there is the problem of the Prince of Wales."

"I don't understand you, Sir Henry. The 'problem' of the Prince of Wales? Of course we must tell Bertie about the Tiara . . . the Crown Jewels . . . his position . . . his worldly advice . . . surely . . ."

"Please, please, Your Royal Highness, do not press me on this. The Prince and I have already had a most curious talk about the Tiara—most curious. He seems to think that it is his. Beyond that I am pledged to secrecy. I beg you to say nothing either to him or to Princess Alix. I beg you."

"Oh, very well, if you say so; but . . ."

"Apart from my own position, ma'am, there is the dinner tonight—Germans, Danes, Russians, French, all looking daggers at each other. If they knew the Queen was wearing faked jewels, there is enough malice there to send the news round the world. . . . Prince William alone . . ."

"Oh, dear me, yes—those awful mustaches. But surely, Sir Henry, Bertie is different. He is one of us. He is, after all—well —heir to the throne."

"We have been frank about the Queen's servants, ma'am. Let

us be frank about the Prince's friends. *He* may be discreet; his *friends* are not, not after a twelve-course dinner, followed by three or four brandies in the Holbein Room."

"They are men of the world."

"Oh, come, Princess, you are being naïve. Can you seriously imagine Lord Randolph, say, or Mrs. Keppel or the Blue Monkey or Rosebery or Mrs. Langtry, or even Dickie Fisher ever *not* telling a secret? It would be told in bed if nowhere else."

The Princess bit her lip. She had no illusions about Bertie, but, like Mama, she was fond of him. She lit another cigarette and once again watched the smoke curling up to the ceiling.

"Sir Henry, there is something else. I hardly know how to say it, it is so difficult . . . it is about poor Eddy."

"None of us, ma'am, can forget the Duke of Clarence. That is an abiding problem."

"In any other walk of life, Sir Henry, one wonders whether he would even be allowed out. . . ."

"Whereas in fact he is always out—from eight P.M. to eight A.M."

"Perhaps I shouldn't have mentioned it, but . . ."

"It had to be mentioned. His vices are unspeakable. So are his debts. So is his cunning."

"His cunning?"

"Oh, dear me, yes! He may sit there with his mouth open, but he can look after Prince Eddy all right. They devise punishments for him. Nothing could be more useless. Madam, I am the Sovereign's Secretary: do you imagine that the Duke of Clarence—second in line of ascent—is not in my mind every day. When I shaved this morning Eddy and the Tiara were dancing before my eyes. Always, however, there is another who must come first. . . . I am her devoted servant."

"Dear Sir Henry, of course. But then we have agreed to tell Mama nothing."

"We have, ma'am. But if she is not to know, then nobody must know. She must not be upset. More important still, she must not be subject to blackmail. She could become the center of a

'Bloody Mary's Earrings scandal' compared with which a flutter at baccarat or another Dilke case would be nothing. The monarchy itself might go under."

"What next then, Sir Henry?"

"Next, we establish our facts. I have just sent for Garrard's diamond expert to examine the Tiara; we do not accept the Maharajah's word alone. Second, may I hope that you will join us for tea this afternoon? Frankly, ma'am, Field Marshal Lord Wilson is now almost *non compos mentis;* but he *may* offer some simple solution. May I tell my wife you will be with us?"

"Oh, please do, Sir Henry. You are a great comfort. Now I must go: Mama will be fidgeting."

"There is just one thing more, Your Royal Highness. I must repay confidence with confidence, even if I shock you—as I am going to do."

"Please . . ."

"It will be a great shock. Yesterday a coachman called Macdonald was supposed to drive me from Paddington to the Tower and back again with the Tiara in the afternoon."

"I remember Macdonald—a very decent sort of man."

"Late last night, ma'am, his body, with the throat slit, was taken from the canal behind Paddington Station."

"Oh, no! How terrible! How very terrible . . . and what does it all mean? What is happening to us all?"

The Princess swayed as if she would faint, and Sir Henry took his brandy flask from his desk.

"But surely, Sir Henry, this complicates matters . . . complicates them a great deal, does it not?"

"It does indeed . . . although I cannot quite see how or why. I should add that the footman was a complete impostor—not an employee of the Household at all. He has vanished—the brougham abandoned in the Buckingham Palace Road."

"But what does it all mean, Sir Henry? What is the link with the Tiara and the diamonds?"

"Well, if it was an attempt on the Tiara it failed. The Tiara is here in the strong room, and I am still alive."

"The Tiara is here, yes; but with faked diamonds."

"True, but it was never out of my sight. The paste replicas must have been substituted for the real diamonds before the Tiara left the Tower or after it reached Windsor—both impossible. I admit, Your Royal Highness, that I am a very worried man. I don't know which way to turn. I need your help. But now, ma'am, Her Majesty will be waiting for you."

Sir Henry rose to open the door for her; she remained seated in the armchair by his desk.

"No, Sir Henry, Mama can wait. It is time for her to learn that there are others in the world. You have something else on your mind. You have just said you needed my help . . . well?"

"Yes, ma'am, there is one other thing. In your kind note, which I found on my desk when I got back from London, you said something which, frankly, shattered me."

"Perhaps I should not have said it . . . better to forget it."

"We can hardly do that now, ma'am. You said . . ." and he picked up the note ". . . you said, 'I suppose the Tiara you brought from London today is the real thing.' Now what, in heaven's name, did Your Royal Highness mean by that? I *must* know."

To his amazement the Princess buried her face in her hands and burst into tears. It was minutes before she could speak.

"Sir Henry, I don't think I can tell you what I meant. And, for the first time, there is something I cannot tell Mama."

"But you must tell me, ma'am. Truly you must. I am your friend and it is your duty to tell me. Please . . ."

"Very well. You know all about the Tiara replicas, the ones that were made for exhibitions."

"I didn't, but I do now."

"Well, naturally everyone assumed that the real thing, complete with Bloody Mary's diamonds, went to the Tower of London, and that the replicas went to—oh, I don't know—Manchester, South Kensington and so on. Anyway, the family also knew that Mama had kept one for the Blue Room."

"That was—well—at least understandable."

"Sir Henry, have you ever been in the Blue Room?"

"In all these years at Windsor, no, ma'am, never. I have never been asked. Mary has been once."

"It's quite uncanny, you know. The Blue Room, not Frogmore, is the real mausoleum. Papa's valet is still in the service solely so that he may put out Papa's clothes, towels, boots and shoes, every day of the year. It is ghastly . . . the deathbed always ready to be slept in. Mama says her prayers there morning and night."

"I knew, of course, that the room had been kept untouched, but all this . . ."

"That's not all, Sir Henry. In the big wardrobes, with their sliding doors, are Papa's possessions—albums, cameras, sketching gear, alpenstocks and so on, as well as decorations, uniforms and jewels. Also . . . also, Sir Henry, the *original* Tiara—the real thing."

"Good God . . . then the one from the Tower was only a replica."

"Oh, yes. You see, Papa having designed the Tiara, it must never, never be touched. It could not even be worn tonight, hence your visit to the Tower, to fetch the fake."

"I see, I see . . . or I am beginning to see. Please go on, ma'am."

"Well, there are only two keys to those wardrobes—golden keys—of which Mama has one. I have the other. Yesterday afternoon, when Mama was walking on the terrace, I acted on impulse; I went to the Blue Room—all the blinds down on that sunny afternoon—and I looked at the Tiara. I had not seen it for many, many years, but there it was, sure enough, in all its glittering glory. Even in that dimmed room it flashed."

"Well, well, Princess, that's certainly a curious story, but, knowing Her Majesty as we do, nothing to worry about . . . all part of the parcel of life at Windsor. And, of course, the whole mystery is solved; the Tiara from the Tower is a replica, the Maharajah was right, and the genuine article is upstairs in the Blue Room. Our troubles are over. . . ."

"No, Sir Henry, I have not finished. Listen. Last night, after my talk with the Maharajah, I decided to have one more look at the *real* Tiara—the Blue Room Tiara. I stayed with Mama, as usual, until she had said her prayers at Papa's pillow, then I used my golden key to open the wardrobe. I suppose I had some hazy idea of comparing the real Tiara with the fake. The original Tiara was well displayed in the wardrobe, under glass on a purple cushion, on the middle shelf. I had seen it, as I have explained, only that afternoon while you were in London. . . . Sir Henry, it had gone."

"Good God! What do you mean, 'gone'?"

"What I say—vanished! The purple cushion was empty. The Tiara had been there, in the darkness of the wardrobe, since Papa's death twenty-five years ago. Now it has gone."

"Wainwright."

"Sir."

"Do you know whether Mr. Bellow is in his office?"

"At this hour, Sir Henry, it is highly probable."

"Ask him to attend upon me."

"Sir."

Sir Henry now extracted a large volume in red-and-gilt morocco from a drawer—the Windsor Guest Book for 1887. He studied it until Mr. Bellow presented himself, immaculate in sponge trousers and fawn frockcoat. Mr. Archibald Bellow, having been superannuated from Bow Street to the sinecure of house detective to Windsor Castle, now spent his days trying not to look like a detective.

"Ah, Bellow, good morning. I have just been studying the accommodation for the Maharajah of Kashgar's party. The Maharajah and Maharani, I see, have the Queen Adelaide Room. Then, let's see, there's Colonel Pinkerton, Miss Nummuggar, two valets, a lady's maid, the numerous gentlemen in attendance and a pansy calling himself the Maharani's secretary."

"That would be correct, sir, apart from small fry in the servants' quarters. Bar Colonel Pinkerton, sir, they are all Indians."

"Quite, Bellow, quite. I shall see that the servants and the eunuch are given tickets for the Abbey tomorrow—there are still some odd seats left in Henry VII's Chapel for underlings. That, Bellow, will leave the coast clear. All the bedrooms must be searched—thoroughly."

"Certainly, sir. And what may I ask is the nature of the documents you are looking for?"

"Not documents, Bellow. Diamonds."

Mr. Archibald Bellow's eyebrows shot up into his bald head. He had envisaged documents. He had done this job before, when the Foreign Office wanted an advance draft of a treaty . . . but diamonds . . . now that was something!

"Indeed, sir—a little unusual."

"Yes, Bellow, two diamond stars, twelve-pointed. You can take your time: nobody can return from London until the evening. But your search must be thorough and leave no trace. I shall expect to find a sealed report in this drawer when I return. Here is the key. I think that is all, Bellow."

"Thank you, sir. That is quite clear."

As a matter of duty and routine Sir Henry had now taken steps to deal with Field Marshal Lord Wilson, with Garrard's of Regent Street and with the Maharajah. He expected nothing to come of any of it, but it had had to be done. Now, at last, for the first time since breakfast, he could sit back and think. When he had told the Princess Beatrice that their troubles were over, that the problem was solved—the Tower of London Tiara being a fake, the Blue Room Tiara being the real thing—he had almost meant it. Now that he was alone the doubts came crowding back into his mind.

Most important of all, the secret must be rigorously kept. The Prince of Wales must get his loan and the Queen must be protected. There was the awful possibility that in one of her 1861 paroxysms of grief she had defrauded the nation. Moreover, grief or not, Sir Henry already knew that she had some very odd ideas about property—to say the least. And when Knollys tried to fix the Rothschild loan for the Prince the truth would emerge. If the Prince was not actually suspected of trying to pass off a fake Tiara on the Rothschilds, which would be absurd, he would certainly be furious at having been made to look a fool. He might even blame Sir Henry . . . "You should have known better, Ponsonby, than to bring back such rubbish from the Tower." He would also be furious with Mama for hiding away the genuine article through the years.

Another thing haunted Sir Henry and shocked him deeply. A fake among the Crown Jewels—and that is how Fleet Street would see it—would be a major scandal, involving the Queen's personal conduct. It would also mean a huge manhunt, while all the time three people, the Queen, the Princess and Sir Henry, knew perfectly well that somewhere in Windsor, in some bureau or chest or even under the Queen's bed, was the real thing complete with Bloody Mary's Earrings, the very things for which the police of all Europe would be hunting.

Of course, as Sir Henry told himself, there was the odd chance that the Princess's story was not true. The Queen's emotional obsession with death may have made her believe, as the years passed, that a replica Tiara in the Blue Room wardrobe had indeed been her own Albert's treasure. At sixty-eight she was already muddled, especially about the dead and the past.

Finally, if the Tower Tiara was a replica, what had been the point of all those goings-on yesterday—the murdered coachman, the sham footman, the boy in the ginger suit, the injury to Black Beauty and so on? If there had been a gang at work—and to Sir Henry it was a big "if"—they too, like everyone else, must have thought that the Tiara from the Tower was the real thing. . . . Anyway, he told himself, thanks to his vigilance they had failed.

He tried to face the problem. His Royal Highness the Prince of Wales was going to raise a loan on a fake, while somewhere in Windsor an obstinate and impregnable old woman had hidden not less than a million pounds' worth of precious stones.

That was the gist of it. In an agony of thought Sir Henry sank his head in his hands. Another complication occurred to him.

Problem piled itself upon problem. There seemed no end to it. What about these upstart South Africans, these Astors and Norths, at the very core of the Marlborough House set? . . . Millionaire diamond merchants, the whole lot of them. These men would do almost anything to get their hands upon the earrings. They would know what to do with them. It was not just that those glittering stars, in Jo'burg currency, were the price of a yacht or a palace; no, it was not just that. . . . Sir Henry might not know much about these things, but he had chatted with these men, specially with Oppenheimer, at Marlborough House dinners, and he did know that the mere release of such diamonds could turn the world market upside down. The South African Diamond Syndicate would pay the Prince a very handsome price indeed for the earrings, not to sell them but to prevent their being sold. . . . If they were genuine, they might even pay him to put them back in the Tower in perpetuity. Diamonds must remain rare. So these men, too, if it came to the point, would be glad to explode the bomb in the Prince's face, to tell the whole world that this famous cache was worthless. Meanwhile the real secret would still be, so to speak, under the Queen's bed.

From his open window Sir Henry looked down upon the East Terrace. What he now saw once again changed everything. What he saw might alter all their lives; it might launch the British Empire upon a terrible—but of course not enjoyable—scandal. The two gentlemen in attendance, Lord Randolph and Colonel Pinkerton, were away on the far side; Sir Henry could imagine their recherché chat. On the lawn beneath the window the Maharajah and the Prince of Wales were locked in talk—head to head. Sir Henry was stunned and furious. The Princess had pledged the Maharajah to secrecy. The Princess and Sir Henry should have known better. The man was clearly incapable of keeping a secret—especially if he could see a chance of the Garter at the end of it all. The Prince now knew that his

Tiara was worthless, that the loan and all possibility of a loan was off. The Royal Family and the nation had been robbed—and in a big way. Sir Henry might be blamed. The Castle would be filled with police. At the Jubilee Dinner that night there would be only one thing to talk about, and they would wallow in it. After all the Queen had been rude enough to most of the clan at one time or another, and all spite and malice would be let loose. Grandmama had been swindled; it would be irresistible. Apart from that, any whippersnapper of a Balkan gentleman-in-waiting, or even some bankrupt princeling, could be selling the whole story in Fleet Street the next morning.

There was a knock upon his door—a loud and peremptory knock.

"Your Majesty."

It had never happened before. In all his long years of service Sir Henry Ponsonby had been summoned to the Queen's room some three times a day, perhaps several thousand times in all. She had once taken tea in the Norman Tower—for his Silver Wedding—and once at Osborne Cottage to see her godchild. She had never visited his office. He wondered whether she had ever before knocked on a door. She sniffed.

"Someone has been smoking here, Sir Henry, and in the morning too!"

"Yes, ma'am. I must admit that when the burden of work is heavy I find a cigarette very soothing . . . in complete privacy of course."

"A cigarette . . . there are three stumps here."

"Yes, ma'am."

"If you can only work under narcotics, Sir Henry, you had better consult a specialist. After all, the work itself must be very light; or do you need more help?"

"Thank you, ma'am, no. But of course just lately there has been the Jubilee. But perhaps it was about the arrangements for tonight's dinner or the procession tomorrow that Your Majesty wished to see me."

"No, why should I? Those arrangements were made weeks

ago, and are in good hands. My confidence in you is complete, Sir Henry. I wish I could say the same about the Home Secretary, but I suppose he understands processions. Sir Henry, I am most concerned about this Tiara. That is what I wish to talk about."

"Certainly, ma'am—the one which I brought from the Tower."

He could have bitten off his tongue—he was supposed to know of no other.

"What on earth do you mean, Sir Henry? Of course I mean the Tiara from the Tower—the Tudor Tiara. There is no other. Really! While you were giving us your dissertation last night, I was pondering upon it. The gems are magnificent, while the setting is of course in perfect taste."

"Indeed, yes, ma'am, we are all agreed about the setting."

"Yes, Sir Henry, but it was, you know, designed to be seen—in the Crystal Palace that is—seen rather than worn, a setting for the display of the Tudor gems. Looking at it again, after so many years, I think that for one my age, and in my sad state of widowhood, it is perhaps a little too magnificent . . . too large. I shall *not* wear it tonight, Sir Henry. The Darmstadt-Hesse Tiara might do very well for this family party, or perhaps better still, the little Coburg Diadem that I wore for the last opening of Parliament . . . but definitely *not* the Tudor Tiara."

"May I say very humbly, ma'am, being no judge in these matters, that I entirely concur in Your Majesty's decision. I will see to it, ma'am, that the Tiara is safely returned to the Tower of London."

"No."

"I beg your pardon, ma'am?"

"I said 'no,' Sir Henry. It must *not* be returned to the Tower. It should never have been there at all. And that raises another matter—the ownership of the Tiara."

"Indeed, ma'am, are there any doubts?"

"One would have hoped not. But if there are, Sir Henry, they must be most firmly squashed. My dear husband brought those gems to England through his own personal efforts, thanks to our wide connections. Others were gifts from old English families. They would certainly not have wished such sacred relics to be exposed to the vulgar gaze."

"Quite, ma'am."

"The phrasing of my Dear One's will, although strictly private, makes the matter clear beyond all doubt. The Tudor Tiara, Sir Henry, is mine, mine personally and not part of the Regalia. Only in the fullness of time, and through *my* will, can it ever go to the Prince of Wales."

"Yes, ma'am. Would Your Majesty wish to have the whole matter confirmed by the Solicitor-General?"

"Certainly not. That is totally unnecessary. Have I not made myself clear? I shall not wear the Tiara tonight. I shall never wear it. It must never go back to the Tower of London—it is private property, not a Crown Jewel. It must today be placed in the Castle strong room. Its case—and I presume it has a case —must be under my seal."

"Yes, ma'am. You do not think that perhaps Field Marshal Lord Wilson may raise difficulties—the Tiara was in his charge."

"That is immaterial; he may be given a receipt."

"Yes, ma'am."

"Then it must be brought to my room within the hour so that I may affix the seal. After that nobody must ever see it as long as I am alive. It is sacred to the memory of a widow. It should never have passed from my care."

"The Commissioners for the Great Exhibition of 1851, ma'am —you do not think that they may ask questions?"

"Mere officials, Sir Henry, administering the funds. I am astonished that you should even mention them."

"I apologize, ma'am."

"Very well. And now, Sir Henry, pray go to the strong room and do as I have said. After that I never want to hear of the matter again."

"Your Majesty will announce, presumably, that the Tiara is

being preserved at Windsor instead of at the Tower—if only to allay curiosity."

"That's as may be. Now about tonight: I have decided to wear the little Coburg Diadem. It is modest and has family connections."

"But it is in the Tower, Your Majesty."

"I know. Fortunately it is barely noon. You will have ample time, Sir Henry, to slip back to London and fetch it. . . . You may even be able to return on the Royal Train if you hurry."

Very slightly, beneath his Jaeger combinations, Sir Henry began to sweat.

"Is that all, Your Majesty?"

"Thank you, Sir Henry, yes."

But it was not all. They were standing in the doorway looking down the long red-carpeted passage. There was a cry.

"Mama! Mama!"

At the far end, rushing toward them, was a towering figure in a Norfolk suit. He was flourishing a cigar. He was crimson with rage.

"Mama! Sir Henry!"

"Be calm, Bertie. In our position one must not get excited: it does not do. Now, what is the matter?"

"Mama, we've been swindled. Bloody Mary's Earrings are a bloody fake."

From the dumpy little woman at his side Sir Henry Ponsonby heard a sharp intake of breath.

"That, Bertie, is quite impossible. And what language! You must not talk nonsense, Bertie. How often have I to tell you that?"

"But, Mama, the Maharajah says that the rest of the Tiara is the real thing, quite genuine, but that the diamond earrings are only paste."

"Nonsense, Bertie. That is quite impossible. I happen to know that it is impossible. The Maharajah should mind his own business. Quite impossible . . . I know."

5

East of Bow Creek

It was Guy Fawkes night—a night without a moon. A thin fog hung with menace over the West End streets, hardly enough to halt the trams or buses, but enough to diffuse the gas lamps into huge stars, enough to make the horses' breath hang upon the cold air, and to make the theatergoers hurry home for fear of worse.

In the Haymarket only the cabbies' noses showed above their mufflers, while the cockaded footmen, for all their little bearskin capes, froze upon the box seats of the carriages, hundreds of them awaiting the fall of the curtain at half-a-dozen theaters. Across the Circus one could still see the blazing lights of restaurants, or the occasional rocket screaming across the sky, but as one went east the fog got worse. Around the Strand, in the little streets between Covent Garden and the River, it was a real fog; far away in Canning Town, so it was said, a man could not see his hand before his face—a good night for an escapade.

In Pall Mall, twenty yards from the Marlborough Club, a most conspicuously inconspicuous black carriage was picking up two late diners, gentlemen in red-lined capes and silk hats. A quarter of an hour later it was setting them down in a very shadowy corner of Wardour Street.

"Well, Serge, that covers our tracks, I think."

"Yes; and now the usual aliases, Your Highness?"

"Of course. You are Colonel Levi. . . . His Excellency the Baron Serge de Staal does not object, I presume."

"Not at all; and Your Highness?"

"Oh, as always, 'Major Chester.' And don't forget that last week you nearly let the cat out of the bag—and at that crowded coffee stall."

"Your Highness has been pleased to tell me so six times."

"Well, one must be careful. It was a miracle it didn't get into 'John Bull.' "

"Anyway, to be frank, sire—'Major,' I mean—it's not your alias we have to worry about, it's your figure."

"Don't be ridiculous, Serge. I'm not the only fat man in London. Besides, just look at me. These bushy eyebrows and this monocle, this touch of rouge, all so easily put on in the carriage. The perfect old buffer—what?"

"I must admit that . . . Major."

"And above all, Serge, everyone knows that after Goodwood no gentleman would wear a silk hat in town—that is the master stroke. Our disguise is complete."

"I wasn't really thinking—er—Major Chester, that you might be recognized in the street. . . . I was thinking of later, at supper or—er—possibly in bed."

"Leave that to me, Serge. I can look after myself. That dear, innocent little Trixie must be told to keep her mouth shut. And I'm sure she will, bless her heart!"

"So be it, if you are content, sire. But you are being naïve, are you not? After all, the Prince of Wales of all men—and you are the only person who just won't see it—to sleep with the Prince of Wales, that is the one secret on earth no woman will ever keep."

"Nonsense . . . and in any case, my dear Colonel Levi, a well-lined pocketbook can do much. But enough—we are here for pleasure."

They had walked briskly through the fog to Leicester Square. The flaring jets outside the Empire cast a curious, shadowless light upon the faces and billboards—a Beardsley monochrome in black and white. It was the second interval, and in the crowded foyer, thick with the blue smoke of a hundred cigars and heavy with the scent of women, they were obsequiously but inconspicuously welcomed. A couple of sovereigns and a couple of envelopes were handed to a commissionaire who, quite clearly, knew what was expected of him. Once, long ago, for the hell of it, they had mixed with the riff-raff of the Promenade. It had been risky to the point of danger. Tonight the Prince sat well back in the box, well screened by de Staal. It pleased them to believe that they were unnoticed.

"Well, Serge, the show is half over, but see how well I have timed it. Behold your own particular friend, little Connie Gilchrist. I confess she's a stunner. I have always said so. You have taste in these matters, my dear Serge . . . obviously."

Down in the stalls and in the circle, to the fury of their womenfolk, men were clapping holes in their gloves for Connie and her skipping rope—so ingenuous, so petite and yet so sophisticated.

"Yes, yes, Serge, I admire your taste. Very pretty indeed, a delicious morsel—but if you take my advice, never sleep with the Talk of the Town. It leads to trouble. You have to share her with other men, and then it gets around. Look at poor Skittles. And God knows what it may do to a man—look at Randolph, a wreck at forty."

"Chacun à son gout, sire."

"Oh, quite, quite. But now . . . here she is. My Trixie. Take the glasses, Serge. Back row of the chorus, second from the right . . . and next to her, her friend—called, believe it or not, Daffodil . . . most extraordinary."

"You forget that I have already met your friend Trixie, and that, for your sake, sire, I have done rather more than meet her . . . all very *très intime* . . . a most respectable girl; she had to be—er—handled."

"Thank you, my dear chap, thank you. I am never ungrateful."

"I am always ready to serve you—er—Major Chester. At least

I can assure you that she will prove as bedworthy as she looks."

"I don't doubt it, I don't doubt it. Always look for them in the back row, Colonel Levi. They may put the old harridans there—they also have their piquancy, you know—but that is also where they train the novices—pretty little innocents from nowhere. Trixie is as pretty as a doll. And for me, you know, that is a great change."

"Yes, indeed, sire. And please remember that you owe a little to my Connie."

"How so?"

"Well, it took Connie as well as me to bring Trixie to the point."

"Why was that, Serge? Surely a 'Major' is enough of a . . ."

"To be frank, sire, she does not like fat men, and, as I have said, she is respectable—positively virtuous."

"Hm!"

"However, Connie demeaned herself by actually speaking to a girl in the chorus. That did it. Trixie is ready for you tonight, sire, when the curtain falls. Our table is engaged at Rule's—the usual table."

"Miss Gilchrist will be duly rewarded, Serge. You know that. But now let us look at Trixie. Of course in the ordinary way give me a beautiful woman, *une grande dame* . . . but also, just now and again, a simple little *ingénue* . . . so easily pleased and no trouble afterward."

"Oh, well, Major Chester, as I say, *chacun à son gout.* I can only hope that it all works out as well as you expect. It has been an honor to serve you, sire."

The curtain had fallen, and as the Empire emptied itself into the fog, the two men mixed with the crowd. They strolled across the muddy square. How the Prince adored these escapades . . . even mud was a novelty! For half an hour they watched the play at Thurston's, that the girls might complete their toilettes. The envelopes had gone to the stage door; the assignations had been made. At midnight, on the corner of Charing Cross Road, Connie Gilchrist, sitting well back in her hansom, awaited her Baron de Staal, alias Colonel Levi, knowing perfectly well that he was the Russian Ambassador. On the corner of Rupert Street, in another hansom, little Trixie, all dimples and curls, awaited her Major Chester, knowing perfectly well that he was the Prince of Wales. Ten minutes later, in Maiden Lane, amid the plush, the gold, the clatter and the rich smells of Rule's, all four were gathered around the grilled oysters and the champagne.

The pubs had closed long ago, but the bars around Fleet Street have their own hours. At one o'clock in the morning, fifty yards up Fetter Lane, the Saloon of The Flying Fish was noisy and noisome with the gentlemen of the Press—mainly editors hanging around for the Paris cables to come in, or for reporters to come back from the country—all very knowing men, passing bets on horses, on actresses, on the next election or the next hanging. There was the occasional pansy, neat and natty, to deal with opera or Society; but mostly these men were hirsute, red-faced, red-necked. Every man's breath smelt of beer, every man's eyes were bloodshot, every man had the night in front of him. The spilt booze, the spittle, the fag ends and the sawdust made a good slimy floor. This was a place of polished brasses, a ship's figurehead, stuffed animals and patriotic chinaware—Napoleon III, Garibaldi or the Iron Duke could see his own image again and again in the cut-glass mirrors. The porcelain beer handles went up and down; the swing door to the urinals went to and fro.

There was another door. Tonight (to the annoyance of the "regulars") it had PRIVATE chalked across it. Beyond it was the snuggery—a cozier version of the saloon: lots of little colored lamps, a horsehair sofa, varnished kegs, a blazing fire and, screening the entrance from Johnson Passage, a large stuffed bear. If the saloon was drowned in beer, the snuggery was drowned in rum. Mrs. Barker—known throughout Fleet Street as "Buffers"—had been bringing in the rum jugs all evening.

A cozy scene should be a cheerful scene; this, in spite of the five men well disguised in drink, was not so. They had reached only the quarrelsome stage, and dared go no further. They would need their nerves before dawn. So, when Buffers brought in the twentieth jug of rum she was told to bugger off. The men wanted the room to themselves.

Tom Shrimp—and if he had another name nobody knew it—lay flat on the horsehair sofa, his yellow ferrety nose pointing to the ceiling, his pink eyes shut.

"The Captain"—and they called him "Captain" since "no names" is a good rule—was stamping around, raising his fists and spitting in fury—waiting for someone who didn't come.

On one varnished keg sat Mr. Wainwright. Scrupulously "mistered" by everyone, Mr. Wainwright had a bare hint of blond whiskers, was dressed to the nines—adenoidal and scrofulous.

On another keg was "Smith"—a very useful name—a toff with an Inverness cape to hide his evening clothes. He had been dining out West (in Mount Street to be precise) but he knew better than to show his shirt front in The Flying Fish.

The fifth man, only the whites of his eyes showing, stood mute and sullen against the wall. He had been born somewhere in the bogs of Sligo but they called him "Cabby." Oddly enough he had once actually been a cabby, years ago before that long holiday on Dartmoor where Smith had made a buddy of him—one hot afternoon in the quarries.

The Captain had stopped stamping around. He stood in the middle of the room, swallowed his last rum of the night, and then swore rather better than a trooper.

"It's after one o'clock. Where the bleedin' 'ell is that bloody bitch? Where is she? Where's Daffodil—blast 'er eyes? She's your doxy, Shrimp. Where the 'ell is she? I'm askin' yer—for Gawd's sake."

"Oh, shut yer great mug, Cap'n. They'll 'ear yer in the saloon."

"Shut yer own blasted mug, Shrimp—with that squeak o' yers—yer li'l rat. Yes, me fine boyho, it's you we'll all swing for yet.

Yes, yer rat—swaggerin' aroun' Paddington in yer smarty ginger suit. I watched yer. That bloody suit cried aloud to 'eaven. Yes, and those great gaudy carpet bags, as big as elephants. Yer might as well 'ave proclaimed us all from the 'ouse tops. Every blasted copper and porter will know yer again—yer young dolt."

"Damn yer bleedin' eyes, Cap'n. What's got yer? The trick bloody well worked, didn't it? We've got the Earrings, 'aven't we? Wot more do yer want—the Crown and Scepter? . . . Yer make me tired."

"We shall see, Shrimpo, we shall see. It's not all over yet—not by a long chalk it ain't."

"Well, four months gone, and not a clue 'ave they got."

"Nah . . . and we ain't got a cent neither. And any day we'll be due for the rope or twenty years 'ard . . . yes, you too, me lad. Oh, I'd like to see you, with yer fancy ways, in broad arrers . . . or standin' on the drop. Learn from yer betters, can't yer? 'Ere's our friend Smith, now . . . discretion itself, if I may make so bold, Mr. Smith. Ho, ho, yes, I liked yer li'l tale of poor Lord Iddsleigh dyin' in the Prime Minister's arms—pulled the wool very nicely over old Ponsonby's eyes—very nicely indeed, Smith. Then there was Cabby 'ere—never even showed 'is blinkin' face. Yer see, the trouble with Shrimp . . ."

"That's more than enough from you, Cap'n. I've told yer already, ain't I, to shut yer mug. Me Daff' is doin' the job fer yer now, ain't she? And I bloody well did it fer yer at Paddington—didn't I now? . . . Come clean, now, did I or didn't I?"

"Arl right, Shrimpo, arl right . . . I grant yer were a cog in me machine. That's wot yer were, kid—a cog, a bloody cog."

"Yer bloody swine. Cog! Cog! Gawd, and to think I did the 'ole job fer yer. These blokes 'ere, Smith an' Cabby, were just common murderers, neither better nor worse—throat slitters. But 'oo worked the wheeze that got that there Fulleylove roight up to Newcastle an' back? Yours truly. I 'ad more brains than arl you blokes rolled into one . . . puttin' one of those blinkin' great carpet bags—bottomless bags—first over one 'at box, in that split second when Smithy 'ere 'ad shoved it on the pavement for me, on the off side of that there brougham, and just when Sir 'Enery was busy with the Station Master, goin' off to piss . . . an' then pickin' up the other bag to show an identical 'at box for the bobby to take to the train. . . . It was all a bloody miracle, I'm tellin' yer."

"Oh, clever, I don't deny it, Shrimpo, but yours weren't the only brains—mine too, as yer very well know. . . ."

"Arl roight, Cap'n . . . and then didn't I create a 'contretemps,' as they calls it, when I nicked Sir 'Enery's nag at Windsor, so as to do that 'at-box trick in reverse, the diamonds —Bloody Mary's Earrings as they calls 'em—'aving been swapped round in the train from their real Tiara to our replica . . . did I or didn't I now?"

"Oh, arl roight, arl roight! 'Ave it yer own way. Christ, the conceit of the kid! But I'll 'and it to yer on one thing: yer a good jooler's boy, nippy with yer tools."

"Good jooler's boy be buggered! That wern't the 'alf of it. An' wot will you lousy bastards give a kid loike me when we settle —a nice pat on the back? Garn, Cap'n, you make me retch."

"Now you just bloody well be'ave yerself, Shrimpo, takin' arl the credit loik tha'. We're all gents, ain't we? We'll play fair with yer an' with yer Daffodil . . . but yer not the only bloody pebble on this 'ere beach—so don't be'ave as if yer was."

Shrimp lapsed into silence. He heaved himself off the horsehair sofa and staggered to the table. He swore at the empty rum jug. Then, standing under the gaselier, in the middle of the snuggery, he started on a fresh tack.

"Arl roight then, Cap'n, fair enough. But 'oo got that fake, that replica as they calls it, of that Tiara out of that there Royal College of Art? Wasn't it me—with a bit of 'elp from Smithy 'ere . . . wasn't it now? Tell me that."

"Not so fast, Shrimpo, my boy . . ." It was Smith talking now. ". . . Not so fast. Arl you blasted well did was to keep a lookout, toimin' the bloody bobby on his beat. Not, moind yer—and I'll grant yer this—that a bloind man couldn't have nicked that college. There was me—conquerin' 'ero of a thousand cracked safes—an' all I 'ad to do was to walk into the place with me jemmy and dark lantern. A little kid could 'ave done it—easy. An' all there was, lads, was a big wooden cupbid with—wot d'ye think—'1851 EXHIBITION REJECTS' painted on it in big white letters. Kind of 'em, weren't it? An' yer could 'ave opened the thing with a penknife—easy! I ask yer! It was dead easy; but it was yer pal Smithy, Cap'n, wot took arl the bloody risks. If that bobby 'ad come along, Shrimpo would 'ave been down the Exhibition Road loik a streak o' lightnin' . . . yer can bet yer bloody boots on that."

The Captain had sat down at last—exhausted with stamping and fuming around the room. He and Shrimp were now side by side on the horsehair sofa. Neither the scrofulous Mr. Wainwright nor Cabby had yet said a word. But again the Captain turned to Shrimp.

"Since yer being taught a thing or two, my lad—an' arl fer yer own good—yer moight note the 'ighly gentlemanly conduct of our friend Mr. Wainwright 'ere—footman extraordinary, as we all knows, to 'Er Bleedin' Majesty Queen Victoria . . . eh, Mr. Wainwright?"

"Oh, not at all, Captain, not at all; only too willing to oblige, I assure you. And very simple too, I might add, given of course a few brains and a little education—Harrow and Trinity, gentlemen, Harrow and Trinity—of a rather higher order than might be comprehensible to our young friend here. Very simple. A message to be left in Sir Henry's dressing room when it was beknown to me that he was not in residence—and I might add that my scarlet coat is the entrée to every corner of the Castle—a swift glance in Sir Henry's closet, and then . . . why, then, gentlemen, an identical hat box from Lock's, the toffs' hatters in St. James's Street. Petty cash due to yours humbly, two golden sovereigns for a high-class billycock . . . as I would have you remember, Captain, at your convenience . . . the billycock being necessary for the sake of the box. Two golden sovereigns plus fares from Windsor, et cetera: say two pounds, ten shillings."

"Mean bastard. An' 'e'll want 'is share of the bloody swag just fer goin' to St. James's and back . . . Christ!"

There were now three knocks on the side door into Johnson Passage; an interval of ten seconds, then two knocks; an interval of ten seconds and then one knock. Like a flash Cabby had bolted the door into the saloon, while the Captain, half hidden behind the stuffed bear, unlocked the Johnson Passage door, letting a whiff of cold fog into the snuggery.

"Oh, Daffodil, we were thinkin' as 'ow yer'd never come. Where the 'ell 'ave yer been?"

"A stiff rum, fer Gawd's sake . . . 'Ello, Shrimp."

" 'Ello, duckie."

There was no rum left, but the Captain had a brandy flask in the skirts of his coat. She had a mighty big swig and then the five men closed round her, mouths set, eyes staring, their lives and cash all at stake.

'Well, Daffodil, wot's the news? Wot's the news, girlie . . . quick."

" 'Ere, not so fast, boys. First things first. I don't know as 'ow ye've told me wot I'm gettin' out of this little spree. Come clean now, Cap'n, or me and my li'l pal Trixie can double-cross yer yet—the 'ole lot o' yer. I'm a 'uman bein' in me own bloody roight, yer know, not just Shrimpo's skirt."

" 'Ell's bells, Daff, we're all gents 'ere, ain't we? *and* all witnesses to each other. But honest, Daff, this is the big game, yer know. Yer'll be arl roight, Daff . . . a lidy fer loife . . . dresses, jools, carridges, the blinkin' lot. It's as big as that, Daff. But fer Jesus' sake, now, tell us the news. We're burstin'."

"Well then, blast yer, she's done it. It's on fer this very noight."

"Done it? Who's done it? What's on? Fer 'eaven's sake, Daffodil."

"Trixie, my li'l chorus mate—she's done it. This very noight, 'ere an' now, she toikes 'Is 'Ighness, Gawd save 'im, to my cozy little plice in Brunswick Square . . . oh yes, the clean sheets are on the bed, boys, and—wot d'ye think?—a foin new chamber pot with the Prince of Wales's feathers on it! What ho! What ho!"

"Oh, Gawd Almighty! Struth! Oh, Christ!" The Captain gave her two smacking kisses and walloped her bottom.

"Oh, yes, they're all at Rule's now—a tête-à-tête supper as they calls it—the four of 'em."

"Four of 'em—oh, Gawd, that buggers it up!"

"Now don't worry, Cap'n. They'll be splittin' up later. There's the Rosshan Ambassador and little Connie Gilchrist. . . ."

"Wot! *The* Connie?"

"Why not? She'll take 'Is Blinkin' Excellency off to Chelsea. And that, boyhos, will leave our Trixie all alone with 'Is 'Ighness. They're as thick as thieves over the bubbly . . . an' our Jo' waitin' for 'em with 'is 'ansom."

"Oh boy, oh boy!"

"Oh boy my foot! You look after Trixie. It's Trix 'oo's sellin' 'er blasted virtue for yer—'er virginity, and not a bloody cent 'as she 'ad, not as yet."

"She will, Daff, she will; keep yer 'air on! Just you wait. Oh Gawd, we'll all be rich forever an' ever, amen."

"Orl roight then, but moind—a moighty big share goes to our Trixie, or you'll swing—an' I mean it—the 'ole bloody crowd of yer . . . see!"

"Only Cabby and Smith are for the gallows, Daff—*not me.*"

"Don't talk such balls, Shrimp—showin' yer ignorance. When I says the 'ole lot of yer, I means wot I says. Slittin' the coachman's throat is nothing. But—an' get this into yer thick 'eads—tonight's work is 'igh treason, assaultin' the heir to the throne. It means the rope."

"We know, we know. We can take care of ourselves. You jest tell us yer story . . . and fer Jesus' sake get on with it."

"Well, I'm only sayin' be fair to Trix. She's a decent kid, livin' with 'er Mum, 'an yer jest don't know wot she's doin' fer yer."

"Come on, Daff—yer story fer the love of Moike!"

"Hm! Well, this is 'er first supper with 'im—and at Rule's. But of course, what ho, it's not jest supper! This is a noight of noights. Tonoight is bed!"

"Where, Daff—fer Gawd's sake . . . an' when?"

"I've told yer, ain't I? An' don't get so darned worked up. Yer'll need yer nerve before termorrer. It's fixed, I'm tellin' yer. When they're through at Rule's an' she's got 'im jest that little bit fuddled, then she'll take 'im off to my place in Brunswick Square—by the Foundling—or that's wot 'e'll think. But—an' this is it, Cap'n—it's our Jo' who'll be droivin' the 'ansom."

"Yes, yes, Daff, good ol' Jo'—but do get on . . . wot then? I can 'ardly 'old meself."

"Well, Cap'n, just by Brunswick Square are some stables, a mews koind of a place, with a dead end. The Colonnade they calls it. It 'as a couple of oil lamps. Yer can bloody well smash those—but quietly, moind. Jo' will turn 'is 'ansom into the Colonnade an' then you bastards will be waitin' with the four-wheeler. I don't 'ave to tell old skunks loike you wot ter do. But, fer Gawd's sake, remember this is not a bit o' common kidnap-in'—it's 'igh treason. . . ."

"Yes, yes, Daff. Don't 'arp on it so, don't 'arp on it. Arl the same, ol' girl, well done. We won't forget yer, nor yer li'l chorus mate neither."

"Then get busy, lads, get busy. They may be another hour at Rule's—she says 'e guzzles—but yer can't tell fer sure. If he's randy he may be wantin' bed more than supper . . . an' yer must be waitin' fer 'im in the Colonnade . . . got it?"

"We've got it, Daff, we've got it."

"Roight! An' the room in Canning Court is arl ready fer yer . . . and no more rum tonoight . . . got that too?"

"Ay, ay, Daff. Come on, boys. We've been on our bloody arses long enough. Shrimpo, get on the box with Cabby . . . the rest can pile inside. . . ."

Maiden Lane at two o'clock in the morning. The fog was really thick now, everywhere, but Jo' as he whipped up his hansom was not worried; he and his mare knew every inch of this great city. He was even laughing into his muffler at the very thought of his passenger; this was the night of his life.

The Prince of Wales was slightly fuddled, a little drowsy and very happy. He remembered now, when he was a boy, the Prime Minister had taken him for a ride in a hansom to see the sights. Papa had demurred but, as Dizzy said, the hansom is the gondola of London; one can see everything from it. He could almost hear the old Jew, so cocky at having coined a phrase. And now, yes, one could see everything—dimly through the fog. Already men were washing down the streets and flushing the sewers. A few early wagons were arriving at Covent Garden. They saw the occasional mail van and once he and Trixie heard the fire engines, bells clanging and harness jingling. In Drury Lane a few prostitutes were still showing their wares—their white flesh—at the windows; children were sleeping in doorways—the Prince thought this an odd thing to do on a November night.

The street lamps flitted by. His contentment was complete. They were beyond Long Acre now and for him this was an unknown world. All real ladies and gentlemen had been left far behind.

"Where's this, Trixie?"

"Tottenham Court Road, sir."

He had heard of it; there was a shopkeeper called Maple who had wormed his way into the Jockey Club. And now the Prince was almost dreaming—half asleep, half awake, savoring the warmth and the smells of the cab—a horsy rug round them both, stable straw under their feet, a scented girl, and brandy on his own breath.

"And this, Trixie?"

"Woburn Place, sir."

He closed his eyes. Woburn Place. Suddenly he seemed to remember who he was. He thought of a great ball, years and years ago, at Woburn. There had been a marvelous Viennese orchestra, but when they danced to the gavotte it had really been to the swirl and rustle of two hundred crinolines. It had been his first dance with Alix . . . but there had already been other women . . . he remembered still the Princess Bourbon Parma (so young and fresh) and the Duchess Caracciolo, the lovely mother of his Olga. Far-off days when he was first tasting freedom. And then he was back in the hansom with Trixie, which, somehow, seemed better than all the glories.

Crossing Woburn Place they had seen an omnibus and a few cabs—probably meeting the Irish Mail at Euston—and then they had plunged into darker streets: Bloomsbury, a seedy, down-at-heel sort of place, all aspidistras and "APARTMENT" cards, all lodging houses for pale City clerks.

Then, quite suddenly, the lamps vanished entirely. The hansom had been driven into complete darkness—a cobbled street without a light.

"Where's this, Trixie? Where are we?"

"My back door, sir. More private-like than the square. It will be warm upstairs."

He helped her out of the cab, out into the dense yellow fog. Clearly it was a mews; there was a four-wheeler alongside them and a general smell of horses. The silence was tense. He could hear nothing except the mare's breath, and could see less.

"A strange place this, Trixie."

"As you say, sir, a very strange place."

Had he detected a change in her tone? She seemed almost to be mocking him. He was handing up the fare to the cabman when, suddenly, something, somebody, knocked off his hat. He thought that the horse must have shied. He saw his hat rolling on the cobbles . . . and then there was something, something warm and suffocating—a rug, a blanket, a coat—it was over his head—and men were clasping his arms.

Nearly a quarter of a century later, coughing himself to death in Buckingham Palace, he was glad that he could be sure of two things—sure that Witch of the Air had won at Kempton Park that afternoon, sure that neither Mama nor the British people had ever been told of this night's escapade.

He never knew where he was taken. The windows of the four-wheeler had been soaped and the fog deadened all sound. On leaving the mews he was almost sure—or so he told the Home Secretary—that they had turned right, which probably meant they had gone east. Later he certainly heard fog signals and ships' sirens out on the river. On and on they went—it seemed hours—sometimes clattering over granite blocks, sometimes slithering over tramlines. Once they all got out and used a most ornamental iron urinal, and then all climbed in again, but from that glimpse of the foggy night he learned nothing. He heard a clock strike four, so that weeks later he had to go with the police to see whether he could identify the chimes of Stepney or Rotherhithe—and much use that was. At one point the horse seemed to be toiling up a short steep slope, and then, with the brakes on, there was a short steep down slope. The detectives thought this might be the hump-backed bridge over Bow Creek into Canning Town—and much use that was.

They hardly spoke in the four-wheeler. As they drove through the night, along these silent and deserted fog-bound streets, they were all mute. It was only in the first few minutes that he had spoken to them.

"I must tell you, gentlemen, that I happen to be a man of high rank. You will pay very heavily indeed for this outrage. For your own sakes I advise you to release me immediately. . . ."

"Stow it, guvnor. We knows wot we're abart. Yer ain't goin' to come to no bloody 'arm—not you, yer ain't."

"Let me go now then, and no more will be said; I give you my word of honor, as an officer and a gentleman. I am no use to you. My pocket is not worth picking. I have a few sovereigns —five pounds at most—take them for God's sake."

He told them that he never carried much cash, that his "secretary"—he had nearly said "equerry"—handled his money.

"Take this sovereign purse, gentlemen; it's all I have . . . there's nothing else."

In fact there was his fob with his garnet; there were his black pearl studs and links; there was his signet ring with the plumes and the "Ich Dien"; there was also the cigar case, that very special present from Cesar Ritz. He prayed silently that these things would pass unnoticed. His prayer was answered. The Captain was in no mood to deal with such trifles.

"It's not yer rhino we're after, guvnor. We're not 'ere to talk 'igh finance. We're 'ere, believe it or not, to talk abart some bloody diamonds . . . Your Most Royal an' Mighty 'Ighness."

So they understood one another. From then on they traveled in silence—not a sound but the clip-clop of the hooves on the granite sets. He reckoned that it must have been about half past four when they stopped in a narrow court, with one lamp.

It was a room without chairs or tables, but it had been prepared for them: a stinking oil lamp on the floor and a blanket nailed over the window. That was all—a room borrowed for an hour. They had pushed him ahead of them into the house and up the stairs. They had put on harlequin masks. Mr. Wainwright and Daffodil had been left behind. They wanted no women, and as for Mr. Wainwright, the Prince had seen him too often at Windsor; even with a mask there was a risk. That left five of them: the Captain, Smith, Cabby, Shrimp and the Prince of Wales. They stood in a circle, their shadows thrown upward, rather weirdly, onto the filthy ceiling.

"There they are!"

With something of a flourish the Captain had taken a handkerchief from his poacher's pocket and laid the two twelve-pointed diamond stars on the bare boards. Five men stared down in silence.

"Well, gentlemen, what is all this about?"

"No good makin' speeches, 'Ighness; three-quarters of a million quid by Tuesday an' we'll take yer 'ome."

"This is ridiculous. This is damnable nonsense. Since you seem to know who I am, however, I might as well tell you that you have the wrong man."

"Nah, nah, none of that. We know yer."

"Oh yes, I'm the Prince of Wales—there's no doubt of that—

but those diamonds are not mine. They belong to the nation. I cannot have any dealings with you. In any case the arm of the law is long . . . there is a murdered coachman to be revenged, and while I scarcely care what happens to me, this night's work, as you must surely know, is high treason—what the law would call 'assault upon a prince of the blood royal.' So you had better be thinking of the gallows instead of talking nonsense. I repeat, the arm of the law is long: you are already in a trap; my detectives shadow me everywhere."

The Prince had blundered. This was pure bluff. He never allowed detectives on his evening escapades. They all knew this —it was common talk—and the Prince could see that they knew it. His first bluff had been called. He was calm—he had been trained to be calm—but a vein in his neck was pulsating.

"We needn't talk balls, Yer 'Ighness. We're all men of the world, ain't we? The sooner we agree the sooner you'll be tucked up in yer li'l bed. Nah, come on, come on. We can't sell those blinkin' diamond stars—not *as* stars, that is—every diamond merchant in the 'ole world knows 'em. On the other 'and, if we break 'em up, they ain't worth ten tharsand quid . . . a tidy sum, I grant yer, but not really worth arl our bloody trouble . . . eh, lads?"

"Very well. I've no more to say, gentlemen. You will be arrested in the morning. We know who you are."

"Nah then, guvnor, nah then, that's enough of yer bluff. We don't want to 'ang around 'ere arl noight, nor don't you. So, we'll break up the stars and get our ten tharsand quid. And then . . . why, then the 'ole bloody scandal can wash over yer, and over yer ol' mum . . . and down yer . . . plus a few spicy bits abart yer boy Eddy, dropped in the roight quarter. An' now yer can blinkin' well walk 'ome—eleven bloody miles in the bloody fog. You've enjoyed yer trip, I 'opes."

The Prince looked left and then right, as if in a trap. His hat had gone. The rug over his head had done him no good. His face had brushed against some cobwebs on the stairs. One false eyebrow had gone. The state of his shirt was unsuitable for the best-dressed man in Europe. Worse still, his famous *savoir faire* was crumbling. The Captain had got him where he wanted him, and knew it.

"Come now, 'Ighness, I'm a reasonable koind o' bloke . . . say 'alf a million. Fair's fair!"

"Hm! Even a prince, gentlemen, does not keep that much cash in his house. How, in heaven's name, do you think you could make the exchange? I could have you watched, followed and spied upon every hour of the day, and then . . . the condemned cell. However, I have a proposal. I admit I'm your prisoner. I will take the earrings—the diamond stars—now. Drive me to Marlborough House with them and, on my word of honor as a prince, I will, within ten minutes, give you a thousand pounds in cash at—well—let us say in the porch of Boodles . . . and there the matter will end, forever. Threats are quite useless, but that is a solemn engagement."

So he was prepared to drive some sort of bargain. He was broken, groggy, like a boxer on the ropes. Well, it had been bound to happen. Now they could put the screw on.

"Nah, nah, Prince, that's no bloody good at arl. Yer word of honor wouldn't count with the loikes of us . . . not on yer loife it wouldn't. Promises to crooks don't count. I know, I know. And Boodles . . . yah! with a couple of St. James's sentries in shoutin' distance. Now then, 'Ighness, our last word: 'alf a million by Tuesday . . . or yer don't go 'ome—not never. No, not tonight nor never. Got that?"

Who was bluffing now? Did they mean it? He could feel his own pulse. He knew his blood pressure was high—he was that kind of man—but this time it was dangerous because he was also frightened. Was this really the end, or was it possible that someone really was still bluffing? What was it to be—death, a long-drawn-out kidnaping, or a hard bargain? He knew that so far as he was concerned the game was up.

"Very well, gentlemen, I have given you a chance to get out of your mess. You have refused. In the end—whatever you may think now—you'll pay for that, probably with your lives. Meanwhile, you may as well state your terms."

"Good! Good! That's more loike it. That's wot I calls business. Shrimpo, my boy, go down and tell Mrs. D. to give yer foive mugs of 'ot coffee. We'll arl drink to this . . . what ho!"

"Your terms, gentlemen? I am waiting."

"Oh, no 'urry, no 'urry. Tike it or leave it—'ere's the plot. As I say, tike it or leave it . . . but you ain't got no bloody choice, really, 'ave yer? 'ave yer? Next Wednesday week, seein' as 'ow yer woife's in Denmark, yer goes up to bonny Scotland to see yer poor ol' Mum. Yer leaves King's Cross at 'alf past ten in the morning, *pre*cisely, with his blinkin' lordship the Proime Minister to keep yer company. They change yer engine at Grantham and again at Newcastle; at Edinburgh yer 'ave a red carpet kind of a do with wot they calls the Provost and a few toffs . . . arl correct, I trust."

The Prince had stiffened visibly. All his plans had been changed that very morning so that he could travel to Balmoral with the Salisburys . . . and already, within a few hours, these men knew every detail. This made the whole affair far more serious.

Shrimp now came clattering up the stairs with a tray of mugs. The Captain laced the lot from his flask and with a mock bow offered one to the Prince.

"Yes, Yer 'Ighness, yer go to Scotland on yer own train, jest 'alf an hour behind the Flyin' Scotsman so that if there's a bloody smash it will be the loikes of us as is killed, and not Yer 'Ighness, eh?"

"These arrangements are not of my making. For God's sake let us conduct our business quickly, and have done with it. I have yet to know why my journey should concern you. Pray tell me what it is all about. Again, I am waiting."

"Then yer need wait no longer. Listen, an' don't yer make no bleedin' mistakes, fer arl our bleedin' sakes. This is the plan . . . these are yer orders, an' if yer make jest one slip then it's all up with yer, an' with yer diamonds . . . so yer bloody well listen . . . now . . ."

6

Ten-thirty from King's Cross

Having emitted three loud puffs of steam and one flourish on its whistle, the Flying Scotsman had drawn out of King's Cross at ten o'clock precisely. In the calm that comes after bustle, the Station Master, a gardenia in his buttonhole, strolled nonchalantly to the Bay. Having got rid of what he prosaically called the "10:00 A.M. to Edinburgh," and having given his glossy topper an extra rub on his sleeve, he now turned to a more exacting task.

This particular royal journey being unannounced, there was no crowd worth speaking of except a crowd of policemen—about three times as many as usual. This was a mystery even to the Station Master. It piqued him: he should have been in the confidence of Marlborough House. At the barriers there was a mere handful of people, a few idlers who had spotted the red carpet. They were a drab lot except for one glamorous and golden-haired floozy. She had been hanging around for over an hour. The Inspector of Police—a Baptist—didn't care for the look of her but had decided there was nothing he could do about her . . . in any case the girl was unlikely to solicit at ten o'clock in the morning.

Here on the Bay, away from the other platforms, the Station Master could look upon the scene with pride. There was not only calm, there was a reverential silence, as in a church just before the coffin arrives. At the far end the big engine, eager to be off, was quietly putting out little jets of steam. There was no bustle, no luggage, no milk cans, no porters. The Marlborough House and Downing Street baggage, together with valets and ladies' maids, had been sent up in wagonettes an hour ago, and was already on board. From one edge of the platform to the other an expanse of crimson cloth was now an empty foreground for the maroon, gilded and emblazoned train.

Ten minutes to go . . . and a City messenger boy, smart and perky in his pill-box hat, was handing a black-edged envelope to the Inspector of Police at the barrier. The Inspector, blushing with self-importance at the sight of the crest, passed it to the Station Master. The glamorous floozy immediately left in a hansom. She had seen all she wanted.

One minute to go . . . At the entrance on Platform No. 1 there was a stir and a flurry, a procession of shiny toppers, of flowered and ospreyed bonnets and of spangled black mantles. The Prince of Wales, swinging his cane, was preceded by the Chairman of the Great Northern, and followed by his two detectives and a fox terrier. The suites, the ladies and gentlemen in waiting, the equerries and the secretaries, plus a repugnant German child in spectacles, velvet, lace and the kilt, all bore the usual self-conscious pose of mutual affability and the pretense that other people weren't there—a pose always to be seen in courtiers.

An acute observer might also have noted two rather more unusual things. First, buried unostentatiously among the various frock-coated gentlemen, were the Right Honorable Henry Mathews, P.C., Her Majesty's Principal Secretary of State for Home Affairs, and also—tremulous with age—General Sir Frederick Rogers, K.C.B., Chief Commissioner for Police. Alongside him, in a short jacket, was a dim, respectable and rather anonymous figure, a Mr. Crawford, a detective from Bow Street. Second, the acute observer might have remarked that although all luggage and impedimenta had long since been stowed on the train, an equerry—a Mr. Cyril Pumphrey—carried a cardboard box, a stout box such as Mr. Poole might use when delivering a suit to a customer. This was doubly odd, both because equerries do not carry cardboard boxes, and because a constable walked within one yard of Mr. Pumphrey's arm.

Everyone was at last collected upon the crimson cloth, now positively heraldic—courtiers sables on a field gules, all proper. The Station Master handed the messenger boy's black-edged envelope to the Prince's Secretary—reverentially.

"Sir Francis Knollys, sir . . . for His Royal Highness."

The envelope, bearing the Queen's crest, had been addressed with one of Ponsonby's new-fangled Windsor typewriters: HIS ROYAL HIGHNESS THE PRINCE OF WALES—EXTREMELY URGENT AND CONFIDENTAL. The Prince ripped it open. His affability vanished. Very curtly he gave it back to Knollys.

"Take this. The bastards have got hold of Mama's private notepaper—the die must be changed of course—and they can't spell 'confidential.' However, I suppose the damned thing gives us our message. . . . Pass it on to Mathews immediately."

Then came the fuss of getting everyone into the right carriages—the usual conflict between protocol and corner seats. The train, as it pulled out at last into the autumn mist on its long journey north, had more dignity than its passengers. Within the central and emblazoned coach, among the palms and the electroliers, the Prince of Wales, the Marquis and Marchioness of Salisbury, the Honorable Mrs. George Keppel, Sir Francis Knollys, and Eddy relaxed in their tapestried chairs. Coffee, brandy and caviar sandwiches were served just before Kentish Town. The luncheon hampers would not be put on board until Peterborough, and one must keep up one's strength—it was, after all, an hour since breakfast.

As the train pulled out of King's Cross one would certainly have noted that the last coach was an "observation car." The observation car had a rear window from which, as the train sped northward, one could watch with fascination the receding perspective of railway lines, or—even more fascinating—the diminishing oval of light at the end of tunnels. Such cars were normally used by engineers for examining the track; this one had been hurriedly supplied with armchairs, a carpet, provender and a slop pail. Locked inside it were the Home Secretary, the Commissioner for Police and the dim and anonymous Mr. Crawford, together with the Honorable Cyril Pumphrey and his cardboard box. While all this was peculiar to a degree, all else was normal—a normal journey such as any royal creature might make to that ghastly castle upon Deeside where Buddha, the spider in the web, was now waiting for her Prime Minister and her eldest son.

From the window of the observation car the two great iron arches of the King's Cross roof were already specks in the distance. It was the Home Secretary who broke the silence.

"Well, gentlemen, here we are, all locked in at any rate until Edinburgh. So far these thugs have kept their word. Here is the message they promised His Highness. It was handed to him at the last moment. . . ."

"Surely the messenger was instantly apprehended, Mr. Home Secretary?"

"The messenger, Mr. Pumphrey, was a small boy in uniform from the Cheapside office of the City Messenger Service. These men are not altogether fools, I imagine. Anyway, here is the message, typewritten on the Queen's Windsor Castle notepaper. . . ."

"By Jove, what damned cheek!"

"Quite, Mr. Pumphrey. Here it is: YOUR SIGNAL—A WORKMAN ON THE LINE WILL MOP HIS BROW WITH A YELLOW HANDKERCHIEF."

The Commissioner for Police, the aged Sir Frederick, gave a hollow cackle.

"Really, ye know, I can hardly see the point of all this nonsense. I suppose we must go through with it now, if only to please His Royal Highness. If only my advice had been sought sooner . . . this journey to Scotland, ye know, at twenty-four hours' notice . . . all most inconvenient and uncomfortable

. . . and quite useless . . . not quite the thing, Mathews, for men in our position, what?"

"The call of duty, Sir Frederick . . ."

"Fiddlesticks! For Mr. Pumphrey here to throw half-a-million pounds onto the railway line—five bundles, you say, of a hundred bank notes each, and each for £1000—is really quite outrageous. I have no wish to be disloyal to His Highness but the thing seems quite farcical, if not criminal. One thing is certain—we shall lose the money and never get the diamonds."

"If those jewels are not delivered to Balmoral within a week, Sir Frederick, it is *you,* you know, who will have to start the biggest manhunt in history. On the other hand, once the diamonds *are* delivered, then the thieves have their money and also know, on the Prince's word of honor, that the matter is closed. They get off scot free, and the House of Coburg escapes a scandal . . . not a bad bargain."

"Very well, Mr. Home Secretary, look at the matter your way. I am only an old soldier but, by Gad, the thing sticks in my gullet . . . this supping with the devil. I abhor royal gossip, but, between ourselves, there is another matter: whence, pray, comes this half million? Popular rumor suggests that His Highness could hardly put his hands on such a sum. I only ask for information."

"Quite, Sir Frederick, quite. I understand that the Prince of Wales spent the weekend with the Rothschilds at Tring."

"Oh, I see, I see!"

Mr. Pumphrey also gave a long-drawn-out "Oh!" The silent Mr. Crawford was content to raise his eyebrows.

"That, of course, is strictly confidential."

"Of course, of course, Mr. Home Secretary . . . not a word to anyone."

"Very well then. Perhaps I may add that I dined at Marlborough House last night. I can assure you that the Prince is determined to avoid a scandal—if only for the Queen's sake. One can imagine the headlines—CROWN JEWELS STOLEN, perhaps; or worse still, QUEEN'S DIAMONDS FAKED. The thought of it is quite unbearable. The institution of monarchy would never survive it, and that is something about which the Prince, for all his—er—conviviality, is much concerned, you know. So I think you may take it, Sir Frederick—as a strict secret—that it is the Baron Ferdy who has put up this vast sum (the actual bank notes were conveyed to Coutts from Threadneedle Street, but that means nothing) on condition that the diamond stars should pass quietly but absolutely to the House of Rothschild—at the Queen's death."

Mr. Cyril Pumphrey brightened visibly. "The Rothschilds, then, are confident that the gang will keep its side of the bargain. They may know something that we don't, but in any case that is surely a good point, Mr. Home Secretary. With all due respect to the Prince's own judgment—and Sir Frederick has just suggested that His Royal Highness is being profligate, reckless and irresponsible. . . ."

"Come, come, Mr. Pumphrey, I meant nothing of the kind. You twist my words, sir . . . really . . ."

"Well, whatever you may have meant, Sir Frederick, we can be jolly pleased that our operation has Rothschild backing. It puts a completely different complexion upon the whole show—what? Does it not, Mr. Home Secretary?"

"Oh, dear me, yes. Certainly, certainly . . . most reassuring."

"And of course the bank notes are all marked?"

"Really, really, Mr. Pumphrey. I have already told you that these men are not fools—desperadoes maybe, but not fools. Part of their bargain with the Prince—and remember that it was made under physical duress—was that the bank notes, now in that box, should be new packets from the Mint, with the seals unbroken. Of course we have their numbers, but what is the good of that? Within hours they will have bought scores of postal orders in a hundred different post offices and cashed them—or possibly changed all the notes at half-a-dozen different *bureaux de change*, in Brussels, Paris, Hamburg . . . who knows? Another part of the bargain is that we must not expect to receive the diamonds for a week—a week for them to change the bank notes and, if they choose, to leave the country."

"Clever devils, Mr. Home Secretary, clever devils!"

"I fear so, Mr. Pumphrey, I fear so. . . . But I see that we are already passing Stevenage. From now on we must be on the alert. Let me summarize our tasks. You, Mr. Pumphrey, must watch, as indeed we all will, for the workman with the yellow handkerchief. As soon as you see him you will open this window here and, as soon as I say 'Go,' will eject your package onto the permanent way. That is clear?"

"Couldn't be clearer, sir."

"That signal—the yellow handkerchief—may come anywhere between here and Aberdeen, or even on that last run up to Ballater. Vigilance must be maintained for every second. Now you, Sir Frederick, have made your dispositions. Kindly explain them."

"Oh, certainly. Positively a military operation. I have two thousand men, drawn from different police forces throughout the kingdom. They are in plain clothes of course. Two thousand may sound a great many, but it is, after all, barely four to the mile. That is enough. Fortunately the mist is thin—a real fog would have been disastrous. The entire track is under observation and if anyone picks up the box of bank notes after the train has passed, why then, upon my soul, an arrest is certain."

"I am glad you are so confident, Sir Frederick. Now you, Mr. Crawford, must watch everything and everybody with your—er—your trained eye. Above all you must have these binoculars at the ready so that when the moment comes we may depend upon you for an identification—some old lag perhaps, or well-known figure from the underworld. I am sure you won't let us down."

"I will do what I can, sir, but identification will be difficult. Our pace is terrific; seventy miles an hour or more. I suppose you will immediately pull the cord and stop the train."

"It was decided, Mr. Crawford, that we would not do that. We were advised that in any case a train of this weight and speed could not stop in much less than a mile. Moreover, the incident might lead to undesirable reports in the newspapers—and all to no purpose. It would also give our protagonists an excuse to break their bargain. No, it would never do. I think we know best, Mr. Crawford."

Mr. Crawford felt he could have managed this affair rather better than either Sir Frederick or the Home Secretary. He also knew his place. He not only knew it, he felt that he was being kept in it, that he was no more than the hired detective. He gazed rather wistfully down the endless perspective of the Great Northern Line, drawn as with a ruler across the level fields of Hertfordshire.

"As you say, sir."

"Quite, Mr. Crawford, thank you. Now I, for my part, gentlemen, am ready to relieve any of you at any time. Meanwhile, I shall go on with what I am doing—ticking off the quarter-mile posts on this schedule of stations and distances. At this moment, for instance, we are precisely one and three-quarter miles north of Stevenage. When the crisis occurs we must be sure of our exact whereabouts—these thugs may have some local hideout or accomplices—someone to harbor them. And now let us all do our duty to the Queen and to the Prince. We have ample viands here, also several bottles of hock. We have an arduous day ahead, some nine hours to go; but my flask and cigar case are at your service . . . now, gentlemen."

They hurtled through St. Neots at nearly eighty. With the sun breaking up the mist, and with the Flying Scotsman ahead, acting almost as a pilot train, the driver barely glanced at his signals. He had surmounted the Potters Bar incline at over fifty —a good start—and was now making the most of these flat stretches of eastern England. He even allowed his bleary but sentimental eye to wander over Fenland spires and the far-off Isle of Ely. Then he looked down the line ahead and spoke to his fireman.

"Wot's up, Jack? They're guardin' the Prince very partikler like this morning, ain't they?"

" 'Ow's that?"

"There's blokes arl along the track—three or four to every mile. Plain-clothes coppers, I reckon."

"Gawd! D'ye think as 'ow it's train wreckers they're afeared of?"

"Nah, just a scare . . . nihilists or Fenians, or jest one of these 'ere dynamite hoaxes. Someone got the wind up. Blowed if I know . . ."

"Not our bloody business anyway."

"Nah. We're ahead of toime—that's our business. Lovely! Lovely! Shovel it on, Jack."

They ground to a halt at Peterborough: seventy-six miles in an hour and ten minutes. The platform had been cleared. The toppers and even the gold lace were paraded, but within the train not a soul stirred. Only the repulsive child in velvet bothered to look out the window. Twenty luncheon hampers were passed to the stewards at the door of the fourgon, and then, drinking their fashionable apéritifs, they were off again, this time through familiar hunting shires with nostalgic memories of runs with the Quorn and the Pytchely . . . and so up the long slope to Grantham. Within half an hour, and with a brand-new engine, they were over the Trent beyond Newark, and skirting the Dukeries—more nostalgic memories, this time of great house parties. And then, with everyone absorbed in the second course of luncheon, Doncaster, although it might have recalled the St. Leger and a night at Tranby Croft, flashed by unnoticed.

At Peterborough it had been possible to ignore the local gentry. York was different. One cannot ignore York. Even though York coincided with the coffee and cognac a moment had to be spared. Bertie and Eddy—successive heirs to the throne—stepped onto the red carpet. The Station Master presented the three Lords Lieutenant of the three Ridings. The North Riding remarked upon the miracle of modern travel; the East Riding said that the mist had cleared. The West Riding, more courageous, addressed himself to Eddy, who said that the mist had cleared. The ladies-in-waiting could be glimpsed in the corner seats of their steamy carriages, dozing over empty coffee cups, their bonnet strings flung back, their veils rolled up on their moist foreheads. It was only Mrs. Keppel who allowed herself a little powder, and a hat which gave cheer to all—a hat which was as if the spring had come. In the front coach four equerries could be seen playing whist; they were playing for ten-pound tricks. In the observation car, the Home Secretary, for reasons best known to himself, had pulled down the blinds—thus starting a fine hare that the dying Emperor Frederick of Germany was being carried north to say farewell to the Queen—perhaps to die in her arms. Then the whistle blew and on the long run up the vale between the Cleveland Hills and Swaledale they touched eighty. Nobody even noticed the towers of Durham.

As they crossed the High Level Bridge at Newcastle—one of the wonders of the age—they might also have beheld the most beautiful and most black of all these northern cities, yet another child of their own time; they snored or gambled.

The four men in the observation car, flushed with hock, struggled to remain alert. None of them spoke until they were past Morpeth. It was the detective who dared to break the silence.

"Excuse me, Mr. Home Secretary, but I think the next half hour is our last chance."

"Really, Crawford, what an extraordinary idea . . . another three or four hours yet, I think, to Ballater."

"The sun sets at Greenwich at 5:20, sir—rather earlier as far north as this."

"Gad, Sir Frederick, the man's right. It'll soon be dark. I never thought of that."

"Nor did I, Mr. Home Secretary, nor did I . . . but why should we? That's Crawford's job. Quite right to tell us, my man, but I can't for the life of me see that it makes a hap'orth of difference. After all, we can't see their damned yellow handkerchief in the dark, so why bother? The whole thing is a mare's nest anyway, eh, Pumphrey?"

"Oh, certainly, if you say so, Sir Frederick. Certainly."

"Of course it is—always said so. The diamonds—the earrings or whatever they call them—have gone anyway. That's that. The Prince must make up his mind to it, eh, Mathews? He's spoilt, you know—between ourselves—and it won't hurt him to have to admit defeat for once in his life, eh, Mathews?"

"Possibly not, Sir Frederick; although the permanent loss of the earrings will, surely, hardly redound to your credit—as Commissioner of Police."

"Pooh! These things are bound to happen, my dear chap. Don't talk stuff and nonsense."

"Anyway, it's not the Prince, it's Ferdy Rothschild who'll be taking the rap. Not, of course, that he'll be losing any sleep either. He will have had the whole thing underwritten by the Sassoons, Barings and all that crowd. They'll all have shares in this robbery, you know. Damned profitable game. Underwritten all over again by the small fry at Lloyd's. Overinsured at the top, underinsured at the bottom. The Ikeys will win—you can stake your life on that."

"Ah! You know a lot, Home Secretary."

"I'm afraid it's true. Nobody is going to thank us, you know, if we do catch these rogues. And I suppose when Rothschilds get the insurance the Prince will take his cut—a kind of commission—that's only fair. No, no, only the Old Girl will be displeased."

"The Old Girl, sir?"

"The Queen, Crawford."

"Oh, yes, sir."

"If she's been told anything about it, that is. You see, Sir Frederick, she doesn't want faked jewelry and she doesn't want a scandal. . . . Everybody else stands to win hands down."

Mr. Crawford was thinking that he would have to tell Mrs. Crawford all this, in bed. He was profoundly shocked. He was an experienced detective and yet it had never occurred to him that people might actually make money out of being robbed. . . . His mind reeled. Mr. Pumphrey now looked around him—east and west.

"Hm, Crawford's right, you know. Sun's almost down. It's jolly well all or nothing now, chaps. The whole thing looks like being a 'no go.' Oh well, at least we'll be able to put our feet up and booze a bit. By Jove we've earned it—what?"

It was almost dusk now, but nobody had thought of lighting the oil lamps in the roof of the observation car. They were running parallel with the Northumberland coast, a few miles inland, about a third of the way from Newcastle to Berwick. There was the occasional hill as at Alnwick, and the occasional rill running down to the sea, where they had to cross some little stream such as the Coquet.

Looking back down the long perspective of the double track, even in the failing light they could see three of Sir Frederick's plain-clothes policemen, widely spaced. Then, suddenly, there flashed into their field of vision a gang of three platelayers—all correct in corduroy trousers and checked shirts, and with the tools of their trade. As the men were on the "up" line they had no need to pause as the royal train roared past them. Two, in fact, kept their heads down. The third stood upright and mopped his brow with a large yellow handkerchief.

"Go . . . Pumphrey . . . Go! For God's sake! Crawford . . . your binoculars."

The cardboard box, heavy with crisp bank notes, whirled into space. Then . . . there was absolute blackness, utter darkness. They were in a quarter-mile-long tunnel.

"Bastards!"

"Bugger!"

"Light a match—for the love of Mike!"

"Damn their eyes!"

"Clever devils—I knew they were. Clever devils! So much, Sir Frederick, for your damned mare's nest!"

It had all been perfectly timed for the twilight. The platelayers, outside the tunnel, could now work on for a few more minutes, unsuspected by the plain-clothes policemen, until it was dark, and time to "go home from work." As for the cardboard box, it had finally thudded onto the line actually just within the darkness of the tunnel, only a few yards from the gang.

And now the train flashed out into daylight on the other side. They had been inside the tunnel and now, quite suddenly, they were on a bridge—a small viaduct.

"Look, gentlemen, look—you see the trick."

Sixty feet below them, waiting in the road which wound up the glen—still just discernible in the dusk—was a gig, the driver looking up as they hurtled by far above him.

"Well, you see, Mr. Home Secretary, you see . . ."

"Of course I see, Sir Frederick. . . . I may be a fool but I'm not a bloody fool. Nor am I in my second childhood. Any identification, Crawford?"

"I do my best, sir, but I have not been trained to see in the dark."

"I didn't suppose you had. You realize, all of you, that that gang can go on quietly working for another ten minutes or so, and Sir Frederick's 'sentries' won't have the slightest reason to suspect them. And then, when they stop work, one of them can nip into the tunnel, pick up the money, come through the tunnel and drop it over the viaduct to his friend in the gig. Most fortunately, however, as we left King's Cross we were told by Sir Frederick that, in the event of the box of bank notes being picked up, an arrest was certain . . . well?"

"Upon my soul, Mr. Home Secretary, you twist my words. Damn it, sir, you twist my words. Reasonably certain, maybe . . . but—er—not this, not this."

"Not what, Sir Frederick."

"The tunnel . . . the tunnel. I never thought of a tunnel."

"I see. Well, gentlemen, as Her Majesty's Secretary of State, I must thank you for your cooperation. It has been a somewhat arduous day, I fear. It is unfortunate that neither the tunnel nor the dusk were foreseen. The whole affair—as I shall have to tell His Royal Highness—has been grossly mismanaged."

"Indeed, indeed . . . and mismanaged by whom, Mr. Home Secretary? Who, pray, is in charge of this—er—this operation?"

"I am, Sir Frederick; and, as you well know, a Minister of the Crown does not publicly blame his subordinates. That may come later. Certainly a most searching inquiry seems to be indicated—an inquiry, Sir Frederick, into the administration of the police. Perhaps there are too many doddering old buffers in charge . . . we shall see, we shall see. Meanwhile we are being whirled toward Edinburgh. His Royal Highness alights for half an hour at the Waverley Station to take some refreshment with the Lord Provost, with the Duke of Buccleuch, the MacGregor of the MacGregor, and with the Lochiel of that ilk. I have, naturally, been invited to join them. You will remain here. The Prince will be impatient to hear my news. And this evening, at Balmoral, Sir Frederick, Her Majesty will doubtless wish to know how her police have acquitted themselves. I am a just man, I hope, but my task will be no easy one. You will now allow me, therefore, to compose my thoughts."

"Most necessary, I'm sure, Mr. Home Secretary, most necessary."

"Enough, Sir Frederick, enough."

Mr. Crawford was thinking that it must have been just like this after the Charge of the Light Brigade. Mr. Cyril Pumphrey noticed that they were now crossing the border: he could see the lights reflected in the river as they thundered over the bridge at Berwick. As a trained diplomat he attempted a *détente.*

"Well, well, let's all put our feet up. Still a couple of bottles left—shall we split one, Crawford?"

"Thank you, sir, that would be most welcome."

"Your first visit to Bonnie Scotland, Crawford?"

"Yes, sir; I am much looking forward to Deeside."

Sir Frederick, having been crushed by the Home Secretary, now saw his chance of vicarious revenge.

"I think, Mr. Pumphrey, that Crawford will be returning to his duties at Bow Street by the first train in the morning."

"I was hoping, Sir Frederick, for a glimpse of Balmoral."

"The Castle, Crawford, is not open to the public. I am sure, however, that the Railway Arms at Ballater will accommodate you. Bow Street is very busy just now—footpads and burglars take advantage of these foggy nights—and a further day's leave would not be justified. And, Crawford . . ."

"Sir."

"I shall be enjoying Her Majesty's hospitality until Friday; you will make no report to your superiors until my return . . . is that clear?"

"Quite clear, sir."

"Hard cheese, Crawford—what?"

"Thank you, Mr. Pumphrey. I am sorry the trip has been such a failure."

"Oh, well, Crawford—not your fault, nor mine. These two must fight it out between them . . . and whitewash themselves if they can . . . glad we're not in their shoes, by Jove!"

Sir Frederick was now both choleric and purple. "Really, Mr. Pumphrey, you go too far. Speaking like that to a subordinate, and in front of the Home Secretary. Upon my soul, I can hardly contain myself."

"It's no good getting in a lather, Sir Frederick. Take it out of poor old Crawford, if you must, but *I'm* jolly well not your poodle, you know. Anyway, two things are now certain. One is that the Home Secretary will have to break the news to the Old Girl sooner or later, and also—in a few minutes when we get to Edinburgh—to our dear Bertie. The other thing is that half-a-million pounds' worth of Bank of England notes are being driven briskly over the Northumberland moors in a gig, and that Bloody Mary's Earrings have vanished forever from the Crown Jewels of England—if, indeed, they were ever there."

"And pray, Mr. Pumphrey, what is the meaning of that last remark?"

"Oh, nothing, Mr. Home Secretary. Only that you and Sir Frederick—both high servants of the Crown, what ho!—imagine yourselves as being given all available information, while I, being only a poor bloody equerry, hear all the gossip."

When they reached Edinburgh the station arc lights were blazing. At the border, at the precise moment of crossing the Tweed at Berwick, the Prince of Wales had taken off his trousers and donned the kilt. The crowd on the platform at Edinburgh, in their fustian—knowing only that the Prince played cards on Sunday—were not amused; the last Sassenach to behave in this bizarre way had been George IV, also no better than he should have been. The "do" with the Lord Provost, although oiled with whisky, was brief; the Prince walked back to the train, along the red carpet, with the Home Secretary.

"Well, Mathews, what news?"

"It happened this side of Newcastle, Your Highness, in the twilight. . . ."

"Go on."

"Three of them—they eluded Sir Frederick's men, sir, in a tunnel which, most regrettably, Sir Frederick had failed to foresee."

The Prince turned curtly on his heel, slamming the door of his coach. All the doors were slammed. The whistle blew. The train moved. The Home Secretary dived into a third-class compartment full of valets playing cribbage.

Outside the little station at Ballater, in the thick mist of a moorland night, eight carriages were drawn up, one with postilions, also wagonettes for luggage and servants. Gillies, on stout ponies, were ready to guide the cavalcade over the rough road to Balmoral. Four of the Black Watch bore blazing torches, their flickering light falling upon the reception committee—His Royal Highness Prince Alfred ("Affie") and Sir Henry Ponsonby, wet Inverness capes reflecting the torchlight, faces almost hidden between mufflers and deerstalkers. Four more highlanders, as the train steamed in, set up a grotesque wailing upon the pipes—a last agony for travelers surrounded by dark, drizzle and mist.

By some mysterious herd instinct everyone remained seated until Mrs. George Keppel had left the train, with her maid, and driven off in a closed brougham, with one outrider. Abergeldie Mains, a ghastly affair of granite, pine and bamboo furniture, was hers for a month. She could not visit Balmoral, a mile away, but the Prince could visit Abergeldie—a convenient arrangement.

Mrs. Keppel disposed of, the Prince of Wales, Eddy and the Salisburys could alight in order to be received by Affie and Ponsonby. The others followed—King's Cross worlds away, nothing ahead but the discomfort and discipline of Balmoral—a loathsome place.

Luncheon at Balmoral was more funereal than usual . . . the whole house, like the Blue Room at Windsor, was an eternal death chamber. The surrounding hills were scattered with cairns and plaques—the larger for Albert, the smaller for John Brown. And now, here at luncheon, in clear succession to Brown, was the Munshi, as catlike and sly as ever, passing round the *petits fours,* while the footmen dropped plates. Even the stags' heads, their glass eyes staring down from tartan walls, were more cheerful than these ladies in rusty black or these bearded gentlemen in kilts.

The dining room was icy. All the rooms at Balmoral were cold. Ponsonby, remembering the disaster of a previous visit, had smuggled an oil stove into the Salisburys' bedroom—those narrow iron bedsteads. "Cold is wholesome." That the Queen's end of the luncheon table should be gloomy was normal. But why, for two whole days, had the Prince of Wales looked like a thunder cloud? . . . "Something has come over Bertie." Hardly had the Prince swallowed his chilly coffee than he beckoned to the Prime Minister and to the Home Secretary. If only for a few minutes he had somehow or other to escape from that grotesque household where people communicated with each other only by notes. Thus, three men in huge overcoats stood on the terrace breathing the cold, damp air, gazing at the distant Cairngorms, white against a gray sky.

"Well, Mathews, this is a pretty kettle of fish. Sir Frederick has left Balmoral in dudgeon. The money's gone, the diamonds have gone . . . what do we do next?"

"I have taken steps, Your Highness, naturally."

"Indeed. I hope they will be successful. Pray explain them to us. The Prime Minister is as anxious as I am to avoid scandal. The House of Rothschild, I might add, are also anxious."

"Quite, sir. I can assure you that the gravity of the situation is not underestimated. Every post office in the realm will retain any person sending any sort of package to Balmoral. If such persons cannot immediately establish their credentials, then the police may retain them for further questioning. All this, sir, is within my powers. It should do the trick, I think."

"Hm! After that farce on the train you can hardly blame me, Mathews, for being skeptical."

"No, indeed, sir. Sir Frederick's conduct was quite incomprehensible. I have already told the Prime Minister that at the next Cabinet I shall demand an inquiry into the administration of the police—have I not, Mr. Prime Minister?"

"Oh, yes, you've told me all right; but by that time, ye know, there may be changes. We don't know, do we? who the Home Secretary may be. That's political life, Mathews—here today, gone tomorrow."

By some magic a footman had appeared at the Prince's elbow, his scarlet coat touched with flakes of snow.

"Yes, McTaggart, what is it?"

"His Grace the Duke of Argyll, sir. His carriage is in the forecourt. My orders are to say that his business with Your Highness is urgent."

"Ask him to join us here."

"Sir." Argyll was a few steps behind the footman.

"Well, my dear Argyll, this is an unexpected pleasure. You know the Prime Minister. This is Mr. Mathews, the Home Secretary. You have had a long drive . . . all the way from Inveraray?"

"Yes, Your Highness. I lay the night in the inn at Pitlochry. A wonderful drive through the glens. Loch Tay was splendid in her winter dress—bare birch trees, golden bracken and snow on the hills. . . ."

"Quite, Argyll, quite—most poetic, I'm sure. But what can we do for you?"

"It's all a little mysterious, sir. Yesterday morning a registered package arrived at Inveraray, with a Newcastle postmark. Inside the package, sir, was this smaller parcel, addressed to you. There was also a scrawled note, in an uneducated hand, asking me to deliver the parcel to you personally—and to trust it to nobody else. I felt it my duty to do this. . . . I trust, Your Highness, that neither of us has been duped by some hoaxer. Here, sir, is the parcel."

"Bastards, Salisbury, bastards! Swine! Clever devils! They'll beat you every time, Mathews . . . every time! Thank you, Argyll."

"Not at all, Your Highness; an honor to be of service. But, really, you know, I don't quite—er—understand. . . ."

"Come inside, all of you. We know what's in here, Argyll. They've used you as a postman—that's all. This damned parcel is worth half a million. At least I hope so. Come inside—you'll freeze here."

In the drawing room at Abergeldie Mains, embedded, as it were, in a great forest of palms, epergnes, easels, Landseers, raffia fans, antlers, pampas grass and bamboo, Mrs. George Keppel was pouring out tea for the heir to the throne. Her coiffure was superb, her complexion divine, her scent discreet. She wore a "tea gown" *à la Japonaise.* Her chaise longue was of wicker.

"Look, Alice, I want your help. You know such a lot about jewels and things of that kind."

"I should. Someone very kind has given me so many."

"Well, this is serious . . . really a sort of state secret . . . I can't tell you quite everything. Ponsonby and Knollys know less than nothing about jewels. Salisbury, for all his great possessions, is no better. Of course I could telegraph for Garrard's man, but

—you know me, my dear: I'm always in a hurry. And I can trust you. Now, just look at these."

And there on the tea table, among the toast and the tea cakes and the scones and the baps and the *gâteaux* and the éclairs and the bread-and-butter and the sandwiches and the jams and the silver cream jugs and the Crown Derby tea cups, the Prince of Wales laid down the two twelve-pointed stars—the stars which the Duke of Argyll had just brought over the mountains and through the glens.

"These arrived today. What do you think of them?"

She barely glanced at them. She had a pretty laugh—a famous laugh—but for once it was also mocking.

"Really, my dear boy, you're not serious."

"I want your honest opinion."

"You shall have it then. The design is magnificent—Spanish of course. The 'diamonds' are quite good paste, better than cut glass. A theatrical costumer might give you a hundred pounds for them."

"Oh!"

"You had better give them to one of your little actress friends. I would expect something rather better."

"I only wanted your opinion, dearest. You are so clever. I never meant them as a present for you."

"I should think not indeed . . . complete rubbish, dear boy!"

7

The Osborne Conference

Skerret, the nonagenarian dresser, and Frau Güttmann, the octogenarian housekeeper—stiff collar and black gloves—were together at an attic window. On this cold, clear January morning, over the tops of cedars and deodars, they could look across an amethyst Solent to see the masts and crosstrees of the clippers in Portsmouth harbor. *Courageous* and *Lion,* lying off Calshot, were an assurance that, under God and the Royal Navy, this world would go on forever.

The two old women, however, were interested neither in clippers nor in ironclads; it was the carriages that puzzled them. One after another the broughams and the victorias, as well as a couple of hired vehicles from the livery stable, had crawled up the hill from Cowes, returning to the quay for a second load. It had been going on all the morning. Mystery was being added to mystery. For one thing, these people had no business at Osborne anyway—Osborne was for the family; and yet here they were—complete strangers—even before the Christmas trees had been dismantled. Why? Skerret and Güttmann had been told nothing.

As each carriage, gravel crunching under the wheels, trotted into the forecourt, disapproval grew. These visitors were not even ladies and gentlemen. They were, indeed, no ladies at all, and several of the men wore billycocks—quite common people. Once, it is true, Skerret thought she recognized the Baron Ferdinand, while Güttmann could swear to the Duke of Argyll . . . but then Güttmann, as Skerret often said, was getting confused in her old age and would swear to anything. Why, for instance, should the Dean of Windsor, not to mention Herr Mütter, the Castle librarian, be here at all? They did not belong—they were purely Windsor. And then, at last, below the window, there was a Field Marshal—in full rig. That was better: he might be hobbling on two sticks but at least he was part of the world they knew. It was something, but not enough; one Duke and one Field Marshal did not in themselves explain the use of the State Dining Room in January. Finally and above all, what was Prince William of Prussia doing here? . . . He must know perfectly well that he was not wanted until August—for the yachting.

The Queen took luncheon alone with the Princess Beatrice—a cup of Bengers, two biscuits and silence. Never had the Queen's mouth turned down quite so much. For three days now it had been one damned thing after another . . . only last night she had had to be told—it could be hidden no longer—that Prince Alfred's reputation in Coburg was unspeakable, and his debts astronomical. Prince Alfred—her dearest Affie—had become almost overnight her "greatest grief," Bertie, by comparison, being no more than "imprudent." It was hard on an old woman, already weighed down with such burdens as were hers. And now, on top of that, and without her permission, there was this absurd gathering of Bertie's in the State Rooms—rooms that were never opened in January, never until Cowes week. This was her house and she was told nothing—that was what hurt. . . .

Downstairs in the State Dining Room, dwarfed by the greatest of the Winterhalters, the Prince of Wales was at the head of the table. There was no hostess. There could be no hostess: this was the Queen's house. Alix, in any case, and as always lately, was in Denmark, while Beatrice was upstairs with Mama. The Prince explained to his guests, first, that this was a "business luncheon"—a most curious phrase—and that protocol might be ignored. Anyone might sit anywhere. This, of course, was nonsense. After a lot of jockeying Prince William got himself on Bertie's right, while Affie, after a tussle with Eddy, got himself on Bertie's left. After that Ponsonby told them all where to sit; it was so much simpler.

General Roderick Sparling, Master of the Royal Mews, was corseted, groomed and spurred to the nines with all accouterments. Field Marshal Lord Wilson, Constable of the Tower of London, sported his Waterloo medal—one up on Sparling—but was blinder, deafer and more arthritic than when Ponsonby had drunk his brandy six months ago. The Dean of Windsor—as always when Bertie was around—had been deprived of his only privilege, the right to say grace. The Marquis of Salisbury, his head as the dome of St. Paul's to other men's molehills, wondered why on earth he had come, but thanked God that, at any rate, it was not Balmoral. The Right Honorable Henry Mathews, looking more than ever like an ugly actor, had become a back-bencher almost overnight . . . as Cyril Pumphrey said, "Jolly decent of him to come at all." Pumphrey himself, having carefully inserted his monocle, did obscene doodles for the amusement of the Duke of Argyll. The Duke, having replaced the kilt with a frock coat, could hardly be recognized as the man who had driven through the glens with the diamond earrings. Sir Frederick Rogers, Commissioner for Police, expecting a wigging from the Prince, and in daily dread of a public inquiry, was more choleric than ever. Sir Francis Knollys simply fussed; he had to look after his master's guests but disapproved of the whole affair . . . totally unnecessary . . . utterly superfluous . . . most inopportune . . . the police could handle the matter . . . a fine body of men . . . second to none. The clichés dripped from him. Sir Henry Ponsonby, as the Queen's Secretary, was concerned with the Household service rather than with this damned conference. . . . The earrings had gone . . . and that was that. He glanced across the table at Rothschild—the Prince had forgotten no one. The Baron Ferdinand was as cool as a cucumber; he had all the figures he needed on a half sheet of note-paper; other men had Gladstone bags full of documents they hadn't read. Mary Ponsonby was really enjoying herself, chatting on her left to Herr Mütter about the Dürer drawings in the library at Windsor, and on her right to Mr. Friedman of Garrard's; he was telling her all the scandals among Regent Street shopkeepers—delicious.

Prince William, giving his mustaches a flourish, started off upon a high-flown oration concerning his beloved grandmother, the great Queen-Empress, and the need to protect her dear name from calumny. Bertie soon put a stop to that, explaining that there must be no discussion until coffee had been served. They would then move into the India Room, to be joined there by eight other witnesses now taking luncheon in the housekeeper's quarters.

When Benjamin Disraeli, in one of his more foolish flights of fancy, gave Victoria the title of "Queen-Empress," there were four things he did not foresee. One was that the Queen would take lessons in Hindustani; the second was that she would take the Munshi—the son of a common apothecary in Agra—and turn him into, first, her personal servant and then her confidential secretary; the third was that the Imperial title would last barely seventy years; the fourth was that the Queen would create the India Room at Osborne. The room became a great landmark in the history of English taste—symbolizing sufficiently its lowest point.

As the lunch, abominably served on Pomeranian porcelain, came to an end, the Prince of Wales led his seventeen guests into the India Room. Princess Beatrice quietly joined them—"Mama is resting." On a bench at the far end were the eight men who had been fed in the housekeeper's room. With a scraping of boots on the Minton tile floor, they rose and bowed. There were two frock coats—Mr. Quennell, the Station Master at Paddington, and Mr. Juniper, the Station Master at King's Cross; they kept together, nursing a common resentment about that housekeeper's room; after all they were in charge of great

London termini, not potty little stations like Ballater and Wolferton. Mr. Archibald Bellow, the house detective from Windsor, in a faintly tartan fawn, puffed out his cheeks in annoyance—he, too, resented the housekeeper's room, but, being inured to royalty's rudeness, knew how to get his own back; only that morning he had raided the Windsor hothouse for a perfectly splendid buttonhole—one up on everybody. Between Chief Superintendent Chambers (Charlie Chambers of the waxed mustaches) and Chief Detective Bertram Riddle (of the Dundreary whiskers) there was also a common bond: both having been on duty at Paddington on June 19, they had been able to concert their evidence while drinking in the bar of the Cowes ferry. Philpotts, the Ponsonby coachman, sat rigidly to attention, his cockaded hat on his knees, his eyes on the ceiling. Mr. Crawford of Bow Street was enjoying his revenge for the Ballater trip: denied his glimpse of Balmoral he was now feasting his eyes upon the polychromatic glories of Osborne—and that nice Mr. Pumphrey had waved to him across the room. Mr. Straw, manager of Lock's, the St. James's Street hatters, was too absorbed in his old game of picking out the real toffs from the dressy riff-raff to bother himself overmuch as to why Mr. Friedman of Garrard's had lunched with the Prince—after all he and Friedman were both warrant holders. Mr. Straw, however, was philosophical about the gentry—he had learned to be. At the end of the bench, dim and anonymous, was Mr. Slattery, a Windsor footman, nervously turning his billycock round and round in his hands, in an agony of apprehension.

In front of the Prince, on an inlaid ebony and ivory and mother-of-pearl table from Mysore, were the two twelve-pointed diamond stars—those useless replicas which, only a month ago, the Duke of Argyll had borne across Scotland, and which the Prince had placed on Alice Keppel's bamboo tea table—to be told they were rubbish. And now, at a nod from the Prince, Francis Knollys gave a tap with his gavel . . . "Pray silence for His Royal Highness."

PRINCE OF WALES: You all know why we are here. Thank you for coming. Balmoral seemed to be inconveniently far away—it often is—whereas Osborne, although accessible, is withdrawn from prying eyes. Secrecy is everything. That, indeed, is why I have called this meeting instead of simply handing the whole horrible business to the Public Prosecutor. That would have let in the press. In effect, you are now behind locked doors. You all know, in a general way, the nature of our business. Six months ago, for one of the Jubilee dinners, Her Majesty decided to wear the famous Tudor Tiara, incorporating those priceless diamonds popularly known as Bloody Mary's Earrings. She therefore commanded her Secretary, Sir Henry Ponsonby, to convey the Tiara from the Tower of London, where it is normally kept with the Crown Jewels, to Windsor. In the course of Sir Henry's journey, by means of a Buckingham Palace carriage and the train, the diamonds were removed from either side of the Tiara and were replaced by clever but worthless replicas. Pray explain to us, Sir Henry, how you came to be robbed.

PONSONBY: Really, Your Highness, really! You embarrass me. With the greatest respect and loyalty I cannot accept your suggestion that I was robbed. Some other explanation must be found. I never betrayed my trust. The white hat box containing the Tiara was never out of my sight—not for a moment.

PUMPHREY: Get along with you, Ponsonby. Old Wilson here must have wined you well—eh, Wilson? Don't you ever go to the lavatory, Ponsonby, like the rest of the human race?

KNOLLYS: Order! Order! Mr. Pumphrey, you forget yourself. There are ladies present . . . the Princess. Dear me, dear me!

PUMPHREY: Oh, damn it all, Knollys, this is an inquiry, ye know, not a blasted levee.

KNOLLYS: There are ways of saying these things, Mr. Pumphrey . . . a man in your position . . . in the Household.

PRINCE OF WALES: Quite, Knollys, quite. You've made your point. All the same, my dear Ponsonby, perhaps you or Mr. Quennell, the Paddington Station Master, could tell us whether anything of that nature did in fact occur. Yes, Mr. Quennell, I think.

QUENNELL: Yes, Your Highness. When Sir Henry's brougham pulled up at the entrance to No. 1 platform, I had already held the Windsor train for some twenty minutes. When the footman opened the door, however, I observed that Sir Henry was—er—somewhat somnolent. It was a hot day. The footman had to tap him on the knee. Upon alighting he was also, quite clearly, in some—er—distress—in need of a lavatory. The hat box, therefore, was handed to Charlie—er—I beg your pardon—to Chief Superintendent Chambers, who, accompanied by four constables, conveyed same to Sir Henry's compartment on the Windsor train . . . Platform No. 4.

CHAMBERS: Correct, Your Highness, entirely correct . . . and at the compartment door we awaited Sir Henry and Mr. Quennell. There was no incident of any kind.

QUENNELL: Meanwhile, Your Highness, I had escorted Sir Henry to my office, where he partook of a thimbleful of the negus which I always keep upon my kettle ring. Then he brushed his clothes, gave his hat a shine, washed and—er—made himself comfortable.

PRINCE OF WALES: Thank you, Mr. Quennell. That is very clear. So, my dear Ponsonby, it would seem that there were in fact some ten minutes or so when the hat box *was* out of your sight. . . .

PONSONBY: Oh, well, sir, of course if you're going to take the matter as literally as all that . . . why, then, I suppose I must say 'Yes' . . . but really! Damn it, Your Highness, even for those few minutes the hat box was in the hands of a senior police officer, with an escort of constables. If that is all . . .

PRINCE OF WALES: It is not all, Ponsonby. It would seem that what with the heat of the day, and Field Marshal Lord Wilson's brandy, you were snoozing in the brougham. You were also attended by two bogus servants—never since apprehended—Fulleylove, the genuine footman, having been decoyed into the North of England, and Macdonald, the genuine coachman, having had his throat slit behind Paddington that morning—with no clues. Correct, General Sparling?

SPARLING: Yes, Your Highness—an unprecedented event in the history of the Royal Mews. I should point out, perhaps, that anyone can buy a fawn coat and then change the facings and buttons—the easiest thing in the world. The brougham was abandoned that evening outside Gorringe's. The two men, since they were wearing the Queen's livery, must have then decamped in a closed carriage which was presumably waiting for them. One suspects a gang.

PRINCE OF WALES: Exactly, Sparling; I have my own private reasons for agreeing with you on that point. And so, coming back to you, Ponsonby—slightly fuddled, you accepted the bogus footman and the bogus coachman without question. . . .

PONSONBY: I was not fuddled. The footman told me some sort of story about having been in service with Iddsleigh. I never saw the coachman's face. You say I took the men on trust—what would you have had me do?

PRINCE OF WALES: They were not the servants scheduled for your journey; you should have driven to the Royal Mews and had the men checked—you had a million pounds in that brougham. Now, after the brandy and the negus, may we take it that you snoozed yet again in the train—including the stop at Slough where your coach was shunted.

PONSONBY: Utterly and completely irrelevant. My compartment was locked. I was locked in with the hat box and a tea basket. And that is that . . . Your Highness.

PRINCE OF WALES: All the same, my dear Ponsonby, while you may not have betrayed your trust—and nobody is suggesting *that*—you seem to have executed it in an astonishing manner.

LADY PONSONBY: Your Royal Highness is wide of the mark. I beg you, sir, not to make a fool of yourself—that would do the monarchy far more harm than a few stolen diamonds. Someone might even point out that the heir to the throne has also been known to snooze after a stiff brandy . . . or two, or even three.

Anyway, it is as clear as daylight that my husband was robbed by the boy in the ginger suit.

PRINCE OF WALES (and others): What! What! Who?

PUMPHREY: By Jove, Mary! Now you've gone and done it. That was a corker for them.

PRINCE WILLIAM: A ginger suit! A ginger suit! What's all this? Really, Bertie, this is all most unseemly and most unroyal. In Prussia it would not be possible, but then in Prussia we have an excellent police force. And all this, Bertie, all this argument, this brawling . . . you actually permit it. Great heavens! What would Grandmama think?

AFFIE: Shut up, Willy. That Tiara is worth a million . . . more or less, according to Garrard's and Rothschilds . . . and they're both here to speak for themselves. I could do with my share, I don't mind telling you. And before you start ordering us all about, just remember that you're not Emperor of Germany *yet*, and that one day you may be very glad of your mother's share of the Tiara money—so there!

PRINCE WILLIAM: Don't be squalid, Alfred. Stick to your violin.

PRINCE OF WALES: Silence, both of you, Now pray tell us, Lady Ponsonby, *who* . . . who on earth is the boy in the ginger suit?

LADY PONSONBY: I haven't the slightest idea—one of the gang, I suppose. The Windsor train, by the time Henry got into his compartment, was half an hour late. There wasn't another train for three-quarters of an hour. And yet Henry was followed onto the platform and into the train by "ginger suit" . . . with two large tartan carpet bags. Now, why?

PRINCE OF WALES: Now, Mr. Riddle, you were the detective on duty at Paddington. Have you anything to say about—er—"ginger suit"?

RIDDLE: I am unable to imagine, Your Highness, what on earth the lady is talking about. You mustn't take too much notice of the ladies, sir; if I may say so they get such fanciful ideas.

LADY PONSONBY: Riddle, Your Highness, was doubtless doing his duty—busy spotting Nihilists and Fenians, although how you recognize them when you see them, heaven knows. Common sense is what is needed. The whole detective service needs overhauling . . . in my fanciful opinion.

PUMPHREY: One in the eye for you, Sir Frederick.

SIR FREDERICK: Really, Pumphrey! Upon my soul, sir. Your Royal Highness, I wish to protest.

PRINCE OF WALES: We'll come to you later, Sir Frederick. Thank you, Lady Ponsonby, for your fascinating evidence.

LADY PONSONBY: And, of course, the detectives have told you there were two hat boxes.

PRINCE OF WALES (and others): What! Two!

LADY PONSONBY: Oh, dear me, yes. I've told Henry a dozen times but he never takes any notice—he doesn't think it's important. Oh, yes—two hat boxes. You may remember a footman at Windsor, sir, a man called Wainwright.

PRINCE OF WALES: Yes, yes, a decent enough fellow—but one could always smell the liquor. What of him, Lady Ponsonby?

LADY PONSONBY: . . . Decent enough fellow—Hm! He came over to the Norman Tower one day in the spring and said he had an order from Her Majesty to leave a message in Henry's dressing room—some nonsense about how to wear the K.C.B. ribbon, or something. I let him go upstairs, but thought it very odd. The Queen doesn't give orders to footmen—she "asks" the Princess to "tell someone"—but *you* know the rigmarole well enough. Of course, after the Tiara furor, I thought back, and became doubly suspicious. Henry wouldn't listen, so I invited Mr. Straw, of Lock's the hatters, to visit Windsor. That's why I wanted him here, at Osborne, today. Perhaps, Your Highness, he might speak for himself.

MR. STRAW: Deeply honored to be here, Your Royal Highness. For one in my humble station of life it is . . .

PUMPHREY: Oh, Christ!

MR. STRAW: . . . On June 25th last, Your Highness, Lady Ponsonby most kindly invited me to Windsor. She arranged that I should—er—hang about in the Castle until, as if by chance, I was confronted by this footman, a Mr. Wainwright. I immediately recognized him as a man who had visited my shop a few weeks earlier. . . .

PRINCE OF WALES: Many people visit your shop, Mr. Straw—I have done so myself. How can you be so sure . . .

MR. STRAW: Oh, I remember him very well indeed, Your Highness. I remember the fuss he made. Many customers, if I may say so with respect, are particular, and rightly so, but Mr. Wainwright was fussy, not about his hat—a very commonplace billycock—but about the box. We have white, black and striped boxes—normal, mourning and racing toppers respectively. This man not only insisted upon a white box, he made a great to-do about it. . . .

PRINCE OF WALES: I see. Obviously Wainwright must be cross-examined upon the matter. All most extraordinary . . .

LADY PONSONBY: Wainwright, Your Highness, within an hour of seeing Mr. Straw, had left Windsor forever. He had been with us for five years and I made Henry ask the Housekeeper for his papers. His testimonials, dated 1882, were absolutely impeccable; unfortunately they had been cleverly forged upon purloined notepaper. In one case the paper had been stolen from the library at Blenheim, and in the other case from Lady Sackville's boudoir at Knole. Nobody called Wainwright, as I soon found out, had ever served either the Marlboroughs or the Sackvilles.

PRINCE OF WALES: I see. Friend Wainwright seems to specialize in purloined notepaper. He wrote to me, as a matter of fact, on Her Majesty's private stationery—very clever. No doubt, Sir Frederick, your men are already hot on the trail. And now, my dear Ponsonby, let us come back to you. Can you tell us what happened when you got to the station at Windsor?

PONSONBY: Certainly, Your Highness. My own coachman met me and, walking at my side, carried the hat box to my own carriage in the station yard. To our amazement my horse—usually a very quiet animal—was rearing up upon her hind legs and foaming at the mouth. Fortunately—whatever my wife may think about him—the youth in the ginger suit was ahead of us and, very kindly, was already holding Black Beauty's head—hardly a criminal act. I suppose, however, on your excessively literal interpretation of my words, sir, I must admit that for a few seconds my eyes were not upon the hat box. I got into the carriage while Philpotts put the box on the pavement so that he could help "ginger suit" calm the horse. I gave the youth a gratuity, Philpotts put the box in the carriage and, within ten minutes or so, the Tudor Tiara was on the desk in my office. I had fulfilled my trust, Your Highness.

PRINCE OF WALES: Very explicit. You can confirm your master's statement, Philpotts.

PHILPOTTS: Yes, Your Highness. I can do that, sir, but should add, in duty, sir, that Black Beauty had been most maliciously injured. On returning to the stable I found the hock of her right foreleg had been cut—an incision with a sharp blade—enough to terrify any horse, Your Highness.

PRINCE OF WALES: Yes, indeed. Thank you, Philpotts. Everything seems to point to "ginger suit." Now, Sir Henry, kindly tell us the next incident in this—er—saga of the Tiara.

PONSONBY: On returning to Windsor, Your Highness, I found a message from Her Royal Highness the Princess Beatrice telling me that Her Majesty had commanded that the Tiara be displayed in the Corridor that evening for the delectation of her guests. With the help of Skerret, the senior dresser, I therefore arranged the Tiara on the onyx table. That would be about eight o'clock; I had been across to the Norman Tower to dress, leaving the Tiara in my office so that Your Highness might inspect it . . . you will remember that, sir. I then left a footman on guard in the Corridor with very strict injunctions to remain at his post at all costs. His name was Slattery. For some obscure reason—at my wife's request, I believe—he is here now.

PRINCE OF WALES: Slattery.

SLATTERY: Yer 'Ighness.

PRINCE OF WALES: Tell us, please, about the evening of June 19th at Windsor.

SLATTERY: Sir, Yer 'Ighness, with 'umble duty. Just after eight o'clock, when I 'ad come on for the evening, the major-domo told me as 'ow Sir 'Enery wanted me in the Corridor. Sir 'Enery 'ad put out this 'ere Tiara and told me as 'ow I was to guard it until 'e came back fer 'is dinner—and on no account ter leave my post. . . . Yer 'Ighness.

PRINCE OF WALES: And of course you obeyed orders.

SLATTERY: No, sir.

PRINCE OF WALES: What did you say?

SLATTERY: I said, "No, sir," sir.

PRINCE OF WALES: But that was most reprehensible, Slattery. Your position at Windsor will certainly have to be reconsidered.

SLATTERY: Thank yer, Yer 'Ighness.

PRINCE OF WALES: But why did you leave your post?

SLATTERY: I was ordered to, Yer 'Ighness. Wot my brother, Yer 'Ighness, wot is in the Royal Fusiliers, says as 'ow they calls "superior orders."

PRINCE OF WALES: Indeed, Slattery; and who, pray, gave you orders which you chose, without permission, to consider so—er—"superior"?

SLATTERY: Beggin' yer pardon, sir, it was 'Er Majesty.

PRINCE OF WALES: Oh! Oh, I see. I shall want your evidence confirmed, Slattery. Which of the ladies was in attendance?

SLATTERY: There wasn't no ladies, Yer 'Ighness. 'Er Majesty were alone.

PRINCE OF WALES: Alone in the Corridor, unattended, an hour before the service of dinner . . . most unlikely.

SLATTERY: But I'm sayin' as 'ow she was, sir.

KNOLLYS: You must not bandy words with His Highness, my man.

PRINCE OF WALES: Leave the room, Slattery.

SLATTERY: Thank yer . . . but I tells yer as 'ow 'Er Majesty was in the Corridor . . .

PRINCE OF WALES: I ordered you to leave the room. . . .

SLATTERY: An' she 'ad a bag . . . a big velvet bag . . . purple . . . I'm only a'tellin' yer. (Departs.)

PUMPHREY: Mary, if you have a pin, drop it . . . they'll think the *Courageous* is firing her guns.

PRINCE OF WALES: Knollys, we may need Slattery again. . . . See that he stays here tonight. Now, I think we should all forget what we have just heard . . . clearly a most insolent servant. . . .

LADY PONSONBY: He struck me, Your Highness, as an honest man in a difficult position.

PRINCE OF WALES: I flatter myself, Lady Ponsonby, that I am, if nothing else, a judge of men. Now, my dear Ponsonby, tell us—when you placed the Tiara in the Corridor you took it for granted, of course, that it was the real thing, *not* one of the replicas of which several had been made in 1851 for the provincial museums.

PONSONBY: Surely Your Highness is not suggesting that sometime between 1851 and today the Tower of London was robbed without anyone being aware of it . . . really, sir.

PRINCE OF WALES: Oh, dear me, no! But I must tell you all that one of the guests at the Castle that night was His Highness the Maharajah of Kashgar—a world expert on gems. . . . You can confirm that, Mr. Friedman?

FRIEDMAN: Oh, certainly, Your Highness. We know him well at Garrard's. I would back his judgment against my own any day.

PRINCE OF WALES: Thank you. Now the Maharajah saw the Tudor Tiara in the Corridor. At the end of the evening he confided to Princess Beatrice—and again to me that next morning when walking in the garden—that while the Tiara itself might be the original, the precious diamonds were so much rubbish, mere paste replicas. So you see, Ponsonby . . .

PONSONBY: It is inexplicable, Your Highness. Or, rather, there are only three possible explanations. One is that the diamonds were tampered with on my journey from the Tower to Windsor; whatever one may choose to think of Mary's "boy in the ginger suit," I think I have shown that to have been utterly impossible. The second possibility which did occur to me was that the Maharajah's aide-de-camp—a Colonel Pinkerton, cashiered from the Indian Army and otherwise disgraced—might have switched the real diamonds for the sham ones. Perhaps, sir, I might ask Mr. Archibald Bellow, the Windsor Castle detective, to say a word on that.

BELLOW: Your Highness, I was assured by Sir Henry that the Maharajah's entire suite—whites and natives—would attend the Jubilee service in the Abbey. Accordingly I gave orders that while they were in London their luggage and rooms should be searched under my supervision. A needle in a haystack would not have escaped us. We drew a complete blank. Whether, of course, the diamonds were in the Abbey, concealed in the Maharani's stays, I don't know.

PRINCE OF WALES: Thank you, Mr. Bellow.Colonel Pinkerton had already been reported to me as being a most unsavory character. I don't think, however, that there is anything more we can do in that quarter. If, by now, the earrings are in India, then they have gone forever. I think, Ponsonby, you mentioned a third possibility.

PONSONBY: Yes, sir. It is this: is it not possible that the Tiara which was handed to me, in good faith of course, by Field Marshal Lord Wilson, was *not* the original which Sir Henry Cole took from the Crystal Palace to the Tower in 1851 . . . thirty-six years ago?

PRINCE OF WALES: Ah! Perhaps Field Marshal Lord Wilson would care to say a word?

WILSON (cupping his ear in his hand): Eh?

DUKE OF ARGYLL (yelling): HIS HIGHNESS SAYS, WAS THE TIARA YOU GAVE TO SIR HENRY PONSONBY THE ORIGINAL—THE 1851 VERSION.

WILSON: Of course it was . . . the man's talking balls.

KNOLLYS (also yelling): REALLY, FIELD MARSHAL, REALLY! YOU ARE ADDRESSING THE PRINCE OF WALES, YOU KNOW.

WILSON: He can be the Prince of Timbuctoo for all I care. He's talking absolute balls. Sir Henry Cole brought the Tiara from the Crystal Palace to the Tower himself, in a Black Maria . . . before my time of course . . . now where was I in '51? . . . let me see, now . . . let me see . . . ah, yes, I was on the Northwest Frontier . . . but about that blasted Tiara—it's all in the books, ye know.

PRINCE OF WALES: So, Field Marshal, we may take it that the 1851 Tiara, the original, never left the Tower until last June, when Sir Henry brought it to Windsor.

DUKE OF ARGYLL: THE 1851 TIARA NEVER LEFT THE TOWER?

WILSON: Of course it never left the Tower . . . bloody silly question . . . except of course in 1861, and then it came back in a few days.

PRINCE OF WALES: What! What's this? I've never heard of this!

DUKE OF ARGYLL: I THINK HIS ROYAL HIGHNESS WOULD LIKE FURTHER DETAILS OF THAT AMAZING STATEMENT, FIELD MARSHAL.

WILSON: Why? It was his own mother had the damned thing sent out to Windsor, or it may have been Buckingham Palace . . . can't remember . . . long time ago. Anyway, it was only her usual fuss, ye know. Ask her, ask her . . . she's still alive, isn't she?

PRINCE OF WALES: Great heavens! Oh, dear! Oh, dear! 1851 . . . 1861 . . . 1851 . . . am I going mad? Poor old chap . . . quite hopeless. But we've got to get to the bottom of it all. For God's sake, Argyll, ask him *why* the Queen had the original Tiara sent to her in 1861 . . . if she ever did.

DUKE OF ARGYLL: HIS HIGHNESS WANTS TO KNOW, FIELD MARSHAL, WHY THE TIARA WAS SENT TO THE QUEEN IN 1861.

WILSON: I've just told him, haven't I? It was his mother's fuss. Her husband had just died—Albert, ye know. She wanted a feller called Martin to write his life, and she wanted to show him every damned thing Albert had ever written or designed . . .

this house, vases, mirrors, all kinds of nonsense. This Albert—I met him once—queer, solemn chap—very German—always mucking about with books and art and pottery . . . never rode to hounds . . . no red blood . . . not much use really . . .

KNOLLYS: MODERATE YOUR WORDS, FIELD MARSHAL. HE WAS THE PRINCE'S FATHER, SIR.

WILSON: Oh, I shouldn't think so. He may have been a blasted intellectual, but very strait-laced over women. I don't know who the hell you are, my good man, but you mustn't believe all you hear, ye know.

PRINCE OF WALES: Let it go, Knollys, let it go. *Non compos mentis,* poor old boy. But it does look as though the Queen may have had the Tiara back to show to Sir Theodore Martin when he was writing his *Life of the Prince Consort.* We shall never know.

PRINCESS BEATRICE: We may. I think I can help, Bertie.

PRINCE OF WALES: You, Beatrice . . . how?

PRINCESS BEATRICE: I was rather hoping to avoid this. It is all so—er—sacred to Mama's sad memories . . . but I do see that I must speak out. Well then, this is the truth. The original Tiara, with all the jewels and diamond earrings incorporated in it, was always—or at least as long as I can remember—locked in one of the big cupboards in the Blue Room. For those of you who may not know, that is the room at Windsor where my father died in 1861. Mama has kept the room quite unchanged—just as it was on that tragic winter night—but with certain precious souvenirs locked in the big cupboards, including the Tiara—Papa's finest design.

LADY PONSONBY: I can confirm that. Once, when Henry and I were bereaved, Her Majesty showed me everything in the Blue Room—including the Tiara.

DEAN OF WINDSOR: And I too . . . I used often to pray with Her Majesty at the late Prince Consort's bedside . . . most heart-rending.

PRINCE OF WALES: Quite, quite, Mr. Dean, but not very relevant. Our problem is still quite unsolved. If Mr. Cole, Chairman of the Commissioners of the Great Exhibition, took the Tiara to the Tower in 1851, how on earth did it get into the Blue Room ten years later?

PRINCESS BEATRICE: Be honest, Bertie, be honest. Face facts. Mama is a very emotional person; also very determined and very direct. What she wants, she gets. Why not say so? . . .

PRINCE WILLIAM: Because, my dearest Beatrice, several people are present who are quite outside our royal circle. All this would not be possible in our wonderful Prussia. It is unseemly . . . some things are better left unsaid. . . .

PRINCESS BEATRICE: Don't be foolish, Willy. As I was saying, Bertie, when Willy interrupted me, for heaven's sake face facts. Field Marshal Lord Wilson has told us exactly what happened. I was only four at the time but I said just now that the Tiara, the real Tiara—and Mama would have had nothing less for the Blue Room—has been at Windsor as long as I can remember. As the Field Marshal has told us, in 1861 the Tiara was sent to Mama . . .

PRINCE OF WALES: . . . And returned to the Tower within a few days.

PRINCESS BEATRICE: Was it? *What* was returned to the Tower? The original or one of these museum and art-school replicas of which no precise record exists? Clearly that is what happened. Mama kept the original, including the earrings, and put it in her beloved Blue Room. And, after all, why not? It was hers.

PONSONBY: Hm! If I might intervene, Your Highness, the late Prince Consort's will was by no means clear on that point. He had the Tiara placed with the Crown Jewels, the property of the nation. I suggest that the Solicitor-General . . .

PRINCE OF WALES: Oh, for God's sake, Ponsonby, forget all that. Stick to the point. After all, what does it really matter? It may even turn out to be a good thing. If Mama sent a replica back to the Tower in '61, in exchange for the real thing, without telling a soul, then that was all the Field Marshal had to give you last June. Moreover, it was all the "ginger suit" gang ever got for their pains when they switched the diamonds round while you were—er—snoozing in the train. However, no harm has been done. The original Tiara, complete with earrings, is safe and sound in the Blue Room at Windsor—as it has been ever since Papa's death in 1861.

PRINCESS BEATRICE: No. No. The Blue Room cupboard is empty. Apart from Mama, I am the only person with a key, and I know. The Tiara, the real Tiara, has vanished. It vanished on June 19th.

PONSONBY: Nonsense, if I may say so, Princess. It has vanished from the Blue Room only because it is now safely in the strong room. Her Majesty commanded me to put it there, under her seal, the day before her Jubilee. I haven't the remotest idea why . . . but she did and there it remains.

HERR MÜTTER: Nein, nein, nein! I am ze librarian only, and ze German secretary, but ze Queen, she trust her old Karl Mütter . . . it ees from Coburg I am. On ze Tuesday before zis Christmas Day—two veeks since only—she say to me, "Herr Mütter, get ze Tiara from ze strong room." Zat I do. I give eet to ze Fräulein Skerret for ze baggage and now, zis very day, it ees here at Osborne . . . oh jah, eet ees indeet!

PRINCE OF WALES: Oh, mein Gott! Mein Gott!

PRINCE WILLIAM: Quite so, Bertie. As I expected, we have all been brought here for nothing. Perhaps, however, now that your grandiose conference is over, you might care to enlighten our curiosity. All the afternoon there have been a couple of twelve-pointed diamond stars on the table in front of you. Might I ask whether they have any bearing upon our deliberations? I have no wish to appear inquisitive. I only ask.

PRINCE OF WALES: Quite so, Willy. I was just coming to these stars although, in fact, our discussion might seem to have made them rather irrelevant. These stars are the alleged earrings—mere paste and rubbish—which were stolen from Sir Henry Ponsonby when he was—er—snoozing . . . one set of replicas removed only to be replaced by another set. . . .

PONSONBY: Quite impossible . . . and in any case you have them back. I am utterly bewildered.

PRINCE OF WALES: On the contrary, my dear Ponsonby, these sham diamonds confirm everything. I too now have something to reveal. I must tell you all that one evening last November, after dinner at the Marlborough Club, His Excellency the Russian Ambassador, the Baron Serge de Staal, accompanied me on a stroll down Pall Mall. I have not invited His Excellency here today because dear Serge always pretends that he can speak no English . . . in private he speaks perfectly. Like all Russians, he loves fireworks and it was Guy Fawkes night. That was why we ventured into the streets.

PUMPHREY: (A long, low whistle.)

PRINCE OF WALES: Thank you, Mr. Pumphrey; your interventions have enlivened our afternoon . . . but enough is enough. To continue with my own story . . . in the course of our perambulations the Baron de Staal and I were accosted by a small group of rough men. I need not go into details. They satisfied me that they were what we have been calling the "ginger suit gang." They even produced their—er—credentials in the form of these diamond stars. I had dispensed with my detective and was not in a strong position. I myself am a trifle stout, and I certainly could not involve the Czar's ambassador in a brawl. In the end, therefore—for a price, of course—I struck a bargain. Mama's name had to be protected at all costs—you would agree with me there, Willy. The money was paid over in such a way that the men could not be traced. . . .

MATHEWS (former Home Secretary): Ahem! Ahem!

PRINCE OF WALES: Surprisingly, Mr. Mathews, the men kept their bargain. These diamond stars were duly delivered to me at Balmoral, thanks to the mediation of His Grace the Duke of Argyll—I need not say more than that, Argyll—but of course the only diamonds the rogues *could* send me were the sham ones which they had stolen from that Tower of London Tiara, while Sir Henry was snoozing in the train.

PONSONBY: It pleases Your Highness to be very persistent on the point. . . .

PRINCE OF WALES: Oh, no offense, my dear Ponsonby—you mustn't be touchy. A lady who is very expert in gems happened, by a most extraordinary coincidence, to be staying at Abergeldie Mains, a mile or so from Balmoral—there is no need to keep whistling, Pumphrey, nor for you, Mathews, to keep clearing your throat—and I was able to consult her. She immediately confirmed my fears, that these diamonds are absolute rubbish—worth a hundred pounds at most, for the skill of the imitation. And that, I can assure you, is the whole story of my transaction with the gang—a very slight affair. And now, ladies and gentlemen, I am sure you are all exhausted. We may, however, congratulate ourselves that the Tiara, complete with Bloody Mary's Earrings, is safely here at Osborne.

ALL: Hear hear. Thank you, Your Highness . . . etc. etc.

PRINCE OF WALES: But, Mr. Prime Minister, we have not had a word from you all afternoon. Would you care to make a—er—a few valedictory remarks, as it were? . . .

MARQUIS OF SALISBURY: Thank you, Your Highness. An admirably conducted conference, if I may say so. I am glad you feel, sir, that it has also been successful and that the Tudor Tiara, complete with those famous diamond earrings, is now quite safe. I have no wish to dampen your pleasure, but may I remind you that the last two prime ministers of the Tudor dynasty were Cecils—the only distinguished members of my house. Consequently in the Muniment Room at Hatfield we have the most complete Tudor records in the world—not least those of Queen Elizabeth when, as a princess, she was the prisoner of her half-sister, Bloody Mary. There are gaps and confusions in the record . . . but be careful, Your Highness . . . be very careful.

PRINCE OF WALES: Nonsense, my dear Prime Minister, nonsense. Those damned earrings went back to Spain with King Philip; but after the Peninsular War, when Spain was piling honors upon our own Iron Duke, they gave him the Holy Earrings, as they called them, and he gave them to my father specifically for the Tiara. There is no room for doubt there, Mr. Prime Minister. No, the time has come to congratulate ourselves, and to drink a toast. Knollys, I think we are all ready for the siphons and decanters.

KNOLLYS: Certainly, Your Highness; but I have just heard a knock on the door. I gave orders that we were not to be disturbed . . . but I suppose it can hardly matter now . . . we have finished our work.

Sir Francis Knollys unlocked the great double doors of the India Room. A footman confronted him—a footman whose face was as scarlet as his coat. Bowing slightly, he mouthed those syllables which the familiars of Windsor, Balmoral, Buckingham Palace and Osborne knew so well how to interpret; they signified quite soundlessly that "Her Majesty is on the way." And indeed she was not far behind. Everyone rose and bowed.

Even as she walked across the room they felt, as always, that in some inexplicable way this diminutive, dumpy and disagreeable widow dominated them all. For the moment there could be nobody else in the world.

"Thank you, Bertie. Sir Henry, a chair for the Prince. You may all sit."

They all sat.

"I have been alone for two hours with that awful Miss Phipps and Jane Ely. I am utterly exhausted."

She placed a large purple velvet bag upon the ivory-and-ebony table. Her mouth was more drawn down than ever. Her hooded eyes barely showed the whites—or, rather, the yellows. Her cheeks had been furrowed by tears. She was as white as her starched cap.

"I suppose you have all been chattering about the Tudor Tiara and those diamond earrings which my dearest husband so skillfully incorporated into its design."

"Yes, Mama."

"Well, instead of chattering and locking me out of my own

State Apartments, you would have done better to ask my advice, and save your breath."

"Yes, Mama."

"Now . . ." and the mouth was set, the eyes closed ". . . now, let me tell you about something that happened some years ago. In 1839 I had a young and unmarried lady-in-waiting. She was accused of being *enceinte.* There was a tremendous scandal. It was all a wicked lie—she only had dropsy. I too was young and unmarried—possibly jealous. I was also very wicked: I supported the gossip and publicly dismissed the lady from my Court. I had to pay the price. In the end I had to admit that I was wrong; I had to apologize publicly—not easy for a young Queen. That was forty-eight years ago and the lady's family have still not forgiven me. Now I have come to tell you that once again—but this time in my old age—I have been deceitful and wicked. I have done wrong."

"Mama, must you . . . is this necessary?"

"Yes, Bertie . . . very necessary indeed."

She was sobbing now. The tiny lace handkerchief was wet with tears; the words came with difficulty.

"Nobody—nobody now living—can ever know how happy I was with my dear husband. Those far-off days in Scotland, the picnics and the expeditions, were paradise. The Great Exhibition—the Crystal Palace—was the epitome of his work."

"Dearest Mama, must you go on?"

"Let me be, Beatrice. In '61, when I was so utterly crushed, when all life had died in me, there was only one material thing that mattered—the objects, the clothes, the books, the jewels which my beloved husband had actually handled and touched. . . . I treasured them even more than my own children. I hoarded them in that dear, sacred Blue Room. Among them was one of the museum replicas of the Tudor Tiara. In the great cupboard this had a special place of honor. Within a few months of the tragedy, however, I sent for the real Tiara from the Tower. I wanted dear Albert's biographer, Mr. Theodore Martin, to see everything Albert had designed. So there, in the Blue

Room, was the original Tiara, the one my beloved and I had seen made, that we had both touched, both looked at, in the Crystal Palace. I surrendered to temptation. I kept it. I sent the museum replica to the Tower of London. . . ."

"It was yours, Mama, to do what you liked with."

"Sir Henry thinks not—that it may belong to the nation. In any case it was very wrong and very deceitful of me, in my position, to change the tiaras round without telling anyone. For twenty-six years, you see, I have allowed the Tower of London to exhibit a forgery among the Crown Jewels."

"Well, at least, Mama, at the time you honestly thought it was yours."

"No. I was not sure. I should have taken advice. I was deceitful. In my overwhelming grief, with the tears often streaming down my cheeks, I did wrong."

"But is that all, Mama? It does not seem so very terrible. Is that all? . . ."

"No, it is not all. I have to tell you something else—something even more difficult for me to talk about."

It was almost dark now. No servant had dared to enter the room. The gaseliers were still unlit. There was only the blazing fire. The men on the bench—footmen, detectives and others—sat with mouths open; in the gloom they had been forgotten. Beatrice now stood with her arm around the Queen. Through the windows, far away, were the lights of Her Majesty's ironclads.

"And now the years have passed. One must love someone. Servants, secretaries, statesmen are not enough—not for someone as lonely as a Queen. There was my dear John Brown, there was dear Lord Beaconsfield—both gone now. In the end I came back to my own children. You, my dearest Bertie, are profligate and imprudent, so that the world thinks that I must disapprove of you. That is nonsense. You may be wayward but you are my son. Anyway, compared with most of our relations you are an archangel . . . you are a dear, good boy. Six months ago, two days before my Jubilee, and on that very evening when Sir Henry placed the Tiara on the onyx table in the Corridor, you came to my room. As usual it was about your debts. For once, however, you had a definite proposal—to ask Rothschilds for a loan on the Tiara. I said you were mad . . . then gradually, in my practical way, I saw the point. I agreed."

"You did, Mama. . . . I was very touched and grateful."

"Nonsense, Bertie. It was nothing more than a good stroke of business . . . both for the House of Coburg and for the House of Rothschild."

The Baron Ferdinand bowed his assent across the room.

"But what was I to do? You see, all the time, I knew that the Tiara which Sir Henry had placed in the Corridor was only the replica from the Tower. If the Constable of the Tower knew, he had never dared to say anything; Rothschilds, however, would not hesitate for a moment. I played for time, telling you not to touch the Tiara yourself but to send it to Hirsch, when I said the word, so that he could negotiate with Rothschilds in a proper manner . . . no hole-in-the-corner business at Tring or Waddesden."

"I see, Mama . . . I see now."

"Yes. From your point of view, Bertie, the wrong Tiara was in the Corridor. That evening, after our talk, I did a very wicked thing and, for me, a very hard thing. . . . I robbed the Blue Room."

"Mama . . . dearest."

"Yes, Bertie. I took the Tiara, the real Tiara, from the Blue Room cupboard, put it in this velvet bag, and then went to the Corridor. I dismissed the footman who was on guard. I was all alone in that huge gallery . . . there was still an hour to go before dinner, and the evening sunlight was streaming through the Venetian blinds. I then, quite deliberately, changed one Tiara for the other. Hirsch and Rothschild would now get the right one. It was very wicked and deceitful . . . but it was all for you, Bertie . . . there are so many calls on your purse, dear boy. A loan from Rothschilds . . . so wrong and yet so sensible. . . . I felt as if I was pawning the Crown Jewels. Above all, I had desecrated the Blue Room, the room where my dearest one had died . . . all for you, Bertie."

"You will feel better, Mama, for having told us all that. We shall also feel better for having been told everything. It is all over now."

"It is not all over. You have forgotten the Maharajah!"

"The Maharajah!"

"Of course—the Maharajah. Oh, I know that the silly man wanted the Garter, but that wouldn't really explain it, would it?"

"Explain what, Mama?"

"Beatrice, you should know. He spoke to you that evening, just after Sir Henry's little lecture. He told you, didn't he? that the diamonds on each side of the Tiara, Bloody Mary's Earrings, were so much rubbish."

"Yes, of course . . . we all know that, Mama."

"Well, don't you see? . . . that was after dinner, after I had changed round the Tiaras. It was the Blue Room and Crystal Palace Tiara, the one intended for Rothschilds, that the Maharajah had been looking at. And, according to him, its diamonds were false. For twenty-six years I had kept that wonderful object as a precious part of my private shrine . . . and now? I collapsed that night. Dear old Skerret had to give me brandy. That I should wear the Tiara at the Jubilee dinner was now, of course, out of the question. The very next morning I commanded Sir Henry to put it in the strong room, under my seal. But now, Bertie, just to round off your absurd Osborne conference, here it is for you all to look at—the genuine Tiara. . . ."

The old woman delved into her velvet bag. She extracted that rich, glittering hideous fountain of priceless stones which nobody had seen since that Windsor dinner party in June.

"There you are, my dear children, the real Tiara . . . but . . . but . . . the Maharajah . . ."

Everyone rose and peered through the shadows at the grotesque object which, in its vulgarity, its intricacy and its excess, was so appropriate to that room. It was Knollys who rang for a footman. Nobody stirred until the blaze of gaslight was reflected from every stone in the Tiara.

For Mr. Friedman of Garrard's—although he had handled crowns and scepters—this was a historic moment. Every one of those stones was known to the trade. Behind his little pince-nez, as the Prince of Wales summoned him to the table, his eyes were popping. He spent only a few moments with his magnifying glass.

"May it please Your Majesty, Your Highnesses. On the basis of a superficial examination, I declare this to be the original Tudor Tiara with all its gems derived from famous items of sixteenth-century jewelry or costume. I regret to say, however, that the twelve-pointed diamond stars, so placed as to be just above the wearer's temples, are quite valueless . . . clever imitations of a very intricate Spanish design, but mere paste . . . value, say, one hundred pounds."

There was a long silence broken only by the Queen's sobs and then, at last, by Bertie's half-choked voice.

"So, Mama, we have all done our best. *We* have the Tiara . . . the gang have my money—or, rather, my dear Rothschild, *your* money . . . but where, oh, where the hell are Bloody Mary's Earrings?"

EDWARDIAN EPILOGUE

A warm January at Osborne . . . but far away the big flakes of snow fell silently and thickly into the streets of Petersburg. The tall railings of the Winter Palace made a pattern of black lines in a white world. A biting wind blew off Lake Ladoga, while across the frozen Neva the tall gold finger of the Fortress of St. Peter and St. Paul was a single spark of life in a dead landscape. A few workmen and peasant women, clumsy figures in thick black clothing, were waiting listlessly as if for something they did not care about. The sentries, deep in their boxes, were muffled to the very icicles on their beards. The Palace itself, its rich baroque all black and white but tinged here and there with a rust red, was withdrawn across a forecourt of untrodden snow.

It was barely light when a gentleman made the day's first footmarks in the Palace snow. He wore a tall ermine hat and a pince-nez on a black ribbon. The peasants just stirred. The sentries presented arms with a click that resounded in the frozen air. The gentleman affixed a small notice to one of the gates and withdrew. Someone was found who could actually read.

At two-thirty-three this morning Her Most Serene and Imperial Highness the Princess Titania Alexandrovna was safely delivered of a Grand Duchess.

Signed: Ivan Ivanovitch Podolski—Court Chamberlain.
14th January, 1888

Two of the peasant women crossed themselves. The sentries stood at ease. The street slowly emptied. The little Grand Duchess, one day to be the Princess Natasha Rostopochin, had entered a very cold and a very bitter world. . . . No wonder she yelled.

The Czar Alexander III had died horribly of Bright's disease. Through the November snows of 1894 his embalmed corpse, with priests and acolytes in the railway coach, traveled in easy stages the seven hundred miles from Sevastopol to Moscow. The corpse lay in state in the Cathedral of St. Basil, by the Kremlin Wall, and then on to Petersburg, to lie once again in the Fortress of St. Peter and St. Paul, by the frozen Neva. For the funeral Petersburg was filled with kings and princes—nearly all cousins, nearly all sharing each other's hereditary diseases. Punctiliously, day after day, they attended long and elaborate masses—punctiliously, although Lord Carrington noticed the curious ability of the Prince of Wales to sleep—like a horse—standing up as the holy taper in his hand burnt itself out. It was in the vast Anitchkoff Palace, where he was lodged, that the Prince first put on the uniform of the 27th Kiev Dragoons. It was in the vast Anitchkoff Palace that he first wondered why the courtyard, and indeed all Russia, was so full of policemen. It was in the Anitchkoff Palace that he first realized that for the new Czar and Czarina, for Alicky, the dearest of his hundred nieces, and for her Nicky, nothing whatever could be done. They were hopeless. She was his "Sunny" and he was her "Little Boy Blue." They read aloud the worst of English novels, *East Lynne* and *Through the Postern Gate,* and on the day that the guards massacred a delegation from the Duma they wrote in their diary that they had "a nice picnic." They were too amiable, too inept, too weak, too hopeless, too credulous, ever to survive—let alone ever to rule over all the Russias. Clearly they were doomed.

It was in the vast Anitchkoff Palace—between one requiem mass and another—that the Prince of Wales first made love to Her Serene and Imperial Highness the Princess Titania. He was really too stupid, too gross, for that very intelligent, very cultured and very beautiful daughter of the Romanovs—but then his attraction for women was always more difficult to understand than theirs for him. This very lonely woman—alone with the little Grand Duchess, her little Natasha, in those huge and echoing rooms—was in any case quite pathetically pleased that he should play with her child. Natasha was six now and the Prince gave her the very best toys in all Petersburg; he telegraphed to Paris for others. He gave her a black-and-silver sledge with two white ponies and red harness. He had always been fond of pretty little girls, and she reminded him of his own Olga at that age—far away in the villa at Dieppe.

The Princess Titania was so delighted that someone—someone other than peasants and servants—should notice little Natasha that one night she kissed the Prince very warmly, and then and there, in the vast and empty salon, allowed him to flirt with her. He was very pleased when she let him embrace her, more pleased than he would have expected to be. Perhaps, to start with, it was no more than a relief after all those requiem masses, but he suddenly found himself regretting that he had to go back to England so soon. And, in the end, when he looked out upon Russia, upon all those starving peasants and all those prisons and policemen, he told Titania—so very much alone in such a dangerous world—that she should bring her child to England before it was too late—too late because an oppressive doom overhung the whole land. He might be Titania's lover and Natasha's guardian, and he would certainly see to it that the mother and child, as well as their fortune and their jewels, would be well cared for. He could do nothing now for Alicky and Nicky—nothing. He knew that truly they were under sentence of death—it was only a matter of years. Quite irrevocably now they were part of Russia. Titania and her little girl were different; for them there might still be time.

The "Bertie" of his mother's Court had become the Englishman's "Teddy"—the King. Teddy was old and Teddy was fat. In 1909, in the June sunshine, high above the valley of the River Test, the gray house was waiting for him. It waited for him in the full sunshine of an Edwardian England where everyone was rich and where it was always afternoon.

The house, in its own curious way, was Ned Lutyens's masterpiece. It was of gray stone flushed with pink. There were thick stone slabs on the roof and long ranges of mullion windows. There were enormous chimney stacks to match the open hearths within. From the carriage drive it was only the chimneys that one could see above the elms. It was on the southern side, with the valley and the winding stream at one's feet, that one beheld and understood the beauty of the place.

There were great flights of steps—a hint almost of Versailles—leading from the broad terraces to the garden. It was a garden that Miss Jekyll had contrived seven years ago for the Princess Titania, that remarkably beautiful woman who was still its mistress. On this Sunday in June the herbaceous borders, the great plat, the water garden, the lavender walks and the dark yew hedges seemed as mature as they were beautiful—they had been planted in the first year of the King's reign when Titania had brought her child from Petersburg.

It was one of those dreamlike houses built by the last generation of the aesthetic rich. After the South African War, having turned their swords into gold shares, they were now basking in the twilight of a culture—of sorts. They got themselves painted by Sargent and Orpen or even, in these latter days, by John; they got themselves dressed by Worth or Doucet; they bought pretty things from Fabergé, and bought each other presents from Cartier. And they got their houses built by Lutyens—the sort of houses where there were always ambassadors in the billiards room and Peter Pan in the nursery wing. This was Heartbreak House or Horseback Hall—Bernard Shaw's "cultured, leisured Europe before the War."

In the heat of the afternoon the three claret-colored Daimlers crackled over the gravel. One was for the King and for Reginald Brett Esher. One was for a couple of equerries and for the scarlet dispatch boxes. The third was for the valets and the luggage. Titania was on the doorstep. Almost any woman seen against sunlight filtered through the distended silk of a white parasol will seem enchanting—and this woman was beautiful with the beauty of maturity, strangely beautiful in any light. If the mass of dark gold hair, the small and freckled nose were rather English—or at least Northern—the almond eyes and high cheekbones were very wise and very Slav. The hair that year was being worn thick on the nape of the neck so that the flowered hat was tilted forward quite deliciously over the forehead. He stood, not a little bewitched, with one foot still on the running board of the car. If French had been the first language of the Court of the Romanovs, German had certainly been the first language of the children of Prince Albert; these two compromised happily with their imperfect English. It had become a strange relationship, the last one of his life—a relationship between a man of the world and a woman of the world—both, in their way, people of many curious adventures. She called him Teddy, which was something allowed to nobody except his parrot. Of all the women he had loved she was the only one who, however remotely, was of the Family; she was allowed to take liberties and she took them.

"Teddy."

"Titania. Charming, my dearest . . ."

"Maybe . . . but you have been neglecting me. Nearly three weeks since you were here—I can't imagine what you do."

"I'm sorry . . ."

"That's not much use . . . but still you've come now. They're all waiting for you of course—out on the lawn—and pretending not to be . . . of course."

"You're a genius, Titania. . . ."

"Don't flatter me; you know perfectly well it's no use. . . ."

"But you are a genius, my dear, breaking the London season with a June party down here in Hampshire. London is like an oven. My God, what a week! Two theaters, four dinner parties, a sitting in the Lords, the Bridgewater House ball, two private views as well as the R.A., the garden party at Holland House and, to crown all, the suffragettes—as if that was *my* business . . . and then you say that you can't imagine what I do!"

"Poor, dear Teddy. Never mind. It's cool out on the lawn and there are lots and lots of perfectly charming people—quite a crowd. Only thirty sleeping here; but five carriages drove over from Broadlands this morning—almost all your friends, with just a soupçon of eccentrics to give the party flavor."

"Hm! Not artists and all that lot, I hope."

"Well, no, not quite . . . stage, not art."

"That's better. . . ."

"But I must warn you, Teddy, a very special sort of stage—not just your Gaiety lot and all that. There's a Monsieur Diaghilev from Petersburg. I am paying for him to bring his dancers here next year. He has a clever musician with him—a Monsieur Stravinsky, who may play for us later, and a quite enchanting and divine boy called Nijinsky."

"Oh. Oh, I see! Hm! And who else, pray?"

"Only my biggest catch of all. You must have met him in the Faubourg St. Germain . . . just think, Marcel Proust is out there on the lawn."

"No, never heard of him. Who else? Some ordinary people, I hope."

"Well, to start with there are the Morells—Phillip and Ottoline."

"She usually has a damned poet in tow."

"My dear Teddy, one must have a little culture, you know. It's done these days, and you really must not be such an old Philistine. It's bad for the arts. But there, don't worry: all your special friends are here too—Tennants and Wyndhams and Harcourts and Mitfords, and even old Cambon and—oh, yes—the Sassoons, with Sybil Rocksavage dripping with diamonds—just fancy, in the afternoon! And there's Dickie Fisher damning and blasting everything; and dear Lady Londonderry telling everyone she's had her legs tattooed . . . she's going to show them me tonight. . . . Do you want—er—another private view?"

"Naturally. Your parties are always marvelous, Titania, and as long as you are there, my dearest, they always will be!"

He gave her a smacking kiss on each cheek. There was a laugh behind them. Natasha was standing at the top of the steps, half shaded by the big curved arch of the porch, looking even more beautiful than her mother. She was very like her mother, but, on this June afternoon, she was a nymph, a sylph of the air—the frills and the ribbons and the quite enormous hat somehow, but miraculously, did nothing to spoil it.

"Nunky—you've come! I just can't wait for my electric brougham—what a marvelous present. You're a dear, dear Nunky."

"Nothing is too good for you, Natasha . . . and I'm told these things are convenient for shopping."

And he kissed her as vigorously as, a moment before, he had kissed her mother.

A valet had approached them as softly as a cat. With rapid dexterity he stripped the King of his dust coat and motoring cap. Beneath was the pearly gray morning suit. The white topper was handed to him, and then together these three strolled through the sunken garden—paths of old mossy stone with cool water lapping their edges. They glanced at water lilies—water lilies worthy of Monet—and at curious exotic fish . . . and so to the great terrace on the other side of the house.

It was an English Sunday. The tennis courts, beyond the walled orchard, were out of use. Even the croquet hoops had been mysteriously whipped away at dawn. The white flannels of Saturday, the boaters and the blazers—blazing with the arms of Balliol and Trinity—had all gone; pale gray or black tails, white hats and spats, and lemon gloves had taken their place.

The befrilled dresses, with their huge sleeves and trailing scarves, were all white, oleander or lavender, as were the long buttoned gloves and the twirling parasols. Everyone moved and revolved slowly across the lawns. These garments, this correctitude, was a tribute either to the King or to the Sabbath—nobody knew which. The Russian hostess had issued no edict. It was all, quite simply, a tribal reaction—something they all knew. Siberia or the mines of the Donbass were further away than the moon—by a million miles.

Tea was being served in the shade of the great elms. Miracles of masculine agility and juggling were being performed with cups and saucers and cucumber sandwiches and plates of strawberries and pairs of gloves; such miracles were admired but it would have been improper to mention them. And then, far away across the lawns, three people could be seen coming down from the terraces—familiar figures. It was almost Chinese: the beautiful princess, the fat mandarin and Natasha—the little Tanagra figurine.

He knew almost everyone; but a *cercle*, a conducted tour—that he might miss nobody and that nobody might miss him—was *de rigueur*. The curtsies on the lawn were as if the petals of a white magnolia were slowly falling. The removing of toppers was as if ordered by a drill sergeant, or—to some—more reminiscent of the raising and lowering of coronets, seven years ago in the Abbey. The garden had until then been filled with the slow but swirling movement of white and gray upon a green floor—enchanting, casual and unordered. Now, quite suddenly, everything had precision; the lawn had become a stage for a corps-de-ballet. Only Diaghilev saw the dramatic beauty of it all; he wished that Degas might be there to paint it, or a choreographer to make it the beginning of an inspiration. He caught Proust's eye and both men sighed at the philistinism of these English who, alas, could not even see themselves.

The intellectuals were given a royal nod. Mama had been persuaded years ago to admit artists and actors to Society—God knows why! It had been a great mistake. She had even given

Irving a knighthood—making honors cheap. Such people were not much good anyway and—worse still—they made one feel inferior. For everyone else His Majesty had the right word, the right quip. For half a century, after all, that had been his stock in trade. They would, every one of them, have taken almost anything from him: to be spoken to was more important than what was said. In fact he gave them all a moment of graciousness in which to wallow.

"Ah, my dear Wyndham, what is a party without you? A party without a Wyndham is unthinkable. And what have you to say? Has not dear Titania got an even more lovely house than your Clouds?"

"I could never admit that, sire, never, but the Princess would make any house beautiful of course—by her mere presence."

"You hear that, Titania. Ah, here is Cambon. *Bien, mon cher vieillerie*—what mischief is Your Excellency up to these days?"

"The mischief is yours, Your Majesty. Have you forgotten our beautiful Paris? . . . It is so long, so very long, since we saw you. Paris is quite *désolée* . . . without her King."

"My heart is there. It always will be. You know that, my dear Excellency . . . but my ministers, they work me to death. And now here is our Margot—your Royal Academy hat, my dear, was totally scandalous. How could you?"

"Sire, it was meant to be scandalous—what is life without scandal? You would agree with that, Your Majesty?"

"Never mind! You should be at Glen this weather . . . and yet what would London be without you? . . . And so this is our little Puffin. And here is General Booth—up to some good, I'll be bound, eh, General?"

"Your Majesty is very gracious."

"Ah, Your Eminence . . ." And it was for the King now to bow low in kissing the ring.

"And Emerald . . . well, well, dear Emerald. This seems to be *your* season. Truly, you know, we hear of nobody else."

"Majesty . . ." and a specially deep curtsy until Titania made the next presentation.

"And here, sire, is our surprise for you—something to make you really happy—the Baroness Meyer."

"Olga! My darling Olga! Yes, this is indeed a surprise. Why, we had tea together only yesterday, Titania, and she never even told me. . . ."

There were no curtsies now—just fond embraces. Everyone on that lawn knew that he took tea at Cadogan Gardens three times a week, but as the father kissed his child there was an inexplicable and slightly reverential silence. He moved on.

"Ah, Sassoon . . . you're entrenched in Park Lane now, I hear. I am told wondrous things about you. Tell me, Philip, when can I come from my house to visit your place?"

"If Your Majesty would deign . . ."

And so round the garden, from sun into shade and back into sunlight, until the dressing gong sounded on the terrace. These curious creatures dressed earlier nowadays. Dinner, it is true, got later and later, but the apéritif hour got more and more sacred. It was their assurance that they were cosmopolitan, that the *fin-de-siècle* was behind them . . . that they were something new . . . their assurance that the King's mother was dead.

The ruin of a great dinner is a marvelous sight. The lees and dregs in all the glasses, the shells of oysters or of plovers' eggs, the bones of quails, ortolans and *gelinottes*, of carp soused in brandy or of crayfish in chablis, the last fragments of caviar, of truffles or *foie gras*, the ruins of iced puddings, collapsed mountains of meringue confections—all this lay littered across the table and through pantries.

Stravinsky had played his last chord. The roulette wheel had turned for the last time. The last card debt had been settled. The last apple-pie bed had been made. The last reputation had been torn to shreds. It was time to move into the "Big Room," time to dance far into the June dawn.

The Big Room ran the height of two stories. At one end, in the broad hearth—whether because the nights were cool or just the look of the thing—big logs were sparkling. The stone canopy above them soared into the roof, carved only with the two-headed eagle of the Romanovs.

"I can only dance quadrilles now, Titania. Long ago, you know, they used to say that I danced very well. Mama approved only of square dances, but later on, of course, there were the balls in the great houses . . . gavottes and polkas then . . . and after I was married, at Marlborough House, night after night we danced the Mandela *valse.* They are playing it now, but, alas, my dear, I am old and fat . . . and I puff. . . ."

"Nonsense, Teddy . . . portly, my boy, not fat. Anyway, I have made my decision. For my sake, and just for a very few minutes, you must start the first *valse* with Natasha."

And he did . . . very slowly they moved round the room . . . alone together on the empty floor . . . everyone watching them. The little Natasha looked up into his eyes. Those eyes were watering and he was looking at her very tenderly—the child of his dearest Titania. He looked into her face . . . he blinked to clear away the tears—again and again. Then, rather suddenly, Natasha knew that she must take him back to her mother. He had begun to cough. That was normal . . . until everybody realized that it was more than just the cough of a bronchial old man. His eyes, now—like oysters in a bath of blood —were bulging, dropping, almost, out of their sockets. The veins, great purple lines, were standing out on his forehead. He was trembling. He laid a trembling hand on Titania's arm.

"Take me away, Titania, take me away. Get me out of here. I'm ill, my dear, ill!"

Very gently she took him up to her boudoir, but he was not really ill—not really. He had had a very great shock.

"The Earrings, Titania, my love, the Holy Earrings! Bloody Mary's Earrings . . . the diamonds. Natasha's earrings . . . tell me."

"My dear Teddy, do be calm. It's nothing to get excited about, or alarmed about. What on earth has upset you?"

"But where did you get them? Where on earth did you get them? Where? When? Why? How?"

"My dear boy, you don't think I could afford to buy diamonds like those—not in these days? I've always kept them hidden from Natasha—ready for the *valse* with you tonight. . . . I wouldn't even let her wear them at the dinner. She's never seen them until now, nor, I think, has anyone now living. You see, as kind of insurance I smuggled them out of Russia. I should be a very rich woman if I'd sold them, but, thanks largely to you, my dear, and to Hirsch, I've never had to use them. I've never even borrowed on them although I did think of taking them to Rothschild when I built this house. . . ."

"Good God! You would have given him the shock of his life. . . ."

"I can't see why. Anyway, I struggled through. There's no mystery about them. After all, the Romanovs have always had the finest jewels in the world. And they have always had the Holy Earrings, at any rate for centuries. . . ."

"Yes, yes. But where did the Romanovs get them? I want to know. I must know, Titania."

"Oh, very well, if you must know . . . but, for the life of me, I can't imagine why you're so upset. The story, oddly enough, does begin in England . . . more oddly still, a few miles away, in Winchester . . . nearly four hundred years ago."

"Yes, yes, yes, that's it. Tell me. . . ."

Very quietly Natasha had crept into her mother's boudoir—the little room with the white paneling, the scarlet curtains and the Paolo Uccello over the mantelpiece. She sat with her back to the candles; she was in shadow except that when she moved the candlelight glinted on the diamonds, first on one side of her head and then on the other. Her mother had lapsed into French now, as she was wont to do in times of emotion. Natasha and the King just listened, her hand on his knee.

"Very well, Teddy, if it will calm your mind, I'll tell you. It's only one of those old stories—legends, call them what you will —that we royals pick up as the years pass. But, yes, if you must know, these really are the fabulous and Holy Earrings which Philip of Spain gave to your Mary Tudor. . . ."

"I've guessed that much—that this was the end of a long story. But why are they here tonight in Natasha's little pearly ears? How did you come by them?"

"Well, Bloody Mary wore them at her wedding—at Winchester, was it not?—her wedding with Philip of Spain. You see, the earrings are very nearly home again."

"Surely, but . . ."

"Keep quiet. Let me tell you. Mary wore them in the Cathedral and she was certain that she would wear them again that night in bed, with Philip. But somehow or other, after the banquet, the Holy Earrings vanished. Mary always said, to the end of her tragic life, that *that* was why she was childless . . . she never bore a child, boy or girl . . . and God knows she tried. She blamed the loss of the earrings. . . ." Titania laughed a little. ". . . You see these diamond stars perform miracles : they make barren women fertile, and fertile with sons." She laughed again.

"But, Titania, never mind that part. How did they vanish?"

"I'm trying to tell you, Teddy. Do listen. You see, everyone wanted the Holy Earrings. Philip thought that once this plain English bitch was pregnant, the earrings were too good for her; he wanted them back in the Escorial. Mary, thinking God had sent them—that she was blessed among women—wanted to put them forever on the altar at Windsor . . . Philip wasn't having that, you know. And then the Imperial Ambassador, Renard, wanted them for himself; he thought that Philip had been pretty scurvy with him . . . that he, Renard, had arranged the marriage and that the earrings should be his perquisite . . . certainly he deserved something, poor man. But above all, it was the Princess Elizabeth, imprisoned at Woodstock, who wanted them more than anyone. She wanted them partly because she was, in any case, the most avaricious woman who ever lived; she wanted them because, when she became Queen, she would put them among the Crown Jewels of England; but most of all she wanted them to frustrate the miracle whereby Mary might have a son—a Catholic heir—and because one day Elizabeth might need that miracle herself. Elizabeth's agents arranged things so that before Philip and Mary could be bedded that night (quite a ceremony in those days) the Lady Clifford—an embittered and disappointed woman—should put the Holy Earrings in a cloth and throw them out the window . . . and she did."

"But Elizabeth never got the earrings. . . ."

"I haven't said she ever got them. She didn't. Something went wrong. There was a plot within the plot. All these people were spies, remember, and all of them corrupt. There was a little hunchbacked girl . . . she was a nobody, but they called her 'Keeper of the Queen's Jewels.' For all her grand title, she was consumed with hatred. She was a crypto-Protestant anyway, and had been ridiculed and ill-treated for her crooked back and legs. She altered the clock that night and the Lady Clifford threw the diamonds out the window half an hour too soon. Under the window the little hunchback had placed her new-found friend, Pétya—Philip's Russian valet, a man devoured by greed as the hunchback was devoured by hate."

"So Philip of Spain had a Russian valet, did he? Russia has come into the story. Go on, my dear, go on."

"Yes. The poor little hunchback, the Keeper of the Queen's Jewels, had found a fellow creature in Pétya. High up in the triforium of Winchester Cathedral, during the wedding that morning, they had planned it all under cover of the music. She gave Pétya the word and he was there that night, under the window, to catch the Holy Earrings. Needless to say he vanished immediately. It is said that he joined some English gypsies. Anyway, he made his way back to Russia, to Kiev where he had been born—probably along the pilgrim routes. It may have taken him years, but he got there all right. And he got a very good price for his diamond stars—Bloody Mary's Earrings. He went to Moscow and somehow wormed his way into the Kremlin. There was a Muscovite lord, a Romanov . . ."

"I see, I see . . . or I begin to see. Go on, Titania."

"This Romanov lord, or princeling or whatever he was, gave Pétya, so it is said, a million roubles. . . . And that, my dear

Teddy, is how they come, this very night, to be in my little Natasha's pearly ears."

"So that was it. Madrid, Winchester, Moscow and now—almost back to Winchester. That was it . . . and to think . . . Papa and the Crystal Palace . . . Mama and the Blue Room . . . the Maharajah and old Ponsonby . . . the Captain and Trixie . . . and Shrimp in his ginger suit . . . and the real diamonds were never there at all. Oh, my dear, dear Titania!"

There was silence between them, and there were tears in his eyes.

"But, Titania, the story still doesn't really work, you know. It still doesn't hold water. What about the Holy Earrings that the Spanish Government gave to the Duke of Wellington, the Iron Duke, after the Peninsular War, and that he gave to Papa in 1851 for the Tiara in the Crystal Palace? . . . The story just doesn't work, my dear—the mystery is still unsolved."

She only laughed.

"My dear Teddy. Don't you see? . . . Poor Mary Tudor went nearly mad when the earrings vanished. God, she thought, must hate her. She was very near to death. To save her sanity Philip had some very perfect copies made. He then told her that they had got back the earrings, and they had caught the thief in Toledo and burnt him alive on a very slow fire. That made her extremely happy; and when Philip came back to England the next year she wore the copies in bed. . . . Ignorance was bliss."

"Well, I'm damned . . . and the Iron Duke?"

Titania only chortled.

"You simpleton. You don't really think, do you, that any Spanish Government there ever was would actually give a million pounds' worth of jewels to an English soldier? As a bribe perhaps—but to reward him *after* the battle was won, that would be pointless. They gave the Duke a couple of enormous estates —arid mountains actually; but diamonds—no. He was just an old buffer anyway who wouldn't know a diamond when he saw it. On the other hand, by 1851 he was the greatest man in

England. Your good Papa had to take the diamonds on trust—as, of course, did the Constable of the Tower."

"I see. So here are the Holy Earrings at last. Ye Gods! No wonder we could never find them!"

He stood up and put his hands very gently on Natasha's ears, feeling the facets of the gems under his fingers.

"Stolen property, Natasha, stolen property . . . Philip of Spain gave them to the English Crown, and Pétya—bless his heart—stole them. I suppose poor Eddy would have liked them. . . . He's dead and gone now. . . . All for the best; Georgie will make a better king, but wouldn't be interested in diamonds. No, no, no . . . They are mine and I give them to you. Keep them, my dear, keep them with my love."

She stood up and kissed him.

"Yes, keep them, my dear. One day you may need them."

"I shall always love them; but 'need them'—why?"

"Well, they are miraculous earrings and if, one day, you were to wear them on your wedding night, then—for certain—you would give the world a Prince."

It was late when Titania had finished her story. Natasha went back to the ball; up there in the boudoir they could just hear the sound of the music, reminding them that the guests must be missing both their hostess and the King. The guests must wait a little longer. The sun was above the Hampshire hills by the time the King had told Titania his half of the story . . . the years came rushing back . . . Windsor, Balmoral, Osborne and a slum somewhere east of Bow Creek. Twenty-two years had passed. There were things he had almost forgotten. And then, at the end, Titania had something more to say.

"I see . . . but what a pity your mother did not live to see the end of the story."

"No. It's better as it is, Titania. Mama, you know, had very curious and very literal ideas about right and wrong, and also about property—not least Crown property. She would think Mary Tudor grossly careless to lose her diamonds like that and to appoint such unreliable ladies-in-waiting. As for Pétya—she would say that he knew perfectly well that he was doing wrong, and would be sorry that the man could no longer be hauled up at Bow Street. With Mama the years would make no difference. No. Bloody Mary's Earrings, my dear one, now belong to your little Natasha. That makes me very happy; but I can assure you that dear Mama would not have been at all amused . . . not in the very least."

Bibliography

BOLITHO, HECTOR, *Albert the Good.* Appleton, 1932.

CHURCHILL, WINSTON, *Lord Randolph Churchill.* Macmillan, 1906, 2 vols.

FULFORD, ROGER, ed., *Dearest Child: Letters between Queen Victoria and the Princess Royal.* Holt, 1965.

HOUSMAN, LAURENCE, *Victoria Regina.* Jonathan Cape, 1934.

LEE, SIDNEY, *King Edward VII.* Macmillan, 1925, 2 vols.

LONGFORD, ELIZABETH, *Queen Victoria, Born to Succeed.* Harper, 1965.

LUTYENS, MARY, ed., *Lady Lytton*'s *Court Diary,* 1895-1899. Rupert Hart-Davis, 1961.

MAGNUS-ALLCROFT, PHILIP, *King Edward the Seventh.* Dutton, 1964.

MALLET, VICTOR, *Life with Queen Victoria: Marie Mallet*'s *Letters from Court, 1887-1901.* Houghton Mifflin, 1968.

PONSONBY, ARTHUR, *Henry Ponsonby: Queen Victoria*'s *Private Secretary.* Macmillan, 1942.

ROTH, CECIL, *The Magnificent Rothschilds.* Ryerson Press, 1939.

STRACHEY, LYTTON, *Queen Victoria.* Chatto & Windus, 1921.

VICTORIA, PRINCESS, *Queen Victoria at Windsor and Balmoral: Letters from Princess Victoria of Prussia.* Allen & Unwin, 1959.

VICTORIA, QUEEN, *Leaves from the Journal of Our Life in the Highlands from 1848 to 1861.* Smith Elder & Co., 1868.

——*The Letters of Queen Victoria.* First Series, 1831-1861, 3 vols., edited by A. C. Benson and Viscount Esher. Second Series, 1862-1885, 3 vols., edited by George Earle Buckle. Third Series, 1886-1901, 3 vols., edited by George Earle Buckle. John Murray.

73 74 75 10 9 8 7 6 5 4 3 2